Praise for
Benchere in Wonderland

Steven Gillis has created an indelible character in Benchere and let him
loose in a slyly subversive wonderland of art, violence, love, grief, greed,
and grand ideals. At once magnificently strange and achingly intimate,
Gillis' novel lingers and burns long after the covers are shut.

DAWN RAFFEL, Author of *The Secret Life of Objects*

Steven Gillis' latest novel once again reminds us that he is not only a master storyteller able to conjure up narrative magic, but it's his lyrical voice
throughout the narrative that's capable of finding the poetry in the most
unlikely places that makes him the 21st century heir to Saul Bellow, John
Cheever, and Stanley Elkin. When you mix Gillis' sad, beaten lyricism with
his continual explosions of narrative surprise, the result is a glorious,
tense luminosity that makes *Benchere in Wonderland* his best book yet, a
satisfying and deeply moving read.

RICHARD GRAYSON, Author of *Winter in Brooklyn*

Steven Gillis' new novel, *Benchere in Wonderland,* is not quite like anything else I've ever read. Surprising, arresting, and electric, it kept me up
a couple of nights in a row. This author has a voice all his own, and it's one
I won't forget. *Benchere in Wonderland* is that rare thing— an original novel.

STEVE YARBROUGH, Author of *The Realm of Last Chances*

Steven Gillis' latest novel, *Benchere in Wonderland,* takes readers into the
Kalahari Desert and embroils them in the stormy clash of art and commerce, politics and aesthetics, ideas, ideals, and the chaos of the human
heart. Anyone who has ever worried over the troubled relationship
between art and the world will want to read this compelling novel.

ED FALCO, Author of *The Family Corleone*

Praise for *Temporary People*

Temporary People is a vicious and compelling storyboard for our time.

JEFF PARKER, author of *The Taste of Penny*

Praise for *The Consequence of Skating*

Steven Gillis possess the rarest of gifts, the voice that seems to flow effortlessly. This guy makes it look easy. Read the first three pages of *The Consequence of Skating* and if you're not hooked, go see a doctor.

JONATHAN EVISON, author of *All About Lulu* and *West of Here*

Praise for *Giraffes*

Gillis' stories are illuminatingly strange, filled with power, electric, and will stay with you long after you think you've gone to sleep.

STEPHEN ELLIOTT, author of *Adderall Diaries*

Praise for *The Weight of Nothing*

Beguilingly mystical.

PUBLISHERS WEEKLY

Praise for *Walter Falls*

An exceptionally well written novel ... *Walter Falls* is highly recommended as a powerful and moving saga of the human condition.

MIDWEST BOOK REVIEW

Praise for *The Law of Strings*

This story collection hooked me from story one and continued to captivate to the end. The expert dialogue and movement and resolution in each piece ... This is a book you could read in a sitting or two. The pace is that swift; the stories are that good.

STEPHEN DIXON, two-time National Book Award finalist

Copyright ©2014
Steven Gillis

Library of Congress
Cataloging-in-Publication Data

Gillis, Steven, 1957-
Bencher in wonderland : a novel /
Stephen Gillis.
pages ; cm
ISBN 978-0-9904370-5-5
(softcover)

1. Artists–Fiction.
2. Widowers–Fiction.
3. Self-realization–Fiction.
4. Self-actualization (Psychol-
    ogy)–Fiction.

I. Title.
PS3607.I446B46 2015
813'.6–DC23
2015001970

Hawthorne Books
& Literary Arts

9   2201 Northeast 23rd Avenue
8   3rd Floor
7   Portland, Oregon 97212
6   hawthornebooks.com
5   *Form*:
4   Adam McIsaac/Sibley House
3
2   Printed in China

Set in Paperback

For Mary, always

Benchere
in Wonderland

A Novel
Steven Gillis

HAWTHORNE BOOKS & LITERARY ARTS
Portland, Oregon | MMXV

Art making is not about telling the truth, but making the truth felt.
—CHRISTIAN BOLTANSKI

Whole sight, or all the rest is desolation.
—JOHN FOWLES, *Daniel Martin*

Ob-la-di, Ob-la-da, life goes on.
—THE BEATLES, *Ob-la-di, Ob-la-da*

BENCHERE IN WONDERLAND

Prologue

AHH BENCHERE, HE THINKS, *I AM THIS*: A BARROSA BULL. American bred. Both eager and unruly. Wayward and thick-headed. Older now, I am the unexpected manifest of my most deliberate ambitions. Hard working yet significantly flawed. I'm the steam kept too long in the kettle. A force of nature, forged in the waters. I am youth gone gray. Unreserved, I am Daniel Boone and George Washington Carver. Deliberate and erratic, foul tempered and temperate, I am a great bustard with one wing snapped hoping to fly. I've gone fat, though am powerful still. Wed to my root, I am the buffalo, am baseball and cool jazz. I am ego and humility. Am charitable and Godless. I am Walt Whitman launched over the rooftops, Lincoln and Jefferson, Action Jackson, Geronimo, John Galt and Joan Jett. I am Harold Brodkey and Harry Caray, Patrick Henry and Harriet Tubman, Frederick Douglass and Mickey Mantle. I'm Mark Zuckerberg, Clara Barton and Benny Goodman, Rosa Parks and Paul Newman, Michael Dell and Billy the Kid, Barbra Streisand, Neil Armstrong, John Paul Stevens, Edmonia Lewis and Arthur Miller. I am Benchere, fickle and firm and quick to howl, *I want,* followed by, *I will!*

I will, I say. *I will,* again.

Book I

I.

IN TIVERTON LAST MONTH, BEFORE GETTING OUT OF BED, Benchere tried to masturbate. He removed the sheet and tugged off his boxers, went with a left grip first, followed by a right, then left again, milking himself until the muscle in his arms gave way and his application was aborted.

Arggh. Ahh Benchere. Way to go. Add this to the list. Without Marti, his cock was a slack slab, indifferent to the effort.

He lay for a while after, rolled on his side, his hand extended toward Marti's half of the bed. A reflex, he mimicked the way he used to touch her, slipping his fingers beneath the surface of her shirt until he found the puff flesh of her remaining nipple. From there he'd move onto the flattened space where Marti's scar snaked across an unexpected hollow. Gently he massaged as the healing allowed.

AT A PARTY on the north end of College Hill, a hundred years ago now. Marti spoke with friends inside the front room. A silver keg sat on ice. Rickie Lee Jones played on the stereo. How come you don't come and P.L.P. with me .... Benchere wore blue sweatpants cut off at the knee, white canvas high tops and a brightly colored Hawaiian shirt. The lighting in the house was lava lamps and candles. Two barefoot girls did toe stands for no particular reason. Marti had on jeans and a purple t-shirt, leather sandals and a green string tied around her right wrist.

Most of Marti's friends were engineering and architectural

students. Benchere had completed his studies in visual arts the year before, was transitioning from favored student to anxious applicant, working four nights a week at The Green Bar – what would become The Scurvy Dog – serving dollar shots and yellow beer. During the day he shared studio space in a Waterman Street loft. A few of his sculptures were placed on consignment at the Dodge House Gallery and Providence Art Club where, through June, only one had sold.

Someone in Marti's group mentioned Charles Jenks' article on the Pompidou Centre in Paris, where Jenks touted the Pompidou as the greatest architectural achievement to come along in a generation, and Marti said, "Please. Where's the achievement? You architects couldn't build a snowman without an engineer there to show you how."

Ha now. Benchere stopped to listen.

One of the other students defended Su and Richard Rogers' design as innovatory, described the 200,000 meters of glass, the exposed coded tubing done up in rainbow colors and maximized flow of light.

"You mean what the engineers did." Marti called the Rogers' effort irrelevant. "They tossed a few ideas down on a sheet of drafting paper then asked Happold and Rice to build it."

Dang, Benchere moved closer. Marti's smile was playful, revealed a confidence rather than arrogance. Undeterred by how little he knew of the Pompidou, about engineering or architecture, Benchere pushed his way into the group and approached Marti with a quick, "Say there, you can't actually believe any of this jabber you're peddling."

Marti looked up.

In his colored shirt, saggy shorts and size 14 Converse, Benchere appeared clown-like, ridiculously large and impossible to ignore. He took another step forward and declared, "You have it all backwards there, Sally. Architects are the ones who deliver the goods. You engineers are functionaries. Like doorknobs and waffle irons. You're waiters and bank tellers, as interchangeable as bullpen catchers. You have a narrow skill-set and no imagination. The best anyone can say is that you enable what others bring to the table. Without architects you engineers would have no career."

"Hey now ... Did he just say ... ?" Those in the group hooted, then formed a circle, turned and stared at Marti in anticipation of her response.

Even as she laughed, could not help, found Benchere's largeness and queer dress amusing, his way of talking as if everything was part of some half-finished lyric, there was a sense of Marti gearing up. Firm of spirit, the second daughter of a third-generation Hillsboro farmer, Marti's temperament was Old Testament, her personal convictions liberal, her nature tenacious, a devourer of fools and false prophets. In reply to Benchere she said, "So engineers have no imagination, is that right?"

"It's true," Benchere defended his statement. "If you guys had some you'd all be architects."

Marti shifted her shoulders. She stood beneath Benchere's chin and asked if he knew the origin of the Panama Canal, the Coliseum, Falling Water and the Pantheon? "What about the Netherlands Delta Works, Hoover Dam and Great Wall of China, the Eiffel Tower and Tibet Railway? All of these were built by engineers from their own designs. Did you know that?"

"Well now ... "

"Imagine," she gave Benchere a tsk with her tongue and handed him her beer. "It's easy for architects to come up with designs when they don't have to worry about function or physical laws. The Pompidou would have fallen in on itself without Happold and Rice."

"Maybe," Benchere answered. "But there would be no Pompidou for you engineers to work on without the Rogers."

"That's ridiculous." Marti told Benchere to "Stop and think. There was no Pompidou before the engineers got involved. Architects draft concepts. They aren't trained to actually build what they draw. Their designs are rudimentary. Sure they have imagination, but so what? Kids have great imaginations, too, but you wouldn't want them designing a building for you."

"Of course not." Benchere countered with, "Kids aren't architects."

"And architects aren't engineers," Marti took her beer back, kept Benchere off balance. Engaged in the debate, her voice rose expressively as she said, "Without engineers, you architects couldn't put two pinwheels together. What good is imagination when you can't even set a cantilever beam or figure out the tension load for a quadrangular Warren truss?" She made a motion with her right hand, suggesting whole worlds collapsing.

Benchere followed the movement, filled his chest with air and held it, gave himself a second to consider how best to reply. His history with woman was well documented, his habit of wading in too fast before gauging the depth of the tide. An overcharge of energy kept him scrambling from one affair to the next. Easily bored by submissive girls, he looked for those aspiring types, became excited by and then competitive with women more naturally ambitious.

Marti moved a strand of hair away from her face. Her inclinations were less impulsive than Benchere's. Never one to wade in blind, her approach was always carefully thought out, her stamina prodigious, her sense of the world in all its abundance. Self-secure, she did not compete with lovers, found most easy prey. As Benchere was not a lover yet, Marti concentrated on their conversation, asked if he had ever heard of I.M. Pei.

"Did she just say … ?" The reference caused the group to yelp again and quarrel among themselves. Marti took Benchere's beer, told him that "Pei was the architect on the John Hancock Tower. You know, the one so poorly designed glass panes actually fell from the façade? This is what happens when an architect relies too much on his own imagination."

"Ahh, wait now." Benchere bent himself forward at the hips, squinted as if he might somehow see Marti's words. He tried to come up with the right response, told himself, Think, Benchere.

"Pei in the sky," he said for no reason, made a quick review of Marti's claims, looked for inconsistencies in her argument. "Here's the thing," he took a stab. "Why when a building fails is it the architect's fault and when it works you want to give engineers all the credit?"

"Exactly. Why?"

"Bah." Benchere swears, "You're cart hopping the horse there, Nancy. You can't blame the architect. Pei did his job. He gave you a blueprint. If you engineers are all that and a box of nuts you'd have fixed Pei's design just as you did the Pompidou."

"But it's not our job to fix mistakes," Marti shot back. "We're waffle irons, remember? We're doorknobs. We're just functionaries connecting the dots you architects lay out."

Benchere rattled, "Who said? Did I say?"

"At least the Rogers gave Happold and Rice something halfway sound. Pei's design was awful and what could the engineers do?" Marti tugged at the front of Benchere's shirt and said, "It's like this. If you go to a tailor and insist he only dress you in Hawaiian prints, you can't blame the tailor for what he comes up with given the limitation he has to work with."

"Whoa," Benchere touched his chest, made a rubbing motion with his fingertips. "Hold on now," despite his effort the conversation had gone sideways. He grunted, "Arghh," stalled then tried to backtrack as Marti reached forward and returned Benchere's beer. "You architects," she said again.

"But, but," Benchere stammered, attempted to think of something clever to say. Who are you? he nearly shouted. Not used to being outdone, he decided to separate himself from the original target of Marti's harass, and said, "But I'm no architect. I'm not one of them."

There followed then a new round of hoots and whistles as Benchere wiped his free hand on his shirt and introduced himself to Marti.

THE WIND AT night in the Kalahari runs across the savannah half warm and half chilled. Unrestrained by anything more than the occasional hills and trees, the motion of the wind is constant as it searches for something to crash against and slow down.

TWO NIGHTS AFTER the party, Benchere phoned Marti at her apartment.

"Ben Cheer?" Marti pretended she couldn't place him, then said, "Well Ben, this is unexpected. I never imagined."

"Good one. Ha to that."

In free-form, they spoke for more than an hour. Marti asked and Benchere answered questions about his work, described growing up in Yonkers, his adventures on Ludlow Street, hanging out at clubs where he first heard Kiki Smith and Fab Five Freddy. Wandering in SoHo and the East Village, he stumbled onto the Park Place Group, Richard Feigen and Paula Cooper, John Gibson and Brooke Alexander, the galleries that came and went, FUN and New Math, Nature Morte and P.P.O.W. where he learned about Brancusi, Botero and Nevelson. Later he discovered *Portrait of Mademoiselle Pogany*, the Sculptural Ensemble of Constantin Brancusi at Targu Jiu, and *Clown Tight Rope Walker.* "And that was it," Benchere said. "After that I was hooked. Does it make sense?"

Marti answered perfectly. "It doesn't have to."

Ahh, Benchere.

The stories Marti told were set in Hillsboro, in Boston briefly and then Providence. Asked how she came to engineering, Marti listed the machinery of her childhood; the subsoiler and chisel plow, seed drill and terragator, baler and topper, backhoe and gleaner all ancient and forever breaking down. She spoke of developing an affinity for repairing the necessity of the invention. "I'm a product of poor design," Marti said and offered her sweet laugh.

Encouraged, Benchere invited her to dinner, was surprised when she turned him down.

He called the next night and they spoke for three hours more. A second invitation was extended, this time for coffee. Again Marti said no. A day later she phoned and asked Benchere to the movies. They saw *The Gods Must Be Crazy,* shared popcorn and a drink but she wouldn't hold his hand and leaned away when he tried kissing her goodnight.

Benchere phoned on Monday and suggested another date. Marti declined, made him wait until she called again and then they went out. They had dinner downtown, shared a smoked carpaccio and later a walk. Benchere expected a parting kiss, but Marti still refused, pushed him off with fingers to the chest. What is this? Benchere went home and paced through his apartment. I … I … I … He could not figure out, What gives?

The pattern continued for several weeks more. Despite their nightly talks and twice-weekly dates, Marti balked at extending Benchere affection. He took her to his studio and showed her his art, tried to impress her with his work, spoke excitedly and rapturously about his vision to create inspired and influential sculptures while redefining the perception of form. He invited her to rallies and public debates, marches and protests supporting the ERA, the ALF-CIO, and nuclear disarmament. He asked her to come drinking at the Green Bar, hoped to entertain her with stories and introduce her to his friends. He gave her every reason to fall for him, to see him in a multitude of lights, and still she kept him at a distance, baffled and unsure.

Say now … Benchere handled each rebuff poorly, regretted how Marti treated him with chilly dispatch. If she was punishing him for what he said the night they met, he apologized and told her his argument at the party was just for show. What did he know about architects and engineers and the whole top dog/bottom dog debate? He fell asleep exploring the tendril roots of relationships and the complication of all things interlinked.

Early on in their non-affair, Benchere went to the library where he read through books on architectural design. A crash course. While logic suggested he educate himself on the fundamental rules of engineering in order to impress Marti, Benchere thought differently. He spent several days studying place and construct, complexity and informed simplicity, points and counterpoints. Relying on first impressions and his own artistic eye, he reviewed the works of Jean Nouvel, Paolo Soleri, Ernest J. Kump and Jack McConnell, Richard Neutra and Ernst May. On the seventh day, he surrounded himself with paper, charcoal and pens and began to sketch his own design.

The house he imagined had roughhewn beams and exposed trusses, beige adobe brick in front, stone cladding to the east, vertical windows arched and cut. Varying rooflines were covered with sculpted clay tiles, set above a stone arch and alder planked door. The flooring was cream colored marble, the rooms with open galleries and sculpted ceilings. Both the library and dining area had a view of the courtyard and loggia. The kitchen was in the west end, the bedrooms and main bath on the second level. The stairwell was sketched as cherry wood, ascending in a circular twist.

Working daily, Benchere made advances, overcame miscalculations and wrong turns. He said nothing about his project to Marti. On the phone, he invited her to dinner, for walks and movies and coffee dates. Each time Marti turned him down, would wait a day or two then tease him with a different invitation.

Frustrated, Benchere tossed up his hands, tried to dismiss his feelings but couldn't. All of his experiences with women and he'd somehow never fallen this hard. In need of diversion, desperate, suffering like a schoolboy with his heart crushed and aching, he resumed dating other girls. A bad idea. In his unrequited pine Benchere was not up to the task.

He sat at the table in his kitchen and added Mocha-glazed maple cabinetry to his floor plan. He sketched granite countertops and stone pavers for the terrace, a dentil frieze, concrete cast doorway, sienna-hued balusters and a maple wood balcony off the master bedroom. Determined not to create a Pei-like pretty mess, he researched the finer points of construction, studied solid-void relationships and issues of circulation, where to place the columns to insure harmony within the interacting elements; establishing asymmetrical balance in an imbalanced world.

Near the end of summer Benchere called Marti as she was coming in from yoga. He asked if she had eaten, if she would like to grab a bite. Marti sighed and said she had to wash her hair. Ten minutes later she called back, invited him to come dancing the following night.

"Now see here," Benchere decided to let Marti know he'd had enough. "Dancing is it? And why couldn't you just say yes to dinner?" He insisted this game of hers was too much, her need to control everything and manage him like some unruly pup. "Isn't it sufficient that you've won?"

He told her how she disturbed his sleep, hounded his head, distracted him constantly. "What is it you want from me?" he asked, then said, "Goddamn it but from you I want everything. Is that selfish? I don't think it is. I don't think you'd accept anything less. Other girls, other girls," he trailed off. "Haven't I been patient?" he began again. "When I call and you don't answer, I find myself worried and need to know you're safe. How strange is that? Very strange for me. And yet here you are and don't you know by now what I want?"

Marti said nothing.

Benchere tapped his finger against the phone, became more animated, spoke of the conversation they had the first night they met and how he realized now how ridiculous he must have sounded. "Here's what I think," he said. "I think it's no different the kind of connection architects and engineers have from what the rest of us want. Everyone knows architects and engineers are inexorably linked, like fish and water, Bert and Ernie, Masters and Johnson, Sears and Roebuck, Porgy and Bess. It's evolutionary," Benchere went on. "We all want to be independent, and then we want to be half of a perfect whole. I wouldn't have admitted this before, but it's the relationship that completes us." Benchere caught his breath, anxious, his large fingers growing hot, he had to wipe them on his shirt while he spoke. He put the phone down on the floor, addressed the receiver as he did pushups and said, "What-point-is-there-to-anything-if-we-don't-act-on-how-we-feel?"

He lay with his belly on the hardwood, his head turned with the receiver cradled in front of him and repeated Marti's name, told her, "I have something to show you, something for you, something I want you to see."

When she still didn't answer, having gone this far Benchere said, "Marti, I … " and waited again for her reply. He could hear her breathing, then nothing more but the click of the phone.

Well that's just great, Benchere. Well played. Nicely done. He climbed to his knees, stood in the center of his apartment and howled until his neighbors banged on the walls. Benchere! A fine kettle, that's for sure. He dropped and did more pushups, more pacing and sweating before walking outside.

In shorts and a BU windbreaker, he cut across the Main Green, circled Lincoln Field, came back around Thayer Street and South Main to the front of his building. Marti stood on the bottom step. Not expecting, Benchere stopped at the curb. He had his keys in his hand and Marti came and took them, went upstairs and unlocked his door.

Inside were books and clothes scattered, dinner dishes in the sink, a radio without knobs, the furniture mismatched and turned at odd angles. "Benchere in captivity," Marti moved toward the center of the room and examined the mess. On the walls were modern prints, Rothko and Avery and Cy Twombly. The smell was coffee and candle wax. The bedroom door was open and the bed unmade. On the table in the kitchen were several large sheets of drafting paper containing Benchere's design.

Marti turned in a circle. Benchere watched, remained silent, tried to ask but couldn't bring himself to say, Why are you here? What now? He still wasn't used to being this way, exposed and at a loss for words. Marti laughed, less surprised. She came closer, rose up on her toes and kissed him. Then she kissed him again, more tellingly, before sliding back down and saying, "Alright Benchere, so what is it you have to show me? What have you got?"

2.

IN THE ATTRITUS, BESIDE A BAOBAB, NEAR A RIVERBED a thousand years dry, miles from the Okavango which flows in the Dorsland as the only permanent body of water, Benchere sits and imagines his whiskey chilled.

The temperatures during the day rise quickly, cool again at night. Harper pours from the bottle. Grains of sand float to the surface of Benchere's drink. He scrapes the sand aside with his teeth, spits then swallows.

South of Maun, equidistant from Serowe and Ghanzi, between Tshane and Kalkfontein, north of the Cape, in the Kalahari seven thousand miles from home. Tonight the fire Benchere's made sends out ash orange sparks. A second fire burns behind the tool tent where one of the new arrivals is smoking *dagga*. Benchere sniffs the air. Jazz chews on a stick while Harper hums and Daimon films the scene.

All the huts and lean-tos in camp are temporary, will be taken down when the work's complete. The common area used for meals and meetings is to the north of the tents, the garbage pit and sanitation unit, straddle trench and burn out latrine to the west. Near the perimeter of the main field, the generator and welding equipment are kept under a tarp when not in use.

Zooie sits out by the other fire, playing guitar. Benchere's sculpture is there in the distance. Some three hundred feet tall, it dwarfs the hillsides and centers the horizon in every direction. Benchere looks across the grounds, thinks about the friction piles used in the foundation of his sculpture. Marti designed the piles to settle the beams the way deep roots hold the trunk of a tree. Without her help, Benchere knows the sculpture would not have survived against the first real wind or any shifting of the sand.

Harper sees Benchere lost in thought. He lifts his glass and tells a joke. "I met this Buddhist once who refused Novocain during root canal because he wanted to transcend dental medication."

Benchere groans and sips more from his drink. Daimon comes over and Harper offers him a cup. At thirty, Daimon is a study in contrasts, his features boyish, his eyes seriously set. Leanly framed in brown safari pants, a blue t-shirt and tan Timberland boots, he's rawboned about the edges with a quick promethean smile and high angular cheeks. In the desert, he looks less auteur than rock climber. A graduate of Tisch, disciple of Errol Morris, professionally seasoned. In the last seven years Daimon has made three feature documentaries: one each on the Chinese activist Gao Zhisheng, the murdered journalist Anna Politkovskaya, and the painter Chuck Close. Hired to record Benchere's time in Botswana, he is still feeling his way along with his subject.

Benchere tosses the stick for Jazz, says of the two tents Daimon and Zooie have put together, "It's a cozy arrangement, but you do know polyester isn't made to keep in sound?"

Daimon laughs. His relationship with Zooie came about unexpectedly. A handful of possibilities, he replies to Benchere, "I hope we haven't kept you up."

"Ha!" Benchere stands. Puffed to his full size he is a man of formidable dimension. A middle-aged *Hermes of Olympus*. The noise he makes when he howls causes Jazz to bark. He sets his drink in the sand, comes at Daimon and wrestles him down, his heavy chest crushing as Daimon offers no resistance, lets himself be pinned.

"One, two, three," Harper rules. Benchere rolls off, gets to his knees, gives Daimon a hand. In the Kalahari the thornbush helps secure the soil. Rising, Benchere ignores the ache in his back. Above him the sculpture rises. Harper smokes. Daimon recovers, brushes the dirt from his face. The ash from the fire blows south. Benchere reaches and pets Jazz. The desert covers 120,000 square miles, goes on and on like a memory.

Harper shifts his shoulders.

Daimon retrieves his drink.

Zooie sings *Hallelujah*, "There's a blaze of light in every word/It doesn't matter which you heard."

Benchere listens. He points skyward. *"Kak,"* he says, and gives the moon fair warning.

AN HOUR AFTER Benchere told Marti he loved her on the phone, after she walked across town, took his keys, came upstairs and asked what he had to show her, Benchere pointed to his kitchen table. Marti sat and studied the design. "Honestly," she asked, "who did these?" Examining the pages further, she told Benchere it wasn't possible to complete this level of work without any formal training.

"Who knew?" Benchere in reply.

Marti found a pen and offered comments, advised Benchere on engineering issues concerning the placement of columns and joists in rooms of a certain size, the dead load and live load to be considered, the interaction between the materials selected and how best to make the relationships engage. All these things were easily fixed, she said, and did not detract from the original beauty of the design.

She stayed the night, made a few calls in the morning, had her architect friends take a look at the drawings. Each reacted the same, did not believe at first. "Who is it?" They guessed Emmanuel Di Giacomo, van der Rohe, Le Corbusier, Gropius and Alto. Marti said Benchere and they laughed. "Bullshit," they told her. "Bullshit to that."

More calls were made. A meeting was arranged at Lerner/Ladds where Benchere's work was reviewed again. The partners at L/L were impressed by the design, yet skeptical when told Benchere was not an architect. They took a day to consider then brought Benchere back for an interview, ran him through some tests before presenting him with an offer. "Here's the thing," they explained how Benchere lacking a license or any formal credentials made his work impossible to sell on his own. What they would like to do, were willing, as a favor, was clean up the design, make it all nice and legal and then sell it under their name. "You'll be compensated, of course," they said.

Benchere weighed the proposal then answered, "I don't think so boys. The work is mine. I didn't set out for any of this to happen, but since it has, here's what I propose." He said he would give them his work to bring up to spec, would let them go out and sell it and they wouldn't have to pay him anything if no one bit. But if his design did sell he wanted 60 percent and his name on the project. If they didn't like the terms he would simply take his work somewhere else.

"Take it then," the partners told him. "We obviously overestimated your grasp of the situation. You clearly don't get it. Do you honestly think you can sell your work without our firm behind you? Do you think anyone else will – what's the word you used? – bite? Go ahead then."

Benchere got up to leave but the partners called him back. Another offer was presented and then a third. Two days later Benchere closed the deal. His first design sold in under a week. Built in Newport, fronting the North Atlantic, the buzz surrounding the house made the partners giddy. They offered Benchere a contract, put him on salary and paid him for future works. He was given an office, a secretary and company car, then told to, "Create!" When his second original sold, Benchere used his bonus check to take Marti to Lanikai Beach.

In the end Benchere did seven originals. He also worked on dozens of ongoing L/L projects, offered his unique creative touch, increasing their value with the inclusion of his name. Keenly aware, the partners helped build the Benchere brand. Private clients sought commissions while Benchere was celebrated in magazines, at conferences and on tv. He took to the suddenness of his celebrity with great ease, was accessible, outgoing and good humored. A popular after-dinner speaker, he came with antidotes and irreverence and kept everyone amused.

Impressive this, and yet as the experience was never planned, Benchere eventually grew dissatisfied and tired of the work. The demands on his time afforded little chance to sculpt. He spoke with Marti, and then the partners at L/L who reluctantly agreed to accommodate his schedule and give him more days off. The arrangement worked for a while and then it did not. Eager to abandon the rigid constraints, the purposefulness, functionality and form of architecture for the abstract inferences and influences of art, Benchere began to wrap up loose ends. After his seventh Benchere original sold, after marrying Marti and having in turn Kyle and Zooie and settling into what he never predicted as his working life, Benchere announced he'd had enough.

What?

Enough.

That summer he gave notice to L/L.

But you can't. No one could quite believe. What are you thinking? You want to walk away from what made you rich and famous?

I do want to, yes.

To do what? No wait, don't tell us.

I was a sculptor before.

So? What good were you? None of us knew you. Think of where you are now.

I have thought, Benchere said. And I want to go back.

Again they asked, *To what? Anonymity? A shared studio and tending bar? You're Michael Benchere. You can't just walk away from that.*

Christ. I'm not walking, he told them. I still am.

Are what? They accused him of trying to manipulate his own mythology by becoming an artist.

Bah, Benchere answered the charge with a quick, If you think I'm living my life in order to get a reaction from you, you're nuts.

So you say. But you plan to show us your art. You'll want to sell us your sculptures. You'll solicit our reviews. Be assured, our opinions won't be neutral. Of Benchere's claim that he was tired of traditional design, of form necessitating function, they asked, *What does that even mean? All your art-speak is nothing more than you looking to make a bigger splash. It's all about Benchere, isn't it?*

Of course it is. Benchere in a huff, barked back, Of course it's that.

Marti listened, let Benchere have his howl, then said he should, "Forget them, Michael. Ignore what they think. Why should you care? Save your energy for things more important than this."

Sage advice. Marti with sound counsel was the voice of reason, unflappable, indissoluble, confident and consummate. Even after she got sick and then sick again she remained fearless and inviolate. Benchere loved her then. He missed her now. As he yelled and snapped, cocked his arms and set his fists, Marti laughed. "Look at you," she said. "All this chirping and who are you fighting? Really now. What's the problem? Who's there to stop you from doing what you want?"

STERN SITS WITH Rose atop the hill. They are 600 yards away from Benchere and the others. The rise is dune-like but with firmer soil, thorny shrubs and grassy patches. Rose's chair has blue vinyl straps stretched out beneath his weight. A red umbrella is stuck in the ground behind them. Even in the shade the temperature this afternoon is over 95 degrees. Stern swats at the termites which swarm and the black flies that are relentless.

Rose uses binoculars to keep an eye on the scene below. Eschenbach Farlux Selectors, German made. "Top of the line," Rose praises the product.

Stern leans over and takes the glasses from Rose. Benchere's sculpture is large enough to be viewed without aid, but becomes resplendent through the binoculars. In the trunk behind Stern's chair is a Crystal RS101x2 computer with Intel CPU architecture, a

Nikon dSLR D700 camera and AF-S Nikkor telescopic lens. All of the equipment, along with the Savage 10FP rifle and Eschenbach binoculars, is government issue. The trunk offers protection from the sand, keeps things cool beneath an insulated lining.

After Marti died, Benchere took a leave of absence from teaching at the Backwater Art Academy and began organizing the details for his Kalahari project. A liberal fellow always, as far back as his days at Brown, Benchere was a staunch supporter of social causes: civil rights, gay rights, workers' rights, gun control and immigration reform, fiscal, environmental, labor and health amendments, communal and political accountability. As he acquired a certain fame, first as an architect and then as a sculptor, his activities came under increased scrutiny, his conduct kept on file.

Twice in the months before flying to Africa, Benchere was visited by representatives from the House sub-committee on African Affairs. His plans were questioned, were discouraged then blocked, his passport suspended until Benchere howled and filed a formal complaint. "Seriously now?" To those who claimed his trip involved a broader agenda than simply making art, Benchere scoffed and said, "I'm going to build a sculpture. A sculpture, that's all."

Rose photographs each person in camp. The shots are digitalized and run through the RS101 for identification. "Nothing to it," Rose boasts.

"Come to data," Stern passes the binoculars back. He lays a flat board across the arms of his chair, produces a folder from his briefcase, clips the pages down and studies his notes. The file on Benchere is several inches thick. Stern reviews the contents daily, searches for clues as to why Benchere's here. "The obvious isn't."

"Unless we're overlooking."

From the hilltop Stern says, "That's funny."

Rose realizes and snickers. "So what do we know?"

Stern reads from the file. Contained within is a detailed history of Michael Benchere at work and play, his personal and political affairs, his involvement in public demonstrations and dissents, civil disobedience, sit-ins and marches. As agitator, Benchere enjoys stirring the waters, his most natural state one of protest, and still he insists in essays and lectures that his art remains a separate beast. Dismissive of the conservative modernists and early forms of progressive modernism, Benchere believes art is meant to inspire the human soul, not issue dictates or dogma. "My art is no roiled fist. I am not some poster maker. My sculptures aren't done up as a stomping boot or raised middle finger to be monopolized and propagandized for any faction, right or left."

"And yet here he is in Africa," Rose says to Stern.

"Go figure that."

"An influential artist."

"Disinclined to influence."

"Or so he says."

"Art and politics."

"Politics and art."

"Benchere claims there's a distinction."

"Is adamant."

"Right."

"Is he?"

"I don't know."

Benchere passes below, wears Bermuda shorts, brown boots and a ratty tan hat. Rose wipes his forehead, points toward the sculpture and says, "She's a big one."

"Monolithic."

"It takes an inflated sense of self to build such a thing."

"Possibly."

"It's hubris."

"Just look at it."

"I can see."

"Who's he trying to impress?"

"That's the question." Rose asks Stern, "Do you think it's what he says?"

"I don't know."

"You don't know, or you don't, no?"

"I don't know if what he says is the real reason he's here."

Rose blows the dirt and sand from the binoculars by using a pocket-sized can of compressed air. He follows this with a gentle rub from a microfiber cloth and soft brush. The excessive care contrasts with the cracks in his boots and the unwashed shirts he wears until the collars fray and armpits change color.

Stern puts the folder back, takes out the Savage and tells Rose, "Time me." He breaks the gun down then reassembles it in under 23 seconds, Rose counting, "One Mississippi, two Mississippi … " As Stern finishes, Rose looks through the binoculars. Stern returns the Savage to its case and asks Rose, "Can you see him?"

"Yep."

"What's he doing?"

"Climbing."

"What?"

"There seems to be something he wants to attach to the sculpture."

Stern shades his eyes, stares straight ahead. Down below a series of rope ladders run off the armatures. Scaffolding surrounds the spine. Benchere scrambles up the wood, reaches the ropes with a sack on his back. Inside is a drill and bit, a bolt and wrench and chime he plans to connect; a wind bell he's brought from home that once was Marti's.

The climb is difficult. The ropes twist as Benchere makes his way off the scaffolding and sets his boots on the narrow rungs. *Too old*, he thinks. *Too fat*. Assigning the task to one of the younger and more agile members of the camp would have been sensible, but then Benchere has no intention of letting anyone else hang the chime.

Daimon stands below and films while Benchere works his way along. The rope sways from side to side before he reaches the top. He sets himself inside a harness, applies the bit and then secures the bolt.

Stern leans forward in his chair. Rose, too, thinks he can

hear as the wind passes through the hollow of the chime and sings out lightly. Both watch Benchere dangling above. "Quite the sight," Rose says.

"A work in progress."

"No doubt."

For a moment Benchere appears as a comet, huge and weightless and nearly in flight.

3.

DOWNSTAIRS, ONCE THE BLINDS ARE OPENED AND THE sliding glass door unlocked, Jazz sprints ahead of Benchere, navigates the back lawn out toward the woods. Benchere walks from the house along the garden path where the perennials Marti planted are in bloom; the bee balm and loosestrife, clematis, bleeding hearts and primrose. A rabbit appears and Jazz gives chase. From a distance, Benchere watches both animals dash into the woods, can hear the twigs and brushwood snapping.

IN THE DESERT, Benchere pounds hammer strokes late, marks the shell. Can't sleep. Others are now used to the sound. Jazz stays near. The lantern sends shadow larks into the field. The armatures of the sculpture stretch out. Benchere grooves the surface of the metals with a ball pein, creates patterns like scar tissue.

Daily now more people arrive in the desert. They come on foot and in jeeps, alone and in groups, in sandals and hiking boots, with suitcases, backpacks and duffles. Many treat the trek as a pilgrimage, while others show up out of curiosity, ready to revel in Benchere's celebrity and be part of the experience. The number of people in camp exceeds expectation. "Party crashers," Harper calls them. Benchere pays no attention to any of this. As best he can, he treats the growing swell as a manageable distraction.

IN THE REAR of Benchere's backyard is a sculpture made a year ago last spring. Assembled during Marti's recovery, composed of blue steel twisted together with overlapping joists, like some recusant vine in bloom, Benchere named the piece *Venus Unraveled*. Designed as a celebration of Marti's resilience, as Benchere wanted to portray her new body as a thing of beauty, *Venus* was hailed as a crowning achievement. The critic Rosalind Epstein Krauss was a fan of Benchere, referred to his discipline as corporeal intuitivism. Celebrated for creating art which provided an alternative to standard perception, dismissing form while observing the world through a lens off-center, Benchere's intended result was tougher to come by in *Venus*, was impossible to show the Marti he saw there. Still, Krauss praised his approach for taking odd shapes and turning them into something revelatory. Moved by the doggedness of his effort, Krauss described *Venus* as a devastatingly intimate piece.

"Devastating sure," Benchere gave his heavy head a shake. Skeptical now, he questioned his ability to represent Marti in the way he wanted. "It's like this," he said to Harper. "She was perfect once, and then perfect again, and how can I show that exactly? There are layers here, do you understand? People see some sort of busted angel's wing and that's not it. Do you get what I'm saying?"

Grass has grown around *Venus'* base, giving the sculpture an even more preadamic look. At auction, S.I. Newhouse purchased *Venus*. When Marti died Benchere bought the sculpture back.

THE NEW AQUATICS Center on Hope Street is only a few blocks away from the Backwater Art Academy where Benchere taught. In order to prepare physically for his trip to the desert, Benchere took up swimming, gave up overdrinking as he had done for several weeks following Marti's funeral. In the locker room, Benchere pulled off his pants and boxers, his shirt and socks, hoisted his belly and tugged on his swim trunks. He approached the pool, kicked off his deck shoes and got himself quickly into the water.

Rather than dive, he dropped down then bobbed back to the surface and began his laps. A modest swimmer, his arms and legs performed efficiently in a synchronized paddle. The water was well chlorinated. Benchere wore goggles but no cap, coordinated his strokes until they established a rhythm. Three laps in he felt the burn, distracted himself with thoughts of Marti and of his children, of Zooie and Kyle.

AFTER HIS SWIM, Benchere drove to his studio. Daimon was there, waiting to film Benchere at work. "Creative context," Daimon called it. "Whatever happens in Africa, we're going to need a preface."

Benchere's studio is an old airplane hangar just outside Tiverton, with high ceilings and a siloxane sealed concrete floor. The front wall is on wheels, the air inside neither heated nor cooled by any constructed system, but subject rather to the whims of the weather.

Benchere wore heavy gloves, a leather apron and clear facial shield. Commissioned to finish one last sculpture before Africa, he spent the morning working on a weld. The acetylene and oxygen tanks were chained together along the side wall, the regulators adjusted, the hoses attached and pressure key turned to blow out any dust. The front of Benchere's face shield was hand painted with eyebrows and a gap-toothed grin. Naveed and Julie assisted Benchere as he leaned in to the heat. The welding rod was set at 6500 degrees, sparked against the metal, while a noncombustible gas protected the vein from the air, kept the seam from oxidizing.

Once the weld was done, Benchere signaled Naveed to turn off the tanks. He holstered the rod, removed his leather apron and mask then walked out in front of the studio. Daimon put his camera back in its case, the case on a strap, the strap set around his left shoulder as he followed Benchere outside. A faint steam rose from the tarmac. Benchere brushed the remaining welding dust from his shirt. He drank bottled water, poured some for Jazz into the palm of his hand.

As a documentarian, Daimon was scrupulous in his research and preparation. In the weeks before, he had read dozens of articles and biographical notes on Benchere, made side trips to visit sculptures and see the seven *Benchere* originals firsthand. He studied the trajectory of Benchere's success after leaving L/L, his effort to win over critics and skeptics, to reinvent himself beginning with works like *Sparrow the Bird* and *Want, Spread, Heart*. He invested countless hours going through interviews, trying to understand Benchere's theories on art, his commitment to causes and the nonnegotiable line he drew between the two. Of Benchere's intent to create an enormous sculpture in the middle of the Kalahari, Daimon confessed, "It's hard to get a handle on your thinking."

"Is that right?"

"The consensus is you're going to Botswana to cause trouble."

"Define trouble."

Daimon answered, "To stir the waters."

"In the desert?"

"Metaphorically."

"The waters now," Benchere laughs. "And why would I do that?"

"I don't know. You're a political person."

"But not a political artist."

"And there's the catch."

"What catch? Why must my thinking be flawed just because you don't understand?"

Daimon stopped here, regrouped, tried to come up with a sound reply. Inside the studio Naveed swept metal shavings from near the sculpture. Julie stored the welding rod, moved the tanks against the wall. Benchere adjusted his sunglasses. Jazz paced at the end of the tarmac. Daimon turned to specifics, addressed the logistics of Benchere's trip and how "Two-thirds of the 53 nations in Africa are involved in some sort of rebellion."

"Fifty-four."

"What's that?"

"There are 54 countries now that South Sudan has split from the North."

"Right," Daimon moved into a small patch of shade. He was also tall, though not like Benchere. He tipped his head just slightly back and said, "Maybe if you told me."

"Told you what?"

"Why you're going."

"To Africa?"

"Yes."

Benchere scratched his ear. "You're asking why?"

"I am."

"Why?"

"That's right."

"No, I'm asking why should you want to know?"

"Because it would help my own work if I knew why you were going." Daimon said.

Benchere in turn, "I'm going to build a sculpture."

"Yes, but why?"

"Why what?"

"Are you going to build a sculpture?"

"Yes I am."

A grassy field lay just behind the studio, off the final runway. At the far end of the field was a shallow pond. Benchere walked around the building, called after Jazz who sprinted ahead then onto the grass. Daimon also came around, removed his camera from its case and recorded Jazz in stride.

Benchere gave the back of his neck a quick massage. His replies to Daimon were more for sport than anything. He did not mind discussing his work, or the reason for his trip, was on record as having tried to explain, even if people refused to believe him. For his final lecture at the BAA, Benchere set his huge hands against the sides of the podium and fielded questions from his students. A purist on the meditation, he taught his classes Vecchietta and Bernini, Rodin and Brancusi, Ann Christopher and Alfred Nossig, among others. When he spoke about the fundamental nature of art, he distinguished such from radical activism; his reputation as a rabble rouser, his temperament robust, his hearty whoofs and howls extreme, his irreverent blasts and iconoclastic indulgence all notwithstanding.

"Anyone can create propaganda," Benchere said. "This isn't

art. Art is not meant to be used as a form of political engagement.
Art is there to influence the individual's heart not provide radical posturing. These sledgehammer strokes aren't real art." He
regarded Goya and Picasso, Ali Weiwei, George Grosz and Marcel
Janco, Zurab Tsereteli and Duncan P. Ferguson, Jewad Selim, Vivi-
en Mallock and Shepard Fairey, as brilliant artists. "But when they
turn their work into doctrinal props, their art becomes cheesy."

"Did you say ... ?" His students asked, "What about *Guernica*
and *The Third of May 1808*?"

"They're both cheddar based."

"And *Dada*? What of 1916 Berlin, the Stieglitz Gallery in New
York, Huelsenback, Hausmann, Heartfield, Ernst and Duchamp
and Dix?"

"What about them?" Benchere agreed Dada changed the
relationship between art and its audience forever, "But the art
itself was a gimmick. Listen now," Benchere believed, "Art exists to
initiate free thought not deliver dogma." He told his students, "If
we blur the line the work becomes imperious, and then it isn't art."

Heidi Hough sat up front, absorbed in the talk, taking notes.
An eager pupil, when Benchere invited questions she immediately raised her hand and wanted to know, "Why then are you going
to Africa?"

Daimon again asked the same.

Benchere left the pavement behind his studio and mashed
down the grass which was soft from an early drizzle. "Why, why,
why?" He answered this way, his heels sinking further into the sod.
"You sound like a parrot."

"Maybe if you answered."

"And told you what?"

"Why you're going."

"But when I answer you don't believe me." Benchere looked
out at Jazz, said without turning, "Wait until we get to the Kalahari.
See if you don't understand then."

Daimon lowered his camera and followed Benchere onto the
grass. The heat after the rain moistened the back of his neck. He

waited a beat, tried to think of something else to ask, some other way to get Benchere talking. He decided on another fact-based statement, hoping to induce a response. "I suppose the Kalahari is a good choice," he said, "given the relative stability of Botswana. I mean it's not the Congo or the Sudan."

Benchere said of this no more than, "It's quiet."

"And isolated."

"Which makes you wonder why I would want to build something where no one can see it?"

"Since you bring it up."

"Why would I? What sense does it make?" Benchere turned to face Daimon once more as he said, "In terms of art, pure art, the art I hope to make, whether or not people see my work makes no difference."

Daimon tapped the center of his forehead with his middle finger, tried to force through a clear thought. Failing, he said, "I still don't get it."

"Then wait," Benchere brought his sunglasses down the bridge of his nose, leaned in and gave Daimon a wink.

Daimon adjusted the strap on his shoulder and rephrased his question. "How is it art if no one sees it?"

"Aaargh," Benchere straightened as if jolted. He grunted low in his throat, his boots in the sod causing a sucking sound as he said, "If a bear shits in the woods and you don't step in it, it's still shit, isn't it?"

Daimon tried again. "Are you saying art exists even if it's never seen?"

"Of course it exists."

"But that makes no sense. Why make art if you don't want people to see it?"

"That's a different question. And I never said I didn't want." Benchere came off the grass. "I said it wasn't necessary." He wiped the soles of his boots on the blacktop, paused to consider whether it was worth saying more, then squared to the debate, offered this as explanation, "Whether or not what I build is seen or not seen has nothing to do with it being art."

Daimon was beginning to wish he had all this on film, something he might review later and show others. He stepped back onto the pavement and asked for an example.

Benchere glanced back toward Jazz who was circling the pond but did not go in. He shifted sideways, said, "Alright," and told Daimon to consider the Aurora Borealis.

"The Northern Lights?"

"What do you know about them?"

"They're beautiful from what I've heard."

"Beautiful right, and they existed millions of years before they were ever seen by man."

"But the Northern Lights aren't art. They're a natural wonder."

"Stay with me here." Benchere asked Daimon next if he'd ever seen *Stronghold*? "Or the death masks of Frederick Delius? Or Sansovino's *Charity*?"

"No."

"Only a handful of people ever have, and yet that doesn't change what they are. Do you get what I'm saying?"

Daimon struggled to keep pace, found talking with Benchere was at times like trying to wrestle smoke. "I get what you're trying to say," he answered. "But before the Northern Lights can be called anything they have to be seen. To say *Stronghold* is beautiful implies awareness. Beauty as a concept doesn't exist without Man."

"You're wrong, Douglas," Benchere used his heel to crush the mud that came from his boot. "You sound like the Florentines convicting Galileo. The world isn't flat because you say so and beauty isn't a concept dependent on anything. Beauty simply is."

"A perception and nothing more."

"Wrong again," Benchere jabbed Daimon with his finger. "Perception is recognition. But to recognize something means it had to exist before. You can't perceive what isn't there."

"And what's there can't be perceived unless someone sees

it." Daimon found this the flaw in Benchere's argument. "When you describe something as beautiful," he said, "you're offering an impression. This is your assessment of the thing you see. Beauty's in the eye, it's not the thing itself."

"You're swimming upstream with that one." Benchere shot back, "A thing *is* regardless of who views it."

"It may exist but it can't be acknowledged."

"Who said anything about acknowledgement? We're talking about what's intrinsically there. You need to quit confusing the two." Benchere lifted his right foot, flicked his ankle and sent dirt Daimon's way.

Daimon dodged. At loggerheads, despite his best effort, he could not convince Benchere to abandon his claim. This idea of beauty and wonder existing on their own seemed more of an academic exercise, asserted as theory, while building a sculpture in the middle of the Kalahari was what? Who knew? Why go to the trouble? To what end? It made no sense.

Standing just off the sod, with the heat from the tarmac rising upward as if from some hidden furnace, Daimon recalled all he had read of Benchere as a vocal advocate for social and political causes. Why then go to Africa and build a sculpture for art's sake and nothing else? "Is there something more to it?" Daimon asked again about the Kalahari. "Why fixate on an idea that seems completely self-indulgent?"

"Jesus," Benchere tossed up his hands and told Daimon, "Stop thinking so much, you're going to hurt yourself." He called for Jazz then started around to the front of the studio. Naveed was inside talking with Julie, his arms behind his back as he leaned his head in closely. Julie smiled, then laughed and touched Naveed's arm. Benchere reached the open door just as Naveed was whispering something new to Julie. He stopped and stared, thought of Marti standing in the same spot not so very long ago and the conversations they shared together.

Julie laughed again. Benchere stretched his hands, rubbed his chin, massaged his neck which remained stiff from the earlier weld. He felt what ached, what had settled there beneath the skin. Once, for a weekend, Benchere flew with Marti to Atlantic City. He left her briefly in the casino and went for a drink. When he came back to the floor, the carnival scene of lights and smoke and people chattering and hurrying about the room, the bells and cheers and groans from winners and losers, monopolized Benchere's view and made it hard for him to find his wife.

He walked around the slots, past the tables for roulette and craps and blackjack. His search triggered his imagination, caused him to see everything as a wilderness; the layout foreign, each turn leading him to something infinitely more regressive and unexpected. It was all harmless at first, and yet the longer he went without being able to find Marti the more troubled he became. Where was she? What had happened? He went so far as to think that he had maybe somehow invented her, that everything was a figment, his feelings a dream with its own face and heart and history. What if she didn't actually exist? What if everything was a creation he had conjured out of thin air?

The prospect unnerved him. How could Marti not exist when everything Benchere felt was so obviously real? Was it even possible for these emotions to survive on their own? Didn't love require some physical host in which to take hold? Or was the opposite true, that love – like art and beauty – existed independently and people were destined to spend their lives searching out a place for it to root?

When Benchere did at last find Marti, sitting there at one of the far slots, her hand exercising the lever, her face a study in sweet concentration as the lights off the screen illuminated her cheeks, Benchere experienced a great wave of relief and let out a loud, "Aaaahh!"

Daimon caught up, held his camera against his side so it wouldn't swing and bang into his hip. He looked at Benchere, at Julie and Naveed and back again. A plane lifted off two runways down and a white tail trail of smoke appeared in the sky. Benchere grabbed a towel from near the door and began wiping the mud from Jazz's paws and belly. Finished, he tossed the towel into the studio. Daimon was set to resume their earlier conversation, but something in Benchere's expression caused him to stop. He avoided asking more questions, spoke instead in supportive terms, did not mention Marti but said rather, "Whatever you're up to, I'm still looking forward."

"Are you?"

"Sure. *Cinéma vérité.* We'll figure it out as we go."

Benchere pushed his sunglasses back, stared at the sky, the blue of it there beneath the smoky scar not yet faded. Cued by Daimon's confidence and keenness, he said in reply, "The trick to figuring things out there Douglas, is not getting too far in front. Circumstances change more often than not and consequences extend well beyond our ability to predict them." Benchere pulled the keys from his pocket and shook them for Jazz.

Daimon watched Jazz run to the car. He understood Benchere's latest pearl was meant as a caution, and yet, having filmed in Xinjiang and Chechnya and other hostile places, he wasn't concerned and repeated, "I'm still looking forward."

"Ha now!" With his back turned, crossing the tarmac, Benchere waved his hand and said, "Fair enough. For the record though, Dennis, we're all looking forward. It's a conditioned response. Unavoidable. We do it even when we think we're not."

4.

INSIDE HIS TENT, BENCHERE SITS LATE. THE OTHERS IN
camp are asleep, or nearly so. Jazz stretches and settles down.
The lantern is dimly lit. Benchere looks at the light for the longest
time, stares until the glow becomes the only thing he can see. He
reaches then and turns it off.

STERN IN THE morning stands atop the hill, watches for signs
of life below. Far to the north, in South Sudan, air raids blast the
hillsides, flatten Abyei, displace more than 100,000 people. In
Nigeria, in the Central African Republic and Chad, rebel forces
clash with government troops. Humanitarian groups, including
the British agency Oxfam, have packed and fled. Rather than report
these incidents, the press prefers to issue updates on Benchere's
project. They cover his story from the perspective of his celebrity,
offer suggestive narratives, fuel the public's curiosity while pre-
tending to fill a need.

"Reporters," Rose says.

"Lazy lot."

"Good for nothing."

"Good for a laugh."

"I blame this whole socialist network."

"Social," Stern corrects.

"Say what?"

"It's social, not socialist."

"Ahh," Rose takes the binoculars from Stern, gives a wry smile and leaves it at that.

A MONTH BEFORE setting up camp in the Kalahari, Harper flew to Africa in order to finalize logistics. An experienced traveler, Harper rented a plane in Maun and flew himself to Kalkfontein. From there he drove south toward Tshane. Directions to camp were mapped, drivers hired and equipment rented from the list Benchere provided from his previous visit.

At the end of his trip, Harper came back through the desert, crossed the border east of Aminuis, detoured into Namibia and the Windhoek Hotel where he planned to unwind before flying home. The Windhoek was an oasis supported by high-end safaris and wealthy adventurers. A casino ran off the lobby. Harper won $416 drawing ten to his jack and queen. He made friendly talk with a woman from Walvis Bay who joined him in his room for a nightcap.

Shedding clothes, they fell into bed where the woman gagged and suddenly became sick. Harper leaped up, helped her to the bathroom before she could barf on the sheets. The rapid onset of her affliction seemed suspicious. Harper imagined someone in the casino spotting him win the cash, and slipping him and the woman an emetic, waiting now to enter the room and rob him. A goddamn *tsotsi*. Worse has been done for less.

In the bathroom, Harper held the woman's head as she puked fetid chunks. "Fuck me," he cursed, then laughed to himself at the supplication. The woman groaned and wiped her mouth. Harper assessed his own symptoms, found that he was fine. As a precaution, prior to traveling, he took all the preventative medicines; Avloclor and proguanil, mefloquine and Malarone. If not an emetic, he hoped the woman's illness was simply a bad meal, not dysentery or malaria, an infection from the bilharzias in the water or a reaction to a parasite. He went to the sink and rinsed his face. The water was cool. He was tempted to drink but knew better. Even at the Windhoek, Africa unfiltered was not a good idea.

He sat down beside the woman and stretched his legs. The

air smelled sour. He thought about the days ahead, about returning to Africa and helping Benchere with his project. When they
first met, more than twenty years ago, Harper was running junkets
out of TF Green for Kelly Transport, doing jumps to Boston, Con-
necticut, Philly and New York. Benchere was newly flush, his sudden celebrity fattening his wallet. Harper flew him up and down
the coast, drank with him on overnight stops. They became bud-
dies, shared a certain anarchistic sensibility, began hanging out
in Tiverton, in Providence and Warwick and New Bedford, where
Harper confided his idea to open his own charter business.

Benchere made a few calls. Coastway Community Bank
agreed to loan Harper the capital for a Piper Saratoga if Benchere
co-signed the note. All these years later and Harper still had the
plane. HighLine Transit now included a Douglas DC-3, a King Air
C90B, and a Cessna Caravan 675. Three HighLine pilots handled
cargo and passenger transport, each licensed for single and dual
props, multi-engine and piston/turbine. Harper flew the larger
crafts himself, was FAA and JAA certified, planned on using the
Douglas to ferry supplies for Benchere into Botswana.

The woman called Harper's name in a voice that sounded
like a sick cat's whimper. Harper heard her stomach growl. The
discs of her spine were visible through her flesh as she hunched
over. She shifted from her knees and put her bare ass on the floor.
Harper wished he had some paregoric to offer. He helped her up
and left the bathroom as she took care of new business.

Tomorrow he intended to fly home, would return in a few
weeks with Benchere. As much as possible, all the arrangements
for the desert were set. Harper found his cigarettes and the open
bottle of Rhum Clément, smoked while waiting for the woman to
finish. The chain on the toilet rattled and soon the shower ran in
the bathroom. Harper scratched at his nakedness. "Crazy this," he
considered the story he'd tell when he got back to the States. Everything served as a prelude to something else. He turned the handle
on the door, tossed his cigarette into the toilet and gave himself up
to what remained of his evening.

ZOOIE ON TOUR. Road warrior. The 23rd of 27 gigs. All 8,000 miles covered in a GMC Savana. After playing the Acoustic Café, Zooie drove down I-95, parked at a rest stop near Bridgeport. Tomorrow she would play DeSoto's in West Virginia. Small venues. On her own, six months after Marti died, she was learning to create distance.

The toilets at every stop smelled of Sanizide, Clorox and urine. In order to save money, Zooie slept in her van. Safe enough she told Benchere when he called and offered to pay for her lodging. A Motel 6 was better than the side of the highway, Benchere said but Zooie refused. Intractable. A Benchere trait. She had her father's spirit, an artist's resilience and preference for adventure over practical concerns. Physically she was more her mother, a slender spring curved through the hips and shoulders, her hands animated as quicksilver. When she spoke her words gathered speed, and when she laughed her eyes stayed wide and watchful.

The shocks on the Savana absorbed little of the road's rough patches. With her were two guitars, an air mattress and pillow, a 34-inch Louisville slugger, one cow bell and a box of her first CD: *Closed Exits*. Of the 750 copies pressed Zooie had sold 212. She did radio interviews in each new city, gave her CD to station managers with the hope of getting airplay. *Quid pro quo.* They invited her for drinks and to see what else she had to offer.

All the miles between gigs were a meditation. On the dashboard, Zooie taped a photograph of Marti. Last week in Pittsburg, slightly drunk, she scratched Marti's name on her arm using the end of a spare guitar string. Each letter appeared on her skin in a puffy pink pattern, settled there for days, traced over until the mark began to scab. Zooie took a picture of her arm and sent it to Kyle who texted in reply, warned against infection.

Just outside Stamford, Zooie's cellphone rang. She checked the number then let it go to voicemail. Daily now, Pete Rayne called and tried to coo in Zooie's ear. A trust fund poet, aspirant of Auden and Ashberry, peddler of promise, Zooie's ex was forever boasting of the verse he'd write, the books he'd publish and teaching jobs he'd get. Tired of the chatter and lip service claims, Zooie ended the affair. In acapella, she sang Roy Orbison's *It's Over.* Rayne could not believe. Convinced everything would be alright once Zooie got home, he tracked her tour on a map of the east coast, asked each time he phoned, "How's the weather? Is there still a chance for Rayne?"

DEYNA IN THE desert paces past the northernmost beam of the sculpture. Bare shouldered, her skin browned, she turns after thirty yards and studies the placement of the foundation deep beneath the shifting surface sands.

KYLE SLEPT AT Cloie's, huddled on a mattress sunk in the center. The springs squealed whenever they made love. Sweating and clinging afterward, folded together and wrapped about as if dropped from a great height, their breathing settled into a binary loop of soft sighs, became synchronized as they drifted off.

In the morning, Kyle showered first. Cloie wore a cotton slipover with spaghetti strings, her skin the color of soft aspen wood; a mixed shade, her mother from Caracas, her dad from Cranston. Cloie's eyes were deep set, intelligent. Native to the south side, the Gabriel Projects, Roger Williams Middle School and South High, Elmwood and Broad Street, RI Hospital, Thurbers, Prairie and Pavilion Avenues, Cloie aspired to a particular matriculation. Concentrating on the prize, she earned PELL grants and a scholarship to Brown. A grad student now in Public Policy, her doctoral thesis on the Providence Plan, she met Kyle last winter at a fundraiser for CWRI – Community Works Rhode Island. Kyle flirted with her until she let him buy her a drink. She waited two weeks before kissing him, then said, "Your tongue tastes like cardamom."

The sun through the window lit half the apartment's floor. Kyle came from the shower and toweled off in the warmth. Tall like his father, more leanly muscled, his arms and legs a taut stretch of jute rope, his hands large and wet hair brushed back, Kyle worked as a project specialist at Maeur Development. His degree was in

Urban Planning, his area of interest the reclamation of South Providence. Single-minded, he looked to wrestle the streets toward repair. Like Marti, Kyle believed in function and form, was more pragmatic than Benchere and Zooie. He met regularly with the City Planning Commission and the Department of P&D, discussed strategies for building better housing, better schools, an efficient infrastructure and reliable revenue stream.

Shortly after 8:00 a.m., Kyle left the apartment and took the stairwell down. The walls inside the Gabriel Project were green with red and yellow lettered graffiti, the trash a mix of pop cans and empty bags of chips, cigarette butts, cotton and tinfoil and burned matches. The heat remained inside the apartments like a sour steam. Kyle crossed the grounds and headed toward his car. A few men were already out front, waiting for a breeze. They watched Kyle pass, saw him each morning now in his suit and tie and said as he got near, "Who you here for, Chief? You sure you're not a cop?"

Kyle laughed and cut across the cement. Sniffing the air as if some scent had him on high alert, he asked, "You smell that? It smells like updog."

The others looked at one another, then back at Kyle and said in unison, "Updog? What's updog?"

"Nothing men," Kyle answered. "What's up with you?"

AT THE BACKWATER Art Academy during spring and summer sessions, students who stayed on campus lived communally in the dorm. Occupied during the day with their sculpting and painting and attending class, they interacted in a collective free-for-all at night, shifting and switching rooms with no doors locked.

Mindy Koyle sketched a picture of Doran Seade inside her room. Doran posed with his tendril arms bent upward, exposing the outline of ribs beneath the near-translucent flesh of his chest. "You're beautiful," Mindy said. Doran smiled and held his pose. Heidi Hough squeezed yellow and green paint onto a large double-thread canvas. The paints were Winsor & Newton acrylics with polymer emulsion. A professional blend. The canvas was a Penelope, laid out in the center of the floor, filling the space between the two beds in Heidi's room. Naked, Heidi rolled through the colors, her shoulders and hips initiating contact with the canvas. She turned onto her belly, pressing flat in a snake-like undulation while the paints beneath her streaked and converged.

Sam Lear specialized in computer-generated art, used an active matrix liquid crystal to accent the pixels; addressing the tactile and corporeal representationally through lights and shadows. The invitation to work with Heidi took Sam out of his element. Lying flat, he maneuvered his hands through the paints, reached and stroked and occasionally brushed up against Heidi while Nan Tyrel filmed.

Heidi's plan was to have Sam take the digital material from Nan and produce fifteen separate one-inch holographic fragments using TFT LCD screens with 4GB of integrated flash memory. The screens would be inserted into the finished canvas as unique loops of action, each lasting ten seconds before repeating. The final canvas would be entered in the BAA's summer contest, where the winner received airfare to work with Benchere in Africa.

The light overhead was a series of white bulbs. The walls a cinderblock painted beige. Heidi's hair was colored red and green. As a student of Benchere, she had studied the Tinga Tinga paintings, Gideon Chidongo, Marlene Dumas and the Makonde sculptures. She read articles addressing the conflicts in Zimbabwe, Somalia and the Sudan. The nudity used to create her painting was explained in donnish terms as, "A way to present the innocence of the human condition as it once was in Africa a million years before."

In close proximity to Heidi, Sam's cock became engorged. Nan laughed and applied more paint. Heidi had her back turned, her head tossed so that her hair struck Sam's face. Rising on her elbow, she checked the canvas in order to determine if they were done. All the paints had run together nicely, every inch of the canvas coated. The result showed the motion of shifting cheeks, chests and knees. Heidi got up while Sam remained on the floor. Unable to stand just yet, he tried covering himself but had little success. He stared at Heidi, the paint on her breasts and bush only making her nakedness more intoxicating.

"Look at you," Heidi noticed and laughed at the extension of Sam's cock. She came and knelt back on the floor. Sam clenched his jaw as Heidi joked about his being a stand-up guy and that she appreciated how hard he worked on the painting. When she reached for him, he shivered. A spontaneous reaction, his painted protuberance aquiver, he wound up adding a final touch to the canvas that could not be helped.

HALFWAY HOME FROM his studio, Benchere stopped at Crossroad Liquors on Bulgarmarsh for a bottle of Turkey and a bag of nuts. "Hair of the dog," he said to Jazz as he got back in the car. Paul Simon's *The Boy in the Bubble* played on the radio. Benchere had no singing voice, had not been in the mood for song in months, but the tune got him thinking about Marti's first trip to Africa and he found himself crooning, *"It was a slow day/And the sun was beating/On the soldiers by the side of the road."*

Years ago, Marti spent a month working with Engineers for Humanity, building water wells outside Serowe, assisting developers on a midsize apartment complex in Ibadan, and correcting the structural flaws of an old clothing factory in Gaborone. Benchere stayed in Tiverton with Zooie and Kyle. Inspired by Marti's enterprise, upon her return he accepted offers to join several new groups, including PinSSE – People in Support of Social Equality – and CARR – the Coalition Advocating Rwanda Relief.

Late in the summer of 1994, Mayor Vincent "Buddy" Cianci, Jr. invited Benchere to help organize a committee looking to bring new business to Providence. A stocky, flat-faced, toupee-wearing Goldwater Republican, with populist support and conservative views, Buddy had the pale patchy skin of an onion eater and the voice of a cracked hinge. At a dinner on the upper-east side, Buddy wore a Platinum Pearlmaster Rolex and a silk Roberto Cavalli tie.

He drank Glenfiddich whiskey, spoke briefly about business then changed the subject and pitched Benchere on the idea of building a sculpture along the waterfront.

"Anything you want. I leave that to you." He offered, "Cash money. We won't use tax dollars, I promise," at this Buddy laughed. The sculpture, he said, would help draw favorable notice to his campaign for re-election. A supportive gesture, Buddy told Benchere, "I won't forget this, Mike. Cooperation goes a long way. Ours is a system of debit. Favors get favored and backs get scratched."

"Do they now?" Benchere raised up high in his chair as if to inspect Buddy from behind. Coming home, he told Marti of Buddy's request. "Can of crap is what it is." He tossed his jacket and untucked his shirt, repeated what he had said at dinner. "My sculptures aren't stage props. I'm no monkey trained. I don't per-form for the highest bid. If Cianci wants promotional endorsement for his political career he can buy bumper stickers and billboards like everyone else."

Marti lay in bed reading. The argument was familiar. Benchere's rant ran along consistent lines each time he turned down a commission; refusing to work with organizations who sought to exploit his sculptures for political use. He quoted Oscar Wilde: "A work of art is the unique result of a unique tempera-ment ... (T)he moment an artist takes notice of what other peo-ple want, and tries to supply the demand, he ceases to be an artist, and becomes a dull or an amusing craftsman." On this point he was hard to move off. Marti closed her book. Whatever sympathy she had for Benchere's resistance, she questioned his logic when it came to reducing the stage for his art, and reminded him here, "Buddy said you could make whatever you want."

"Did he?"

"You just told me."

"Doesn't matter."

"Think now," Marti said. "Consider what you're rejecting. A sculpture by the waterfront."

Benchere went, "Bah." He dropped his trousers and strutted around in his drawers.

Marti groaned. Such childishness, she thought. Benchere's attitude, his firm conviction and absolute certainty as it pertained to his art, was all singular by design. Not that she didn't find his devotion endearing. His love was the same; innocent and absolute. As an engineer, Marti's system of faith relied on rules meant to offer security and stability, while Benchere's favored edict was that rules could not be trusted. Between them, they effected a balance. Marti kicked back the sheets, wiggled her toes and said, "Buddy wouldn't have contacted you if he didn't respect you as an artist."

"That's a stretch." Benchere maintained, "Buddy isn't interested in my art. He only wants to use my name."

"You're being stubborn."

"Am I?"

"An artist has to be aware of his public." Marti asked Benchere to tell her, "What would be so bad about doing a sculpture for the city?"

"You mean other than Buddy?"

"Forget Buddy," Marti stared at Benchere as if he was ignoring something essential. "Just think about the people," she said. "What you need is to build a sculpture so amazing no one thinks about Buddy at all."

Benchere walked to the bathroom, gave the suggestion some thought only to come back again and say, "It doesn't matter what I make, Buddy will claim it."

"So let him. People aren't going to care about Buddy when they look at your work." Marti turned her pillows upright and shifted back against the headboard. Benchere bent over and gave his back a stretch. Marti waited until he was standing straight again, his big body bear-like in the center of their room. Knowing she had little chance to win this debate, having played this game before without luck, she asked nonetheless, "What would happen if you made a sculpture in support of someone or something you actually liked?"

"Liked?"

"Liked. Like Greenpeace, or Tom Harken. Would it be so bad? What if you made one for Gerry Brown or, I don't know, the National African Congress?"

"The *NAC*?" Benchere's position didn't change. "It would be the same regardless," he said. "It's still not art. It's hype and dogma either way."

"Art," Benchere tossed his hands up in the air, shouted and beat his chest as if words alone could not do justice.

Marti laughed at the spectacle. "Ahh Benchere," she hooted again and patted his side of the bed. "What am I to do with you now?"

The following spring, Marti created a duel-mass supplementary damping system for the Bloomberg Tower in New York. The system stabilized the structure's 54 floors, its glass façade, six-story canoidal skylight and backlit mechanical screenwalls; offsetting movement caused by high winds, quakes and tremors. Proud of her effort, Marti said to Benchere, "How's that for art?"

"Ha!" Benchere dismissed Marti's use of the term, referred to her industry as calculated efficiency, said, "Function is a stogy old bench sitter. Art is what puts the muscle in your arm. Without art there's no Bloomberg. Art is your leap of faith, your imagination brought to life. Art is the only thing original in all your narrow treatments."

"Did you just say?" Marti's amusement became something else. "There's nothing narrow about giving people a safe place to live and work. How does art help with that?"

"Let me tell you," Benchere turned the question around and said, "If practical concerns were all that mattered, this would not be much of a life, now would it, love?" He stepped closer, brought Marti into his meaty arms and held her tight.

AS SOON AS the front door opened, Jazz dashed down the hall to the den, from the den to the stairs, up and down again, still expecting to find Marti. A habit now, he circled through each room, cut across the wood and tiles until some buried dog memory kicked in and he remembered.

Benchere went into the kitchen and made a drink. His own habit, he stood by the island in silence and waited for ghosts.

The house was open arches, cavernous, a grand sense of space, the roof beams raised high. Marti favored earth tones and Benchere had included Brazilian cumaru wood, stone inlays cut for the fireplace, additional limestone for the patio and, terra-cotta tiles in the bath and sauna. The island in the center of the kitchen was a Madura gold granite. The table cherry wood.

On the shelf above the sink were Marti's pills, the Anastrozole and clonazepam, tamoxifen, pain meds and digestive aids, homeopathies and hardcore pharmaceuticals; a potpourri of would-be curatives. Benchere left the meds as they were, left Marti's clothes and books, notes handwritten and hanging from a magnet on the fridge, her slippers and soaps, magazines and voice on the message machine. "We're not here to take your call ... "

He played the message, thought how purgatory wasn't really a property of the afterlife, where dead souls waited in the grey for a final determination on their eternal selves, but rather the paralytic pause those left behind stood and stuttered through during moments like this.

"Aargh." Benchere kicked his left leg straight out, breathed in twice deeply, mocked himself for throwing such a pity party, then jogged around the island and back into the hall. An African mask hung near the stairs. A gift from Marti's friend, Jev Butar. Benchere gave the mask a quick look, began walking back toward the den. He was thinking how, in Africa, the Kalahari translated as *the big thirst*, when Kyle opened the front door carrying two bags of Chinese and a long cardboard tube.

Kyle called for Benchere, left the tube against the front wall, brought the food into the kitchen. For several weeks now, following the fall and then the winter, in what was for everyone a period of adjustment, once Benchere convinced Zooie to go back on tour, Kyle began bringing dinner out to Tiverton each Wednesday. The gesture was appreciated. Kyle took his suit jacket off, rolled the sleeves to his dress shirt nearly to his elbows. He was, at twenty-seven, a long wire framed by lean shoulder muscle. Composed of contradictions, he was both eager and evaluating, practical and unrealistic, fully subscribed to the value of function and form yet impatient with his expectations. As a boy all the universal wonders amazed Kyle and he wound up overwhelmed by the abundance of possibilities. He developed a tic, contemplated his every move as if the slightest mistake might prove fatal; went from building castles and model cities with Marti to spending months in a sullen retreat.

When that stage at last passed, Kyle came out the other side with a renewed sense of purpose. Athletic, he won awards, was recruited for lacrosse, played and studied at Providence where he explored his interest in Marti's work as it applied to urban planning. A romantic, though he would deny, at Maeur Development he presented ideas for rebuilding the south side. Idealistic in his application, he relied on leaps of faith, his self-buoyance and liberal determination delighting Benchere and allowing him to love his son with something bordering on glee.

They spoke over egg rolls and orange chicken. Kyle asked about *Helix at Rest*, the sculpture Benchere was working on at his studio, was to finish before Africa. The commission was from the Pare-Mathus Institute, the unveiling scheduled for next week. For a while they spoke of Zooie, compared notes, weaved in stories about Marti. Throughout they checked to see how the other was doing. As Kyle knew there was no chance of changing Benchere's mind about Botswana, he no longer tried. The adventure was needed, the project a part of providing, if not closure, a final offering. Kyle had seen the design for the work Benchere and Marti dreamed up, had joked with Zooie, imagined the sculpture in the desert and said, "Goddamn."

Benchere added ice to his drink. He asked about Cloie, about Kyle's project on Prairie Avenue, the one he had partnered with Carla DeStefano, executive director of SWAP – Stop Wasting Abandoned Properties – to convert the old Federated Lithographers into a public health clinic. Inspired by the theories of Oscar Newman, Peter Eisenman, and Sergio Palleroni's BaSiC Initiative for sustainable communities, the clinic was an extension of Kyle's attempt to develop new housing below Broadway. In the last year, Kyle had worked with Carla and Maeur Development, among others, to refurbish no less than eight facilities for new housing projects.

A noble plan. Benchere supported Kyle's effort yet questioned the wisdom of concentrating on housing first. "To pay for properties people need jobs."

"Sure, but to bring businesses back to the south side we have to rebuild the infrastructure."

"That's bass-akwards." Benchere enjoyed having the debate as a form of diversion from his night. "You can't rebuild without people working," he said.

"That's not true." Kyle insisted, "The jobs will come when the housing's in place."

"Eggs and chickens," Benchere shot his elbows out like wings.

Kyle rolled his eyes, turned to statistics in order to make his point. "The demand for low income housing in Rhode Island is up 365 percent over the last five years," he said.

"Because there are no jobs," Benchere tapped the table three times with his middle finger. "Your point proves mine."

Kyle in dissent said, "It doesn't at all. The truth is housing will stimulate the area toward productive growth."

"It's wishful thinking."

"It's progressive planning."

"A house of cards."

"Not hardly. It's a process." Kyle was certain, "The larger companies, the regional stores and manufacturers, even the mom and pop shops will return once we rebuild."

The gap in Kyle's claim seemed glaring. Benchere wasn't used to being the voice of reason, but felt a paternal need to make his position clear. "Listen," he said, "mom and pop aren't coming if people don't have money to spend. If people aren't working, the places you build won't rent. And if the places don't rent, you're sunk. The loans you take out to build will come due and then what? A shit storm."

"If if if and what what what," Kyle sang. "Since when did that ever stop you from doing what you thought best?" He stabbed at his chicken. Such debates with Benchere were a challenge as they required both factual support and a need to be clever. Everything was timing and delivery, when to engage and when to pull back. Kyle leaned forward and recited the developer's edict, "You have to build things to change things. Look at Harlem, Tampa and Cleveland," he drew comparison, provided a list of other cities that had made a similar comeback.

"What do I know about Cleveland?" Benchere conceded as much, refused to argue and focused instead on additional concerns. Experience had taught him, "Function guarantees nothing. When you build things there are lots of moving parts and people looking for ways to cash in." Years ago, while still working at *L/L* and wanting to offer something back to the city, Benchere was asked to help design a project on Thurbers Avenue. The facility, a twelve-story high rise both subsidized and privately funded, was meant to offer affordable apartments to low-income families.

The complex was championed in the press, hailed as an alternative to the more dangerous projects out on Roger Williams Green and near Cranston. Naïve then, focused on completing the work, Benchere failed to take into account the back door deals, the contractors and subcontractors skimming from the budget, using cheaper materials in their work, paying off inspectors who further compromised the integrity of the design. Less than two weeks after Angle Rite Apartments opened, a six-year-old girl named Natashi Moore fell to her death when the screws mounting the fire escape to the brick broke free.

"Did I tell you she was six?" Benchere could not get over. Here was what came from putting one's faith in function and form.

Kyle had heard the story before, said in reply, "There's

always a risk in every deal. The tragedy's not in our effort. You know that." He lifted his fork and told Benchere, "If you're really worried about us, why don't you help?"

"Help?"

"You know the row houses we're developing on Broad Street?"

"I know them."

Kyle said, "Carla and I thought you could look over the design, let SWAP attach your name as a consultant and sell the project with your endorsement."

"Wait," Benchere stared back across the table. "Slow down there, captain. You want me to do what now?"

"If you're concerned about us selling the spots."

"You want to use my name?" Benchere moved his plate to one side, hoisted his hands behind his neck and said, "You realize I don't do designs anymore."

"We're not interested in a design. Just a touch or two."

The request came from the blindside, caused Benchere to sort through all possible answers. Kyle knew what Benchere was thinking and addressed the matter directly. "I'm not asking for a sculpture," he said. "This is business. It's leverage. Putting your name on the project is resourceful. It's practical. It's just that." He slid his dish next to Benchere's and left the kitchen, went out to the hall, returned with the tube which he carried into the den and leaned against the desk. Coming back to the kitchen, he said of the tube, "I can pick it up in a few days, either way."

In the den after Kyle left, Benchere stood near the glass door and looked for Jazz. The moon overhead was orange-silver, the flowers in the garden yellow and blue. Jazz trotted along the edge, seemed to know not to disrupt what Marti had planted. Benchere turned and went to where Kyle had left the tube. He stared for a minute, imagined the reaction from the press and others if he resumed any sort of design work after all these years. What a twist. The question was one of probity, of whether lending his name to Kyle's project was different than the restrictions he applied to his art. That Kyle had never asked a favor of him like this before did not so much clarify the situation as provide the tipping point. "Ahh hell." The decision became foregone. Benchere tossed his head back and laughed.

He finished his drink, opened the door and whistled for Jazz. Reaching then, he went and popped the lid on the tube and slid the contents out. The prints unrolled across the desk. The design showed sixteen row houses, two sets of eight units facing one another on a single block. Benchere noted their plainness, considered what was needed. Using a white marker he revised the positive and negative space, applied informed simplicity and the solid void theory to reconfigure the entrances, moved columns to enhance the circulation path, reconciled complex patterns into one coherent arrangement, adjusted the program/core space and reevaluated the rooms for light.

The job took less than thirty minutes. Even after all this time Benchere's ability to visualize structural design came easily. He signed his name on the side of the prints, slipped them back into the tube and leaned the tube against the wall. *Done and done.* All he had to do now was ask Kyle to keep quiet until he'd left for Africa so he didn't have to deal with anyone making more of things than they should.

Jazz came from drinking water in the kitchen. Benchere moved to the center of the room, stood listening to the silence of the house. He pictured Marti in bed, told himself she was there and then that she wasn't. There was a Joni Mitchell song that Zooie sang, "Down to You." *Everything comes and goes* ... Benchere knew the first verse. He went back to the open door, stuck his head outside and howled. Jazz came over. The breeze from the yard warmed Benchere's cheek. He closed the door and pulled the blinds. Bending down, he picked up Marti's slippers, walked back through the hall, turned off old lights and felt along the wall for new ones.

5.

IN THE KALAHARI, ATOP THE HIGHEST BEAM, THE WIND moves the chime recently set. The sociable weaver birds fly through the beams and check out the source of the sound.

BENCHERE IN THE morning woke and swam. Halfway through his laps Marti asked, *Are you ready?*

Am I ... ? He gave the question some thought, arms over shoulders and belly down in the water, legs set to kick as he turned and churned back through his wake.

STERN STANDS ATOP the hill, peers down and says to Rose, "Look at it, will you."

Rose stares as well, hesitates then says to Stern, "Yep."

LEAVING NAMIBIA, HARPER flew the red-eye home. Sixteen hours from point to point. He bought paregoric as a preventative, determined to keep his belly from souring the way the woman's had back at the hotel. The dose he took did the trick, inspired sweet opium dreams out over the Atlantic.

ON HER WAY from Beckley, Zooie drove north along Route 119. Seven weeks on tour. A long time gone. She sang, "It's been ... "

Her two final gigs were in State College on Friday and at Maxwell's in Jersey Saturday night. Rayne took the train down, showed up to surprise Zooie while she performed. She resented him for coming, his arrogance and persistence. Still, when her final set ended, she went with him to the room he'd rented. The walls were soft green. The bed king-sized. The carpet plush. There was a mahogany framed mirror and flowers in a red vase.

Rayne waited to see if Zooie was pleased, then pulled her toward him, moved her hair and kissed her as she let him. She kissed back for no reason other than she wanted to feel something. On tour she'd abstained from sex, did not indulge with any of the other musicians, the club managers or men from the audience who came on to her. Kissing Rayne was different, was casual now, reminded her of things that had nothing to do with him.

In bed, Rayne tried to talk but Zooie told him to be quiet. His desires were not her concern, his expectations not her responsibility. She let him do things he knew she liked. No guesswork, their time together worth something. She closed her eyes, anticipated, was interested only in the payoff, the shiver shake that came as she did.

Rayne slept deeply after that. Zooie dozed. When she woke the early light in the room was sandy grey. She found her clothes, found her way to the door, opened quietly and went out. Back on the interstate, she pictured Rayne waking and waiting for her. *Silly boy*. What did he expect? She decided to text him in an hour, took I-95 further north and made it home before Harper.

DEYNA DRINKS WITH friends at McCabe's Tavern in Colorado Springs. A professor of anthropology at the University of the Rockies, she teaches graduate level courses when not in the field. Tomorrow she leaves on sabbatical, is eager to depart. The semester has left her antsy, she feels more at home on the road. Peripatetic by nature, and now by occupation, she has lived in Haiti, in Mesopotamia and Iran, has studied the Indus Civilization and its earliest incantation of urban planning pre-2000 BCE, has done peyote beneath a Tibetan moon with Paul Farmer, explored cultural phenomena with Marko Lebel, lived with a Russian poet in Minsk, been drunk on dandelion wine while conducting research on the

Sumerian Settlement in Iraq, tended to the broken femur of a colleague while visiting the Bnot Ya'akov Bridge on the banks of the Jordan River, avoided seductive advances from Naama Goren-Inbar while charting the social significance of man's move from Africa through the Levantine corridor. Lately, she has spent additional time in Africa, studying the San Bushmen and Ju/'hoansi of northwest Botswana, has postponed offers to continue her research this summer as she's become intrigued by something else.

A toast to her travels. A friend tells a joke about an anthropologist working in South America who is told by a tribal *brujo* that the leaves of a particular fern are a natural cure for constipation. The anthropologist had his doubts, though the *brujo* insisted, "Let me tell you, with fronds like these, who needs enemas?"

The first time Deyna heard of Benchere's plan to build a sculpture in the middle of the Kalahari, she also thought it was a joke. She pictured the San coming upon a 300-foot tall monolith in the flat of the desert and what would they think? There are over 47,000 San in Botswana, each living in small cooperative groups, nomadic in their search for water. A San village is rarely more than 60 people. Deyna lives on her own. The apartment she keeps near campus has her bed and books and stereo, some dishes in the kitchen, the tools of her trade packed and ready. The last lover she lived with left almost a year ago. Despite her professional training to evaluate the past, Deyna rarely thinks of him anymore.

She offers a toast of her own, "Here's to experience." In the Kalahari, she will be close enough to the San to resume her research should she choose. She has read additional stories about Benchere, older interviews and newer articles over the last six months. Curious, she can only imagine in a broader context what sort of impact a sculpture like this will have; autonomous in its construct, independent in its intent. She has also read about Marti, and again of Benchere, has weighed the potential for what will come, made arrangements and in the morning flies to Maun.

BENCHERE WORKS WITH Naveed and Julie putting Helix at
Rest on a flatbed truck for delivery to the Pare-Mathus Institute.
The unveiling is scheduled for Saturday. The forklift Julie borrowed
is painted bright orange, has an automatic alarm which sounds
each time the gears are put in reverse. Benchere backs the truck
into place, then helps Naveed keep the sculpture balanced as Julie
raises the lift and slides Helix into the bed.

"Everything that rises," Benchere says and grunts against
the sculpture's weight.

Before he traveled to Africa for the first time, Benchere had
a dream about the desert. This was after Marti first became sick.
He saw himself there alone, the wildebeests and hyenas watching,
the vastness of the Kalahari making even someone as large as he
feel small. He wandered in search of what he could not be sure, the
sense of something missing so acute that when he woke and found
Marti beside him, he wailed with relief.

Two nights later, he presented his plan. "Here's what I'm
thinking," he said and spoke of the desert, expressed a desire to
merge their talents, both sculpting and engineering, to create in
tandem an *objet d'art*. Desperate to not lose Marti, still haunted by
the fear from his dream snaking its way through him like a shiver cold shot, Benchere convinced himself as long as he and Marti
were working together no harm would come to her. The plan was a
fiction at best. He did not confess this part, went ahead and draft-
ed a sketch of a sculpture that would stand above the desert like
the myth of Akhenaten.

Marti reviewed the dimensions, calculated the size and
weight, resolved the bracing of the armatures, how to balance the
base and set the foundation as firm as the roots of a ziziphus tree.
Since first volunteering with Engineers for Humanity and aug-
menting the water wells, Marti had gone back twice to Africa. She
had always wanted Benchere to come with her and visit the spots.
Ready now, Benchere and Marti together began to prepare.

All went as planned until Marti's cancer returned, forcing
them to postpone their trip. Benchere took the news poorly, insist-

ed at first there must be some mistake. Ultimately, he regrouped and addressed the reality, got Marti through treatment, through surgery and recovery and what came after that. Reporters writing of Benchere began publishing updates on Marti's decline, reduced her role in the project to that of a spectral muse, her mastering the constructional demands of the sculpture's scale dismissed. Benchere argued otherwise but the reporters were there to sell papers, took the story in another direction. More and more Marti was described in mournful terms, marginalized and eventually eulogized. As Benchere remained determined to complete the project, Marti was given the title of his dear dead wife.

HARPER LANDED AT Logan and drove the fifty-two miles to his apartment in Bourne Mill. Since his divorce he lived in a fourth-floor apartment on the east side of the city. Connubial downsizing, a consequence of the consequence, he regarded his failed relationship as pilot error, a turbulence his instrument panel had warned him of. "Fucking radar." He blamed himself, "I should have seen it coming."

In his apartment, Harper showered and shaved, slipped on clean slacks and a shirt, went through his mail and messages before calling Abby at HighLine.

Abby Berecht was HighLine's comptroller, ran the office when Harper was away. Creole, Louisiana born, Dutch-based, a Berecht of the Morgan City Berechts, her first language was pidgin, her first husband a landscaper from Medford who left her for a florist from Laredo. An original hipster, Abby's cigarettes were hand-rolled, her brown hair worn in large braids. Her figure was round, not gone to seed but gaining in a proportional expansion at forty-seven. Expert at keeping HighLine's planes on schedule, Abby's occasional dates with Harper did not compromise their professional relationship. "Don't flatter yourself, little one," Abby teased. At their age nearly everything, including sex, was performed casually, without drama or expectation.

Harper spoke with Abby about business, then said, *"Mwen*

sonje w! So *cheri,* did you miss me?" They made a date for later. Harper phoned Benchere next and arranged to meet for dinner. "The cat is back," he told him and settled on Stonebridge at seven.

KYLE'S APARTMENT IS on the Upper South side, near Dudley Street and the Davey Lopes Rec Center. A two bedroom with cherry wood floors, secondhand retro Alphaville chairs, a dresser and table bought from Brian Furniture near Oxford Street. Last night, Benchere delivered the row house designs to Kyle's apartment, was given hearty hugs from both Cloie and Kyle in thanks for his support.

A bottle of wine was opened and glasses poured. Kyle raised his arm and offered a toast, "To things to come."

DAIMON PARKED BEHIND the white van in Benchere's drive. Mid-morning. He brought two large coffees, freshly brewed, black and hot. Burnt offerings, he rehearsed the joke, slipped his camera over his shoulder and carried the coffees toward the house.

When the doorbell rang, Zooie was sitting in the kitchen reading emails off her laptop. Two days back, she had yet to sleep at her own apartment. She pictured Marti in the chair next to her. Yesterday as Zooie walked from room to room, she found Marti on the couch, in the fixtures and photographs and shadows on the wall.

Daimon wore his hair short. He had on blue cargo shorts, a grey t-shirt and brown Hamilten boots. He introduced himself and asked for Benchere.

Zooie recognized Daimon's name from what Benchere had told her. She had somehow expected an older man, had pictured one of those sun cragged documentarians in hiking boots and a canvas safari jacket, smelling of Pall Mall cigarettes and road dust. For whatever reason, she didn't tell Daimon her name, said instead, "Mr. Benchere isn't here. Do you have an appointment, Mr. Daimon?"

"I was told I could come by this morning." Daimon handed

Zooie the coffees, showed her his camera case, explained about the film.

Zooie left the door open, stepped back and said, "If you'd like to come in and wait." She turned and walked down the hall.

Daimon followed her to the kitchen, stopped on the near side of the island and took his camera out. Zooie set the coffees down. The familial resemblance made it easy for Daimon to determine who Zooie was, and curious why she'd yet to introduce herself, he went ahead and asked, "And you are?"

"Housesitting."

"No, I mean," he took note of all the Benchere traits; the cockiness and confidence, the playfulness which seemed at once an amusement and a blood sport. He smiled then said, "Ok. So, Ms. Housesitter, how do you know Benchere?"

"Mr. Benchere."

"Mister, sure," he began filming. "How do you know him?"

"What's that?"

"I asked … "

"No, what are you doing?" she pointed at the camera.

"I'm filming." Daimon stated the obvious, explained no more, asked only, "Does it bother you?"

Zooie took the lid off one of the coffees and sipped. "I've known Mr. Benchere for years," she answered Daimon's question this way.

"Are you a family friend?"

"I'm close to the family."

"And you also work for Benchere?"

"Mr. Benchere."

"Sorry."

"I do, sometimes."

"Beyond housesitting?"

"Yes."

"So you are what, a personal assistant?"

"Something like that."

"And you're working now?"

"I am working," Zooie pointed to her computer.

Daimon continued to film. He asked more questions, zoomed the camera in until Zooie put her coffee down, put her hands on her hips, pushed her head forward and told Daimon to stop. "Why are you filming me?"

"Shouldn't I be?"

"I'm not Mr. Benchere."

"No," Daimon moved the camera around the kitchen, panned the space then slid back onto Zooie before giving up the game and saying, "But you are close enough, aren't you?"

Zooie had her father's laugh, a quick horn blast of a sound which rose fast and gave notice. She looked at Daimon closer, tried to see what she hadn't yet, considered the way things went from one point to the next without ever stopping really.

"HALLO BWANA." HARPER was waiting at the bar, called out as Benchere came into the restaurant.

A hostess led them to their table, introduced them to their waiter. The dining area was to the left of the bar, the windows in the rear of the restaurant fronting the water. Wicker chairs lined the deck. Over drinks they discussed Harper's trip. The route to camp was now mapped, the distance from point to point, the driver hired to truck the supplies down from Maun: the food and water, tents and sheds, generators, sanitation and refrigeration units, medicine and tools. All the metals Benchere purchased, the derrick crane and 2,500 pounds of unmixed cement, were set to arrive by ship at Walvis Bay or from Rianburg & Associates in Johannesburg. Harper calculated the cargo space and fuel load of his DC-3 to transport the other supplies.

"Here's to," he raised his glass, suggested bringing extra bottles of whiskey and rum to the desert. "For medicinal purposes, malaria and scurvy, snake bites and scorpion stings. Maybe a crate or two more for personal consumption," Harper quipped. During their first trip to Africa, in search of the perfect spot to set up camp, charting the landscape from Kasane to Nata, Rakops to

Kayne, around the parks near Chobe and Gemsbok, all the distant dots of towns miles removed from where Benchere planned to build his sculpture, Harper had an idea to fly in extra goods and sell them in the untapped markets.

"Consider the potential," he made a list of what to hawk, included crates of whiskey and cigarettes, canned meats and vegetables, soft drinks and tuna, toothpaste and aspirin, toilet paper, salts and sugars, soaps and socks and powdered milk, all mixed in with Benchere's provisions to avoid taxes and tariffs. "It's supply-side economics," Harper said. "Everything is vendible."

"Maybe so," Benchere didn't doubt, "though trade in Africa's a different animal. It's not the same as buying fertilizer and foot spray at Walmart. Beating the competition has a different meaning."

"Yuk yuk." Harper moved the collar away from his freshly shaved neck and said, "Not to worry. Try thinking of what I'm doing as a humanitarian effort. I'm bringing in goods not otherwise available."

"And peddling them," Benchere addressed the flaw in Harper's statement. "Since when do humanitarians sell their supplies?"

"Since the Battle of Solferino. Foreign aid is a booming business."

"Can be. Either way," Benchere said, "it doesn't matter. You won't sell a thing. I know you, Harp. You'll pay to bring in all this extra product then give it away. You're soft as soup."

"Soup is it?" Harper flung his fingers out as if to mirror a splash. "Let's bet," he said. "I'll make a profit or you don't have to cover costs for flying your stuff over." He gave Benchere his hand to seal the deal, said of the opportunity to pitch goods in Africa, "It's the land of milk and honey. It would be blasphemous for me to not take advantage." He signaled the waiter for a fresh drink, described his plan as part of the post-colonial free-for-all. "Everyone there wants to be independent but there's no infrastructure. Most trade is still black market. Out where we're going folks don't even have basic staples. That's where I come in." Harper boasted,

"My supplies will feed the free market. I'm expanding the base of people's choices. If they don't like the product they don't have to buy. Bingo bango. That's it. Ultimately everyone pays for what they want."

The declaration, more than anything, was hard to argue and Benchere let Harper know, "That's the first smart thing you've said tonight."

AFTER DINNER, HARPER followed Benchere out to the deck where they sat and looked at the water. A white winged tern circled the lake and searched the shore for a place to land. Benchere finished his drink, put his glass down on the deck, leaned back in his wicker chair and thought about the last time he was here with Marti. They sat outside together like this, in the warm grey dusk of a near set sun, until Marti tired and he took her home.

How long ago now? The time was somehow impossible to measure.

Harper glanced at Benchere, could see the way his jaw was set and knew what he was thinking.

After a minute, Benchere took the ice from his glass and threw it toward the water. The ice dissolved and disappeared. Action and reaction; everything was this. The physical world was calculable and contained, could not be denied, and yet when it came to the human heart, to free will and deed, what was rational rarely entered the equation. How could one *want* and be rational at the same time? *Impossible*, Benchere knew.

The thoughts in his head were like welding sparks. He compared the grind of the last year to Sisyphus with his rock. The image did not appeal to him however, and he startled Harper by groaning, "Bah!" Despite his misery without Marti, he held fast to his resolve, accepted the daily doses of melancholy but fought against a full spiritual collapse. His temperament was upbeat, if damaged, his nature expectant. Whatever rock there was to push, Benchere was determined to believe the effort was worth it.

He considered this in more detail, thought of purpose and

reason, the responsibility of living an authentic life, as Kierkegaard first examined. If the world was absurd what was there to do but persevere, passionately and sincerely? The *facticity* of our details was set but did not define us. We alone define who we are. This was what Benchere attempted to show in his art, to avoid the existential angst and celebrate the meaningless as a way to invent our own revelations and exalt in our charge. His love for Marti was this, his commitment a part of his own creation.

A dragonfly hovered just off the deck. Benchere watched the insect in flight, how it hung above the water, raced off and returned. He thought of Africa and the purpose he attached to completing the project. His determination was not a search for meaning because the meaning was already established. This he understood. The fact that, after more than thirty years with her he was heading into the desert without Marti was a reality he could not change but was attempting to live with.

"Hell," Benchere breathed in deeply, looked across the water for the white tern. "It's all a cliff dive," he said to Harper, saw the things people hustled toward and the way they did it, some with heads down and others with arms extended. "The outcome is unpredictable regardless. What matters is the approach." He said this as if Harper should understand, stopped himself there and rubbed at the underside of his chin. If his sculptures achieved anything it was to demonstrate the universality of the human will. Meaninglessness was meant as an expression of freedom not grounds for inaction. The metals in his works showed this, each turned and welded, the stretch and reach of angles forged and flowing, all in an effort to represent the beauty and potential of what was otherwise absurd.

A couple leaving the deck spotted Benchere as they went past. Benchere acknowledged them, was pleased to be recognized, though for reasons having nothing to do with ego or celebrity, but as confirmation that he was still here. He flipped his empty glass over, thought once more of Marti in the chair, then said to Harper, "Tell you what."

In that moment he felt he should be grabbing hold of things, gathering in what he still could, after having already lost too much. He took inventory, considered the totality of his options, then pointed and said, "I'll make you a deal. You want to bring in extra supplies to sell off. I'll give you that if you do something for me in turn."

"A favor?"

"Right," Benchere said. "I need this."

Harper listened before answering, "Sorry. What you're asking is not a good idea."

"I never said it was a good idea. I said it's what I want."

"Ha!" Harper ran through the list of complications, the regulations they'd have to circumvent, the false papers needed and what the authorities would do if they got caught. "It's not like smuggling in a bag of chips. There are rules you know."

Benchere watched the shadows on the water. He could feel the last of the day's warmth passing as Harper warned him about the desert beasts, the lions and snakes and deadly heat. "Sure, sure," he didn't care. The voice in his head howled, *I want!* followed by *I will! Everything comes with risk. If I'm being selfish, so be it.* He spoke of what he had and didn't, of what was gone and what was left and said, "Damn it, I know Harp, but listen to me. Here's the thing."

He rose from his chair, lifted his head, and speaking with clarity and instruction said, "What it comes down to, at the end of the day, what matters is the company we keep. Who is here and who isn't, and what can we do about it, Harp?"

"Yeah but ... "

"What? Hell, you have to know. I know you do. Times like this, what good is a man without his dog? Do you get what I'm saying?"

Book II

6.

STERN DOES CALISTHENICS. NOTHING TOO STRENUOUS because of the heat. A mix of yoga and push-ups to keep the body from turning to mush. He stops after a time and stares down the hill. "Soon," he says to Rose who remains anchored to his chair and answers, "Soon is what I'm thinking."

THE MAIN TERMINAL of the MUB Airport in Maun fronts a circular drive. The building is brown brick decorated by a glass façade cut into triangular panes. The runways are asphalt, the planes international. People pass through the terminal carrying boxes, LV and Tumi Vapor bags, suitcases strapped with ropes and belts. Benchere and Daimon walk outside. A copy of the Botswana Gazette is tucked under Benchere's right arm. *Kitso ke Maalta.* On the third page is a reference to his scheduled arrival.

Harper and Naveed have flown out ahead in the DC-3, brought Jazz and the supplies from the States. Everything is loaded now onto two rented trucks. Naveed and a man named Dawid Nawer drive the first truck to camp, while Harper remains with the second, waits for Benchere and Daimon. *"Dumela,"* Harper in aviator sunglasses, a pair of green shorts and grey Boston Red Sox t-shirt, has learned to say hello in Setswana.

Jazz sits in the truck, head out the window, barks as he spots Benchere.

"Hallo, hallo, hallo," Benchere opens the door and lets Jazz jump.

Earlier Harper toured the open market where he bought carrots and beets, onions, oranges and grapefruits. The desert fruits have a tortoise-shell rind, insulating the juice within. A crate of turnips was also purchased. Naveed has read up on how to preserve root vegetables in the desert; burying them in the sand and keeping them fresh for weeks with a sprinkling of waste water.

The duffles are tossed in back of the truck. Daimon stores his equipment, climbs into the cab of the truck between Harper and Benchere. Three days ago, he drove out to Valley Falls with Zooie where he filmed Benchere's sculpture *New Cue 2*. On the way home they stopped for a late lunch, split a pizza at Ralph's Bull and Claw. Zooie squeezed Daimon's elbow as she got out of his jeep and Daimon felt her grip throughout the meal.

Jazz is put in the bed of the truck, behind the crates. The heat of the day passes 100 degrees. They drive south. The road outside of Maun is a rough patch of uneven terrain. The shocks compress beneath the weight of the supplies, absorb little of the bumps. Daimon films through the windshield. The scenery is brush and rock and sand done up in three shades of brown. Two hours into their drive Harper stops the truck and everyone gets out. Harper adds gas to the tank. Daimon does situps and pushups near a ziziphus tree. Benchere gives Jazz water, walks away from the truck.

The temperature turns the air into cooking steam. Benchere concentrates on the landscape. Some twenty hours ago he was at the Pare-Mathus Institute, unveiling *Helix at Rest*. A good crowd had gathered. Drinks were served by waiters in black shorts and red bowties. Tables with white linen offered large platters of fruit and assorted finger foods. Many of Benchere's old students came down; Mindy and Cherry, Sam and Doran, Heidi and Nan. Cloie and Kyle spoke with Zooie and Daimon. Pare-Mathus was built on five acres of grassland on the southern tip of Bristol, near Mt. Hope Bay. Benchere's flight to Africa was a few hours off. He stood between the maples and said his goodbyes. Rather than have Kyle and Zooie drive him to the airport, he gave an excuse, made other arrangements, rented a Ford Focus, tossed his duffle in the trunk and drove east along the shore of the Seekonk River, away from the airport and out toward Swan Point.

The grounds were freshly mowed and decorated with an undergrowth of laurel. Steeply banked ravines lay on the river- side, with curved pathways cutting through two hundred acres. Benchere parked and walked. Many of the headstones at Swan Point dated back 150 years. Marti's stone was a white and tan mar- ble Benchere carved himself. He moved to the side of the stone and placed his hand on the surface. The marble was cool to the touch. Benchere leaned in and whispered to the stone. Kneeling then, he pulled some grass from the lawn and put it in his pocket.

Thirty yards from the truck now, in the sands outside of Ghanzi, Benchere took the grass from his pocket and let the piec- es float free in the air.

Harper came over with a mango. Benchere took the fruit. He watched the grass drift along the surface of the sand further out into the desert.

LINDA DARLING WATCHES herself on the monitor. Digitalized, shot through filters and shades, she is a one-time Emmy and Gold- en Globe winner, re-imagined now as a star of reality tv. In its third season, *The Darling Hour* had been created to re-launch Linda's career. Instead, the show has reduced her to self-parody, chroni- cled her tabloid persona, cashed in on her misadventures. Recent episodes showed Linda dumping 200 boxes of Jell-O into an ex- lover's pool, using a Peng lighter to set off the fire alarm in the Tri- bere Hotel, and driving in reverse across the Throgs Neck Bridge at two o'clock in the morning.

Life imitating art imitating whatever else was going on. In March Linda mixed X with gin and MDMA, Adderall and ketamine before passing out in the men's room at Club Zeal. Catatonic, she was taken to Emergency, down for the count, her body tempera- ture nearing that of a lake trout, her skin the color of chilled topaz. The entire episode was caught on film, earned a 3.2 share on cable.

In the kitchen now, pie-eyed from a night of Sobieski and Dexedrine, her makeup smeared and panties in her purse, the camera has to work twice as hard to capture less. Linda does a line of perico. The others do not care that Linda is digesting the parrot's beak at four o'clock in the morning. For next week's episode Linda will be confronted by friends at a staged intervention. The dramatic arch is aimed at getting Linda into rehab. The whole device is bullshit. Linda knows if she ever really went to rehab there would be no show, and if there wasn't a show no one would care if she went to rehab.

The crew breaks down their equipment. Linda's house is in New Paltz. A *Benchere* original, one of only seven. The hallway is travertine, the walls Spanish stucco. Linda bought the place back when she was flush. Only *The Darling Hour* keeps her now from foreclosure. She knows nothing about Benchere except for what she's read and what she read convinced her to buy the house. She pours a drink. On the counter in the kitchen is a Victorinox Swiss army knife, three tea bags, an ashtray with eight cigarette butts, two glass jars and an open box of Saltines. Linda cuts the perico with a steak knife. Upstairs she has Lunesta and zolpidem, zaleplon and clonazepam, Zoloft and trazodone. A potpourri. She will take something when she's ready to sleep.

Out in the hall, panty-less, Linda kicks off her shoes, her dress drawn to the heat of her pudendum. Her hips sway in a sort of hoochie-coochie twirl as she calls, "Good night, good night," and blows a kiss as the crew heads to the door. Toward the end of the line is a young gaffer, mid-twenties maybe, dark haired, carrying a Mickey-Moles lamp. Linda didn't notice him before, stops him now, has him wait until the others are gone. She calls him Mickey, tells him to put down the lamp, asks if he'd like a drink. "Do me a favor," she sings the line from Elvis Costello, wants him to help her, "Take off that party dress."

Upstairs, Mickey sets the light so Linda can frolic. Resourceful, a want to one day make films of his own, he is smart enough to understand the alchemy between opportunity and invention.

Using the camera on his smart phone, he sees what he needs, what Linda likes and is like. He gives it to her, the what-for and where she asks. She shows him all, how she lifts and separates, makes room, takes in, turns and gives him every point of view. Afterward he heads home, replays the clip, downloads the action, makes a few calls, weighs each and every offer.

HARPER REFERS TO the heat inside the truck as "oven baked. Like putting wheels on a sauna." Flies find their way inside the cab. Other insects explode across the windshield, require surgical removal beyond the wipers.

They drive until dark then stop and camp for the night. Dinner is the dried meat Harper picked up in Maun. They take turns afterward sleeping and guarding. Harper has purchased a Win 300 Mag rifle, standard fare, he says, "Better safe than eaten." Jazz keeps Benchere company. When it comes his turn to sleep, Benchere dreams of the distance travelled.

In the morning they roast potatoes with onions and drink some of their bottled water. Daimon checks his phone for messages from Zooie. The irony of Africa is that, despite its level of poverty and political chaos in nearly all 54 of its sovereign states, the skies overhead are filled with sophisticated satellites, carry communication across the continent into the Middle East and Europe. Benchere dumps the sand from his boots. Harper tends to the fire. Jazz eats a bowl of Purina One Benchere sent over with the early supplies. Grease from the potato roast is also poured into the bowl.

The day warms. Back in the truck, Harper drives first. The route they've taken has them within a few hours of camp. Just beyond Kalkfontein, Harper turns from the road and heads into the desert. Benchere sits in the passenger seat, reviews the sketches for his sculpture, reads through the handwritten notes Marti added.

When the campsite comes into view, Daimon is driving. It is by now early afternoon. Daimon spots the first truck and honks the horn. Two tents appear in the foreground. One of the generators has been set up. Crates and other pieces of equipment are stacked in close proximity, protected by a tarp Naveed has thrown over the top. Four hundred yards west of camp is a series of hills. The vastness of the area tricks the eye into visualizing a beige undulating ocean. Naveed and Dawid walk toward the truck. Behind them, three more people Benchere doesn't recognize are watching.

ROSE SPOTS THE truck first and calls to Stern. Together they observe the scene below. "How many now?"

"Eight."

"Including our man of the hour."

They take note, take photographs, make data entries before resuming the unpacking of their jeep, which is parked on the far side of the hill. Everything is carried up. They work individually at first and then together. Stern takes the lead, pulls while Rose puffs and pushes from behind.

"Long way."

"What's that?"

"I said it's a long way to the top."

"Always is."

"And a long way down."

"Quicker though."

"True that."

"A gravitational inevitability."

"What goes up."

"You said it, brother."

DANCY MUND ARRIVES at the Sun Hotel in Gaborone along with his wife Gabriella and eleven pieces of luggage. The bellboy brings up the bags, helps Gabriella unpack, fills drawers and handles hangers. Dancy tells the boy – who is actually a man, a Barolong tribesman and chronicler of Tswana fables – to open then close the window, to check beneath the bed and in the bathroom for any prowling scorpions or spiders. He insists the *boy* stock the refrigerator with preferred drinks, provide the room with extra towels and soaps and lotions. For this, Dancy offers up a dollar, stands sternly by the door and waits to be thanked.

In the dining room, in the spa, on the nine-hole golf course and at the casino, Dancy and Gabriella enjoy the fruits of their travels, occupy the Kwanzaa Suite for two nights before packing up again and heading into the desert.

LAST MONTH HARPER convinced Benchere to sell six slots to people interested in working on the project. "Think Tom Sawyer," the plan was to raise capital while acquiring free labor. As the cost of building the sculpture was high, Benchere gave in to the idea. The Munds applied and paid their fee; arrive now with all eleven suitcases in tow.

"Well now, well now," Dancy approaches the truck as Benchere and the others park. "Hello, hello." He comes at Benchere with hand extended. "A pleasure, sir. What is it the natives say? *Sannu! Hallo. Le kae?*" He is not tall, is sensitive to his height, is also burdened by a slight limp in his right leg, a product of a hip disorder. He attempts to compensate by displaying a gymnasium physique, bought and shaped with the help of a professional trainer. He moves swiftly, says again, "A pleasure Mike," his voice pitched to boom. He has trim Anglican features, dark hair colored against the grey and deep black eyes.

Gabriella steps forward and introduces herself. Her voice is measured, tamped down, less ingratiating than her husband. She says, "Mr. Benchere." Standing an inch or so taller than Dancy, slim like a Q model, narrow through the hips, with dyed orange hair covered in part by an Abercrombie and Fitch pith helmet, she has a practiced smile, intelligent and well fixed. Cool with her conversation, when she talks her voice contains insinuation and when she laughs her sharpest teeth show through.

Benchere greets the Munds as if he's pleased to see them. In truth, he's forgotten they were coming. On their application, the Munds wrote of being longstanding admirers of Benchere's work. "Huge fans," Dancy adds now. Together the Munds own Daybreak

Motels, a chain of econo-lodges stretching in coordinated inter-vals through the panhandle, New Mexico and Colorado and fur-ther west. Since opening their first Daybreak in 1992, Dancy and Gabriella now own 112 motels, refer to themselves as impresarios of the interstate, intrepid investors, products of the dream, hard-working disciples of Lincoln and Reagan, reverential toward Adam Smith and Friedrich Hayek and the capitalist ideal.

"We won't keep you," Dancy Mund says and grabs for Benchere's hand again. "Go unpack. When you have a moment we can talk. We have some thoughts," he looks toward his wife. "But not now. You go and get settled. A pleasure, Mike," he repeats. "We are looking forward."

KYLE, AS PROMISED, waits until Benchere lands in Africa before letting others know about the revisions to the Broad Street prints. He calls Carla at her office, starts her off with small talk then says, "So here's some news."

HALFWAY TOWARD THE hills, Deyna digs in the sand. She has on a sleeveless t-shirt, brown shorts and dark work boots. Her shovel is a KS-D all-steel spade. Benchere stares in her direction. What is she doing? He can't decide. She digs shallow holes, inspects the soil and moves then several feet off. When the truck arrived, Deyna did not join the Munds to meet the others but kept on dig-ging. From a distance, the shovel shines when turned to the light.

BENCHERE HELPS HARPER, Naveed, Daimon and Dawid unload the truck. The Munds remove yellow Flylow work gloves from their back pockets but otherwise don't join in. Once the truck is unpacked, Benchere and Daimon set up their tents. Benchere has brought a General Purpose army surplus with a poly webbing grid attached to the fabric and connected to the poles for addi-tional support against high winds. With a hip roof design, Benchere thought the ceiling would be tall enough, but the poles are just six feet, leaving him barely able to stand hunched inside.

He exits his tent and walks to an area a hundred yards north of camp. Jazz follows. The sun is white. Benchere's shirt sticks to his skin. Sand covers the ground like a surface carpet. Shallow fissures run across the baked earth beneath. The seasonal rains have come and gone. Benchere paces fifty strides west, marks the spot with several kicks of his heel. He paces off another fifty strides south, then north and east, before going back to camp for a hammer and stakes.

When he returns, Deyna is walking toward him. Benchere pounds the first stake into the southernmost corner. Deyna's hair is brown, pulled back and tied away from her face. Her features are Mediterranean, sharply cast, her cheeks high, her eyes warm and assured. She has the sort of shape which suggests orderliness, is trim through the arms and lower legs, a look of discipline if not restraint. There's a fleetness about her though she does not appear rushed, is agile and familiar with the demands of outdoor work. Despite the heat her bare shoulders are not burned. She steps to where Benchere is crouching and says, "Hello."

"Hello yourself."

"Who's this?"

"This is Jazz."

"Hello, Jazz," she gives the dog's head a good rub, looks at Benchere again and introduces herself.

Benchere stands, moves the hammer from his right hand to his left. Deyna is an inch or so taller than Zooie. Benchere gestures toward her shovel, is curious still, tries placing her name on the list along with the Munds, assumes she is part of Harper's select six, attempts to recall some bit of information provided, is about to ask what she was doing digging earlier when Deyna questions him instead. "Is this where you plan to build?"

"My sculpture? Yeah it is."

Deyna scans the area then asks, "Why here?"

"What do you mean why here?"

"You're miles from the nearest water source, the rivers and reserves, Lake Ngami, the Okavango River delta, Lake Xau, the seasonal ground flows that connect the natural reservoirs. This will get you some privacy, but the Kalahari is 120,000 square miles. There are thousands of sites you could have chosen." She asks again, "Why here? What do you know about this place?"

Benchere shrugs and says, "What's to know?"

"If you have to ask," Deyna puts the blade of her shovel firmly into the ground. "Have you checked the soil?"

"For what?"

"Sand and clay beneath the crust. Granite, gneiss, basalt, manganese deposits, fossils, signs of uranium, chrominium, cobalt, platinum."

Benchere takes the claw of the hammer and scratches his head, pretends for just a moment that the question has thrown him then answers, "The depth of the crust we'll dig through to set the foundation won't come near to hitting any mineral deposits. Clay maybe, sure, but we'll add a concrete footing and stabilize the ground before we place the columns. This area of the desert is pretty much the same for three hundred miles in any direction. A few feet either way won't make a difference. Now if we were closer to Francistown, to Selibe Phikwe, Gope or Lerala, we'd have to think differently about what we might unearth."

Deyna releases the shovel's grip and places her hands above her eyes. Shaded from the sun she is able to see Benchere more clearly. "Listen to you," she says. "What's to know? I'm impressed."

"Don't be." Benchere turns and paces off to the next corner where he sinks the second stake then walks west and sinks the third. "I've learned what I had to," he says about the desert. "What I just told you is pretty much all I have."

He stays on his knees, rakes at the sand with his fingers, thinks of Deyna's original question – *Why here?* – and then of Marti. "My wife," he says, can't help, wants to answer Deyna now in broader terms, tells her how Marti first visited Africa, about the work she did near Serowe, Ibadan and Gaborone, and the way she described the area, *Here is the root. Here is the origin of everything.*

"It's true," Deyna lowers her hands.

Benchere gets up and brushes the sand from his knees, asks Deyna if she is an archeologist.

"Anthropologist."

"But you like to dig?"

"I do. It helps with the process, knowing where things are buried."

As they've only just met, Deyna's sense of Benchere is raw, comes mostly from what she has read. That he has spoken of Marti serves notice. *Here is the root*, Deyna thinks. Her own reason for coming to the desert includes a curiosity toward the study of social phenomena. She anticipates probable developments, the draw of Benchere's celebrity and the location of his project likely to cause a convergence, throw everything into the social soup.

She takes her shovel, walks to the center of the field, stands in between the stakes and calculates how tall the sculpture will be if the metals are set at 45 degree angles. She tips her head straight back and studies the distance. When she looks for Benchere again he is still standing on the far side of the field. She waves at him, not urgently but expressively, and says, "For something this big you're going to need a spine."

"What's that?"

"A spine. Something to hold it all together."

Benchere finds the statement perfect, has not expected her to say anything quite like this. "Seriously now," he answers. "Who are you? A spine you say?" The suggestion gives Benchere back his good spirits. He slaps his thigh, calls out laughing, "Damn it all, don't I know? Without question, we're going to have one. A spine and then some, no doubt."

7.

ZOOIE SITS IN THE YARD. THE GARDEN IN THE EARLY evening appears ripe with color. *Venus* is on the far side of the lawn. Zooie sips her beer, plays guitar. She thinks of Daimon, of Benchere and Marti, Harper and Jazz, Kyle and Daimon again. Two days before Daimon flew to Africa, she slept with him at her apartment. Afterward Daimon spoke of the Kalahari. Zooie refused to consider, put her mouth to Daimon's ear and sang softly, "Ain't no thing but a momentary fling."

She sings a different tune now.

The shot in her hip is sore. She checks the time, rubs at her leg. Her duffle is stuffed with clothes brought from her apartment. When Benchere packed for Africa, he put a pair of Marti's slippers in his bag. That morning Zooie woke in one of Daimon's t-shirts, his scent on her skin. She finds Daimon's t-shirt now, puts it in her own bag, moves her duffle and guitar to the front porch where she waits for Kyle to come and drive her to the airport, thinks *crazy, crazy, crazy* the whole way there.

"BUSY BEES," STERN says to Rose.

"They do like to swarm."

"Where is he now?"

"There," Rose points.

Stern wipes his face with a towel. He squints through the sun, looks for Benchere and asks, "Do you think he knows?"

"About us?"

"Us? No. He knows about us. I've seen him wave."

"He doesn't seem to care."

"He probably thinks we're reporters."

"Or soldiers."

"Here to protect."

Rose says, "We could be with the *BDP*."

"The BMD, BCP or BNF."

"Could be," Rose follows Benchere with the binoculars.

Stern changes his shirt, comes and sits in his chair beside Rose. "I don't think he knows," he says and Rose agrees.

THREE DAYS AFTER Linda's adventure with the gaffer, she is called in by the network. They are, in a word, distressed. This is the word they use. They do not say disappointed as that would imply expectation. Hope has let them down before. They had hoped Linda wouldn't screw up, had hoped she would employ some discretion and not make a sex tape that wound up on the internet. "We had hoped," they say but know it's too late for that sort of wishful thinking.

What are they to do now when the footage has already been viewed more than a million times online? One point three million hits in 36 hours, they tell her. An injunction after the fact? A civil suit? Why bother now? The bag has no cat. At best they can attempt a follow-up response on *The Darling Hour,* show a contrite Linda, or perhaps a brazen and indifferent one. The consensus, however, is that there is no point. A line has been crossed. Advertisers have bailed. Drugs are one thing but this? The tolerance toward Linda has faded, the spin impossible to doctor, what career she sought to salvage has dissolved into sludge. The exposure – ha! – is all too much. Protesters have gathered, demanding the show be cancelled. Those from the network shake their heads collectively and say, "Ahh Linda, Linda, Linda. What have you done?"

HARPER FINDS BENCHERE'S laptop and logs on through the VSAT LinkStar Geostationary satellite system. Across the internet, on the *Huffington Post,* the NY and LA *Times, Slate* and *Cold Hard* and elsewhere there is reference to Benchere's arrival in Africa. In chat rooms, on blog posts and Twitter, keyboard theorists debate the significance of Benchere's trip. Here in Africa, in Europe and the States, in the markets, cafes and on the street, people discuss the project, are fascinated by the whole idea. Is it art for art's sake or something else? Motivated by their curiosity, two men from Madrid and a woman from Tanzania arrive at camp late that second morning. A clockmaker, poet, and pastry chef, they are drawn by an interest in Benchere and a want to be part of the scene.

IT TAKES TWO days to prepare the grounds; the storage area and cooking space, digging the straddle trench, the garbage pit and burn out latrine. Benchere works with Harper, sets the field for his sculpture, makes sure the generators and sanitation unit are hooked up, the equipment inventoried, the food well stored and metals on their way. Each night the temperature cools. A fire is made with the wood Naveed and Daimon gather. The loose drifts of camel thorn and bamboo crackle as they burn.

ON TUESDAY THE winner of the BAA Contest is announced. Heidi pools her prize with Mindy, Cherry and Sam, Doran and Nan, mixes the winner's pot with what the others can afford. Together they buy six tickets, head to Africa with $141 dollars remaining between them. Landing in Maun, they go outside, bags in hand, and negotiate their ride.

ROSE SAYS TO Stern, "The last time I was in Africa I came this close to contracting dysentery."

Stern looks at Rose, who is holding his thumb and index finger a half inch apart, and asks, "How could you tell you were that close?"

"Believe me," Rose answers with absolute certainty, "There are things you know just by feel."

NAVEED HAS WRITTEN out instructions for Skype. Benchere finds the piece of paper, tries Kyle, hits contact, sees his face in a small section of the screen. Unclear what to do next, he taps the surface and says, "Hello? Hello? Is anybody there?"

SHORTLY AFTER HER sex tape appears online the network officially cancels *The Darling Hour*. "We've seen enough," the comment is delivered without irony. The press is less kind, lampoons Linda with, "Nice Golden Globes," and "Talk about screwing your career." Linda reacts to the ribbing with middle finger raised. In search of a place to regroup, she stumbles upon the Kalahari project, reads about Benchere's travels. As owner of the seventh *Benchere* original, Linda interprets the timing as fate. She checks the airlines, visits her doctor for the necessary shots, packs a bag and slips past the paparazzi camped outside in the middle of the night.

THAT AFTERNOON THE final three paid workshop participants arrive in camp. Each is in their middle twenties, from Iowa City, a woman and two men traveling together as RIPPLE Africa volunteers. They have arranged to stop and work with Benchere before spending the school year teaching English and mathematics in Gaborone. Naveed welcomes them, brings them out to where Benchere and Deyna are finishing the straddle trench. Benchere pulls off his gloves, extends his hand, offers them a chance to dig.

IN ZIMBABWE, DEMONSTRATORS protest the result from the recent election. In the Congo, members of M23 launch coordinated attacks across the county, while in Kenya, Uganda, Somalia and Chad grassroots protests and rebel attacks have each country on the brink of war. In the Sudan, airstrikes ordered by al-Bashir continue to drive people from South Sudan into the Nuba Mountains.

Out where the first metals purchased from Rianburg & Associates have arrived by truck, Benchere discusses the situation in Africa with Deyna. He takes a rag and the Weiman polish he's brought from Tiverton and works the surface of his future sculpture until the steel beams glow.

ZOOIE ARRIVES IN a bush plane flown by a man running junkets from Maun to Kgalagadi Transfrontier Park. Daimon comes and embraces the surprise. "Well now," Benchere too, hikes in from where he and Deyna have been preparing the beams. He takes her bag, gets Naveed to find an extra tent. Later, Benchere and Zooie walk out in the direction of the acacia trees a hundred yards west. The day is more than hot and Benchere is wearing a tan safari hat, broken in and beaten down so that the crown collapses and the brim sags across the front. "Where did you get that thing?" Zooie can't remember seeing it before.

Benchere touches his head. He is still processing Zooie's arrival, is happy to have her; the familial bounty, not quite Marti but in its own way perfect now. He tosses an arm around Zooie's shoulders, says in answer to her question about the hat, "It's Daimon's."

REPORTERS DRIVE TO the desert hoping to land an interview. Benchere is affable, careful not to turn them away, mindful of their influence yet focused on the work at hand, he leads them around camp, shows them the field where the sculpture will rise, the metals laid out and waiting. He talks of his project as they want him to, denies that he has come for any reason other than art. "It's all I know." He challenges them to answer in turn, "What other reason could I have?"

FOUR NEW PEOPLE arrive that evening: a teacher, taxidermist, day trader and mechanic. Each is eager to become part of Benchere's project. They approach and ask to be invited into camp, deliver personal appeals, pledge their talents. Benchere takes a headcount, surveys the area, says, "Let's see here," and turns the new folks over to Harper.

IN THE MORNING, an orange mini-van appears and Heidi and the other BAA students pile out.

Rose and Stern watch from the hill, take photographs of each new arrival. They conduct searches through the database on their computer, identify and record everyone. "Heavy traffic," Rose says.

"A reunion," Stern notes.

"Looks like," Rose scrolls, checks the list.

8.

BY THE FIRE, DEYNA WEARS A SANDSTONE JACKET, BLUE
sweatpants and brown hiking boots. Zooie is there with Daimon
and the BAA students. Benchere sits in one of the deck chairs Harper brought. Scuff-whiskered, already his muscles have begun to
ache. Tomorrow he and Deyna, Naveed and his students, Zooie and
the Iowa three will dig the second and third foundation holes for
the sculpture. When not filming, Daimon will help as well. Naveed finds an empty wooden crate to sit on. He talks of Julie, is anxious to see her, wants to arrange a special dinner for the night she
arrives from the States, is thinking antelope.

"Go on then, bwana," Harper slaps Naveed's knee, pictures
him with the rifle shooting wildly into the desert. In the morning
Harper will head back to Maun, return one of the trucks and pick
up the Maule he's rented. He'll then fly Julie out to camp along
with a crate or two of fresh supplies.

The new arrivals have placed their tents a hundred feet to
the west of the common area. The Munds remain further off. Their
tent is a double ridge dome, shaped like an igloo, made of Gore-
Tex with curved internal rods that lift and round the roof. During
the day, the Munds wander back and forth from their tent to the
work areas, chatting up whoever is near while avoiding any real
labor. Tonight, as at every meal, they wait near the wooden picnic
table Naveed assembled while the others cook. When the food is
ready they fill their plates.

Dancy joins the fire now. No longer dressed in shorts, he's

changed into corduroy slacks and a leather Burberry bomber jack-et. He unfolds a canvas chair, places it to the right of Benchere. There's a hint of aftershave, a sweet manufactured smell, miscast against the dry and feral scents of the desert. Dancy acknowledg-es the group, extends his hands toward the fire and comments on how quickly the air has chilled from the 100 degrees it was a few hours before.

"It's the sand," Deyna explains that sand is easily heated by the sun but has a very low capacity for storing energy. "At this time of year when the sun sets and the air cools, the sands chill and the temperatures drop fast."

"The sand is it? Well what do you know?" Dancy looks at Benchere and asks, "Did you know that?" He laughs as if the fact is remarkable, then points in the opposite direction, out toward the staked off field, and says to Benchere, "This is exciting, isn't it, Mike? This is great. Look at all of this, will you." Animated, Mund's energy appears part of his genetic coding. Even as he sits there's a sense that he is moving. He says of the desert, "I love it. Where better to build your sculpture? You have no competition. The Kala-hari's yours for the taking."

The comment is old corn. Yesterday, and the day before, the Munds proposed developing the area around Benchere's sculpture, transforming the grounds into a desert oasis. "People are going to come to see your work, Mike. Why not give them a place to stay?" Mund repeats all this now. Resilient against dissent, he disregards Benchere's objections, refers to the sculpture as "a marketer's wet dream. We'll call the hotel African Daybreak, an all-inclusive built right here with your sculpture at the center."

Benchere refills his cup, passes the whiskey back to Harper, treats Mund's suggestion as just so much prattle, of no interest to him, he lets Mund know, "Never going to happen, Dan."

"Now Mike," Mund raises his shoulders, resets his hip, says, "Never is a long time." He recounts the research he and Gabriel-la have done, how there's money to be made in Africa if one has their wits. "The problem in the past," Mund says, "with the Brits and Frogs and all the others who tried to plant their flag, is they approached things as imperialists and not as businessmen. Think how much better Africa would be economically if she embraced a modified form of colonization."

"Just bend over and take it, is that what you're saying?" Heidi stands with Mindy, their backs to the fire.

"Not at all," Mund attempts to laugh.

Deyna has the sleeves of her jacket pulled down over her hands, is holding her whiskey against the leather. Skeptical, she asks, "How do you see modifying what has already been rejected a dozen times?"

"I'm glad you asked," Mund shifts forward in his chair. "As a business model," he explains, "terms and conditions would be negotiated with the focus on cash money. Right now it's all a mess. Africa has over 3,000 ethnic groups. After 10,000 years the entire continent is still a tribal culture. It's primitive. Its nation-state design is inherently flawed. It survives not on industry but on the kindness of strangers. All these liberal charities and foreign subsidies providing handouts rather than incentives, it's glorified welfare. The strategy has killed Africa's development, has created dependence while perpetuating bad business."

"Hold on now," Mindy as a reflex takes offense. "These liberal charities have brought clinics and schools, created farms and social awareness."

"To what end?" Mund turns and looks at Daimon who is standing with his camera filming. "Good business is forward thinking. Good business serves American interests right here."

"Wait. American interest?" Zooie doesn't let the comment pass.

"Of course," Mund moves his bad leg away from the fire. "What serves America will ultimately serve Africa," he says. "Who's going to help Africa advance if not the west? It's a jungle out there," Mund can't resist. "Look at Rwanda in the days after Habyarimana's plane was shot down. Look what went on without intervention from the west," he does not pause. "Without American investment, Rwanda's controlled by gangsters running their black market through the RDB. Without American business there's no stability, no economy."

Deyna's features are lit by the fire. She finds Mund's charge naïve and says as much. "You're not discussing reformation you're talking exploitation. Rwanda's corrupt because of American interests. Starbucks and Google, Mobil and Exxon and Standard. American business makes oil and mineral deals with the OGMIR and ignores human rights violations."

"Apples and fish," Mund has an answer prepared. "Americans are trying to bring business to the region. It's the locals who are exploiting one another and killing themselves off."

"Hold on," Daimon sets his camera hip high, finds talking with Mund is like playing slap paw with a cat; it may seem cute at first but the eventuality is never pleasant. "You can't just call out *the locals* as if that's all there is to it," he says. "It's more than tribal clashes. It's corrupt governments. In Zimbabwe, Somalia and the Sudan, Kenya and South Africa, there's no support for current regimes. The people want change."

"All the more reason American business is essential," Mund insists. "American interest provides jobs, creates an economic market and social stability."

"You make is sound like stability is a western concept." Deyna argues, "Right here in Botswana the people have put in place a stable democratic government."

"Please," Mund waves Deyna off. "Compared to what? You're measuring Botswana against Zaire? The C.A.R.? The GNP of Botswana is less than North Dakota. The schools stink, the number of AIDS cases is higher than almost anywhere in the world. The reality is this," Mund says. "Africa has three things going for it: oil and minerals and tourism. Now maybe you want to argue this is how American business likes it, that without stability America can wheel and deal as it pleases. I'm not here to say otherwise. I believe in self-interest. Propping up illegitimate governments helps America extract a country's resources. It's efficient. If along the way putting unqualified people in power creates politicized plutocracy, so be it."

"What do you mean *so be it?*" both Zooie and Mindy together.

"I mean there's no reason to expect anything different." Mund says, "Let's be clear. There's nothing altruistic in what we're discussing. Business is business and that's the first rule. It's not the fundamental nature of capitalism to do any sort of nation-building. Reclamations are only worthwhile if there's a profit to be made. Sure a stable socio-economic culture can grow out of a capitalistic venture but capitalism first draws cash to itself before anything can be put back in. That's the bottom line. Remember the Mensheviks thought capitalism would naturally evolve into socialism but that was just pie in the sky nonsense. Capitalism serves its own god." The statement causes Mund to grin. Emboldened by his own bluster, he faces Benchere and says, "You know what I'm talking about, don't you, Mike?"

"Sure I do, Dan," Benchere wags his finger and thinks to howl but does not want to give Mund the satisfaction. *All this yakking.* He wipes the sand from inside his cup then stands. The size of him rises above the fire. What there is to know about Africa Benchere has learned from Marti. He does not romanticize the continent, is aware of the conflicts, the brutality and setbacks, the issues with Omar Bungo, Musevni, Kaggme and Mugabe, Mapinduzi and Nguema, Kabila, Jammeh, Deby and Guebuza. He has championed causes, raised money for UpNow and Doctors without Borders, is familiar with the complications and not so callow as to dismiss everything Mund is saying. Still, taken as a whole, it is the personal effect of Mund's misapplications which feeds Benchere's current irritation.

He rubs his chin, leaves his drink beneath his chair, readies himself as Dancy rocks forward and declares, "We're all capitalists, Mike. We can't help. Even your art is commerce. This is not an insult. All great works have commercial value." Mund notes the million-dollar selling price of Picasso's *Nude, Green Leaves and Bust* and Giacometti's sculpture *L'Homme Qui Marche 1.* "Everything's for sale. This is the beauty of the marketplace. Everyone has something to sell. A man like you, an artist with your reputation, when you make a sculpture you're creating value. That's what we're looking to tap into here. That's what we're after."

Benchere in reply speaks censoriously, with caution in his tone, a hint of buildup in the message as he repeats the question back, "What am I after, Dan?"

Mund responds in a way he hopes will curry favor. "You're here to make a great work, Mike. I know that. You're here to build your *David*, your *Hermes and the Infant Dionysus*." He sets his hands in his lap, folds them, says nothing about Marti or the verisimilitudes of art, concentrates instead on convincing Benchere, "We both want the same thing. We're here to make your sculpture a success. A resort will get your work the attention it deserves. Think Anne Norton and Gustav Vigeland. It's all about amplifying the value of your art."

Such blabber is meant to convey solidarity, but instead Benchere is even more put off. He moves beside the stack of wood where he searches the pile for manageable sticks. Gathering what he needs, he arranges the twigs at angles, binds them together with a loose bit of twine, mounts his effort against a larger length of wood then thrusts the base end into the sand. "There you go, Dan," he says. "A bit of desert sculpting. How much do you think its worth, this one-of-a-kind, freshly minted and first of the African series? What do you suppose, Dan?"

Mund stares, knows he is being mocked, is no fool, and yet who is to say the piece does not have value? He thinks, *Why not?* and begins to reach, considers the offer.

"You like then?" Benchere touches the top of the piece.

"Like?" Mund hasn't thought of it in those terms and looks more closely now. "Well yes, I do. Of course I do," he says.

Benchere remains beside his creation, keeps Mund from taking hold. "What do you like, Dan?"

"What?"

"When you look, what do you think?"

"Well now," Mund considers, again squirms back in his chair, can only come up with, "I think it fits your oeuvre perfectly. It is a raw extension."

"Isn't it though," Benchere moves behind the sculpture, all cobbled together and rising to his waist. He examines his effort, inspects the sticks and string, the placement and positioning, then shakes his head and grips the center post. "Nope," he says. "Not quite right," and here he pulls the work out of the sand and tosses it into the fire.

For a second, Mund nearly comes out of his chair, a reflex to save what Benchere has wasted, but again he knows enough not to play the fool for Benchere's demonstration, and eying the fire, he says, "Better luck next time then."

Harper cracks loud along with Mindy and Daimon who has caught the scene on film. Deyna watches Benchere who is watching Mund now differently. He imagines what Marti would have made of Mund, all his talk of Africa and American influence and reducing everything to its commercial effect. He looks at Zooie, gives a wink, thinks *Right, right, right. What to do with such a man?* Jazz barks and Daimon flips his camera off. Benchere stretches and says goodnight, turns and walks back to his tent.

9.

LINDA DARLING CATCHES THE SAME RED-EYE THAT JULIE is on. Five hundred milligrams of Ativan lets her sleep all the way to Maun. She clears customs, clears her head, goes outside where Julie has offered her a ride.

Harper spots Julie and waves. Linda has her sunglasses down, two bags in tow. Harper hesitates for only a second, can't help, has seen the post online and says, "Linda Darling in the flesh." He laughs at this, laughs again as he imagines Benchere's reaction. He takes a cigarette from his pack and gives Linda a smoke.

DAWID HAS TAKEN the second truck to retrieve the final shipment of metals now docked at Walvis Bay. Benchere uses the materials already in camp to begin work on his sculpture. Each of the foundation beams is brought out to the field by the crane Benchere's rented. The posts are huge: eighty feet long and over 1,800 pounds as they are laid out on their sides. All of the foundation holes have been finished in preparation for placing the beams in the ground. Twenty-five hundred pounds of cement arrives along with 100 gallons of river water. The foundation holes are filled halfway with cement mix then secured by reinforcement bars to keep the base from cracking.

When the cement dries the beams will be placed on top, bolted down and the holes then filled completely. Long sheets of copper and nickel, bronze and brass are laid out beside the beams.

As they wait for the cement to dry, Deyna, Mindy and Naveed work with Benchere detailing the sheets which will then be welded to the beams as an ornamental second skin.

Benchere kneels over the metals, teaches Deyna how to use the pliers and ball peen, describes how he wants the copper and bronze sheets to look. Deyna holds the hammer between her thumb and forefinger; rolls her wrists like a xylophone player. The work gloves she brought from the States are Kevlar. Her hair is turned up, not in a bun, but folded and clipped for convenience. She wears boots, grey socks and shorts. Her shoulders and face are a perfect golden tan while Benchere is more red, his flesh forever threatening to peel.

They talk as they work, fall into a steady back-and-forth. Deyna is like Marti, practical-minded, methodical, appreciative of the empirical, of order and form and logic. She also has a fearlessness about her, has flown to Yemen in the middle of the night to study the findings of a piece of farming equipment uncovered and dating back some 12,000 years. As a scientist, her creative instinct contains a rational approach, differs from Benchere's wild hare way of addressing the world by creating abstract works drawn directly through chaos.

Deyna asks Benchere about his sculpting. She is interested in the genesis. He tells her as he did Marti years before about SoHo and the East Village, talks as well now about his mother, about Amelia Benchere, a designer of landscapes. An adherent to the primal call, large in body and spirit, Amelia worked the grounds like a natural aesthete, filled her sausage fingers with black soil and squeezed the dirt into Benchere's palms. Full of humor and frankness, she more than anyone exposed Benchere to the significance of art and encouraged him to embrace the mystery of creation.

"My dad," Benchere said, "provided a different sort of influence." B. William Benchere was a Keynesian capitalist, follower of Robert Smith and James Tobin, he made his money selling industrial chain link fences, took his company national, became involved with global trade, with bringing product overseas, opening factories and employing workers at salaries less than he paid in the States before exporting his product back to Yonkers and all points west. A mixed bag, Benchere's parents were counterparts, contrary in their views yet somehow managing to merge well. As a couple they were happy, gave balance to the other, laughed loud and embarrassed Benchere with open affections, dances through the living room and high squeals from private quarters. As progeny, Benchere was the mutt made in the stew.

Deyna likes this, says to Benchere, "Everything is part of something else. Eventually all things connect as they should." She tells him about a study she read a few years ago, where photographs were taken of a hundred different faces. The photos were then cut in half and reconfigured so that the right side of each face was duplicated and matched with itself. The process was repeated left to left. The result showed that in matching right to right and left to left no one looked at all like themselves. "It was only when people were composed left and right together that they became again who they are: a sum of the parts."

Benchere says, "It's all a grab bag mix."

"Yes, but it's not chaos," Deyna in reply, describes anthropology as the search for reason, the seeking of clues in what already exists. "All things happen by design. The study of history reveals this," Deyna says and applies the ball peen to the metal.

Benchere taps the surface of the sheet which he has heated with a handheld butane torch to make the copper more pliable. Now that construction is underway his mood is singularly directed. As always, the process of creating art causes him to internalize his focus, removes him from his outward self. He replies to Deyna in a matter of fact tone, "History comes after the fact but doesn't help us in the moment."

"You're wrong. Experience teaches us everything. The study of history allows us to predict what is going to happen now. For example," she says, "to understand your project we need to wait and see how people react. But by looking at history we can begin to predict beforehand." Deyna puts this out there for Benchere to process. She doesn't challenge his view of art, or dismiss his intent to build a self-contained sculpture in the Kalahari, is convinced just the same that something is going to happen because of his work. "Nothing occurs in a vacuum," Deyna says. "The moment you place something in the world, there is consequence."

"There is always consequence," Benchere remains defensive, is wary of those who offer comments about his project. "The tendency is to think of consequence as an *if-then* dynamic when in reality it's constant. Doing nothing causes consequence, too."

"But you're not doing nothing," Deyna insists Benchere focus on that. "If you didn't build your sculpture here, things would happen in the desert regardless, that's true. But you are building here, and so what happens is the consequence you caused and that should interest you."

Benchere strikes the metal, says as always, "I'm only interested in making my sculpture. What comes of it comes of it."

"That's an avoidance. You need to take responsibility for your work," Deyna surprises him. She uses the thumb of her glove to wipe sand from her forehead. "Bringing your art to Africa creates a consequence that will eventually find its meaning. That's what interests me."

Benchere has stopped hammering. He listens as Deyna tells him about a dig she joined last year in Central Africa, Cameroon and Chad. "The World Bank sponsored an underground petroleum pipeline, but as they started digging they began to uncover all these amazing archeological finds. Eventually, more than 470 sites were unearthed. To date the artifacts uncovered prove this part of Africa was settled over 3,000 years ago, much earlier than we first thought, with people living in sophisticated communities. We found tools and art and ways to store food. Near Chad there were burial grounds and signs of ceremonies performed."

Deyna says, "This is what you have to understand. Coming to Africa you can't just rootle around and build things wherever you want and ignore where you are. Africa doesn't need your sculpture," she says. "You chose the desert. You're a guest. Africa's beautiful without you. Right here is our matriarchal soil where Man's civil and social natures evolved. The connection between present and past is everywhere. Everything is here, all parts of then and now."

She surprises Benchere again and says, "It's like art," and compares his sculpting to an anthropological exploration. "You're searching as you create, never completely sure what you're going to find and yet knowing, if all goes well, you'll discover something amazing in your work."

Hunched over the metal sheet, Benchere takes in the sum of what Deyna is saying, squints into the glare of the sun as reflected off the copper. In contrast to the Munds, whose self-serving blather turns Benchere choleric, Deyna's chatter leaves him thinking of ways to reply. He wants to talk of Marti again, to say to Deyna that maybe she's right and the significance of history is how it impacts the living, what came before and where this leaves him now. He thinks to discuss Africa and Tiverton, consequence and connections, beauty and need, but he decides against, prefers to let things sort themselves out on their own.

Deyna has the sun behind her. Benchere settles back on his heels, his knees in the dirt. The color of the desert passes from brown to gold, with darker veins in the sand laid out below. The sun holds white, the sky a pale shade of blue. Benchere returns his attention to the metal. Warming the surface, he slaps at the copper with the ball peen. A moment later Deyna does the same, lifts a chipping hammer and taps the sheet. The pounding from their hammers echoes into the desert, creates a rhythm. Benchere feels the tempo in his hands, sets his strokes inside of Deyna's. He thinks again about what she said, thinks until he can't anymore. Resting his hammer, he places his hand flat on the copper and tests the surface for heat.

THAT EVENING, A man from Bangalore and two women from Quebec reach camp by way of a rented van that departs shortly after. The total number of people in camp is now approaching thirty. New articles appear in the papers and online, offer another round of speculation regarding Benchere's project. They describe what is transpiring in the desert as at once mythological, political, egocentric, artistic, invasive and inventive. Blog posts issue commentary and invite new debate.

Benchere pays no attention.

The Munds approach all the new arrivals, introduce themselves, discuss Benchere's project in terms of their idea for developing the grounds. Benchere dismisses the noise, refuses to worry about the Munds, has his own concerns and sets his mind to more immediate tasks.

IN HER TENT that night, Deyna writes in her journal. She has rinsed her body in the makeshift shower she and Naveed have jerry-rigged with water reused through a filtered drum. Naked beneath the blanket she has wrapped over her shoulders, she can make out shadows on the outside of her tent, her lantern illuminating the handful of people still moving about. She thinks of the conversation she had with Benchere earlier, thinks of the designs he showed her how to make on the copper skin that will be affixed to his sculpture, smiles at the image of him there on his knees, in the sand, bent over so intently, like a child.

KYLE WAITS A week then hits the banks with blueprints in tow. He shows the letter Benchere has provided as proof of his involvement with the Broad Street houses. *Well now, yes, this is a different colored horse,* the loan officers tell him. Institutions once hesitant to provide capital are suddenly eager to revisit applications. Word spreads. Soon a list of potential purchasers starts to form. Reporters call and want to talk with Kyle. He sorts through the messages, returns calls to those who have treated Benchere favorably in the past, leaves the others to write what they will without any quotes or accuracy to their story.

AN OLD CHEVY Bel Aire pulls up with several more people inside.

Suitcases and backpacks are unloaded. In jeeps and trucks the process repeats itself over the next two days. The articles in the papers and online continue to generate interest, draw people from San Cristobal and Texas, from Madrid and Frankfurt and the Ukraine. Among those now in camp is a biochemist, three artists, two business owners, a dentist and engineer, a physical therapist, horticulturist, horse trainer, puppet maker and a political activist from Denmark recently released from prison in Peru. Benchere treats the influx as a flattering sort of mystery. He shakes his head, speaks with Harper and Deyna about how to keep everyone fed and sheltered without letting them distract him from his work.

Linda Darling proves a pleasant surprise. Resourceful and engaged, she asks for assignments, rolls up her sleeves and dives into each task. Spirited, she jokes with the others, starts a friendship with Harper, follows Benchere's instructions as she would a director on set. A marked improvement from her first night, when she disappeared after dinner, reemerging stoned. Benchere took her aside then and said, "Listen, Darling, this is not celebrity rehab. You want to get fried, have at it. But if your being here fucks with my work, we'll put you on the next truck back to Maun."

Linda smokes now, whatever cigarettes are on hand, puffs with a fury, fitfully, has taken most of her pills and tossed them in the straddle trench. With Benchere she jokes, likes to needle, shows her thanks by telling him of her zolpidem, her Lunesta and zaleplon, "I pissed them away for good."

ONCE THE FOUNDATION beams are ready to be raised and placed into their holes, Harper mans the crane. Benchere moves to the first hole as Harper activates the chain and brings the post forward. Massive, once the beam is near enough, Benchere wraps his arms around the middle and muscles it into position. The chain is then lowered and the beam bolted down. The rest of the cement is poured into the hole and topped off with dirt and sand.

It takes a full day to get all four corner beams set and the cement added. A fifth hole dug in the center of the field is deeper, the spine heavier and taller than the other beams; cast with crooks and curves as part of Benchere's design. The middle post forces Harper to be careful when lifting. Adjusting the crane puts the joist at risk of swaying as Harper shifts the levers and draws the slack out of the chain.

Once the crane is close enough, Benchere begins to bully the beam into position above the hole. The post is too heavy however and won't be budged. Benchere grunts and tries again, first pushing from the front then pulling from behind. Both efforts fail. The hole is less than two feet away. Harper hollers from the cab of the crane for Benchere to stand back. "I can put her in myself." He raises the chain and the beam begins to move erratically, side to side across the hole like a giant pendulum. Harper shifts the arm and moves the beam too far left. He decides to start again, drives the crane a few inches forward, attempts to lower the chain but instead hits the lever which raises the arm and sends the beam skyward.

Everyone hollers as Harper shouts, "Shit," and reaches to disengage the lever. As a reflex Benchere leaps and tries to tug the center post down. A foolish choice. He catches the beam with his arms and legs, clings as the crane continues to rise. By the time Harper finds a neutral gear, sets the lock and cuts the engine, Benchere is thirty feet overhead.

Hell, Benchere scrambles onto the base posts at the bottom of the beam, stands and assesses the situation. Flummoxed, Harper holds his hands away from the levers, tries to decide what will happen if the engine is restarted. Will the arm and chain let go and send Benchere crashing to the ground? The wind picks up suddenly, gives the chain additional sway. Zooie yells. Benchere sets his feet, finds balance, stares down.

The four posts set earlier appear like petrified trees sticking out of the sand. Naveed runs back to camp for a long piece of rope Deyna wants to toss up to Benchere. The idea is to have Benchere tie the rope around the base plates and dangle low enough to jump. Daimon suggests creating a sand dune beneath to soften Benchere's leap either way. *Ridiculous,* Benchere finds his circumstance, can't help but let out a loud "Haah." *High art,* he thinks. *Lofty ambitions.* What now? Who knows? Jazz runs in circles and barks.

Benchere changes his view, stares across the desert. The vegetation in the savannah is a series of yellow-brown stalks that shift with the breeze. The beam turns on the chain, swings in half circles, sends Benchere east where an old school bus can be seen approaching from the distance. The bus is yellow with black lettering and patches of brown rust. A sand cloud rises up from beneath the carriage, creates a tail of gold and white which fans out as the bus comes nearer, parks a few feet from where the others are standing. Benchere watches as fourteen new people climb out of the bus. The driver is a short Motswana in a white t-shirt and brown leather sandals. He appears after the others get out, stretches his back, points up at Benchere and asks Deyna, "Why he do that?"

Harper remains inside the crane. The driver walks over, reaches in, starts the engine, disengages the lock and slowly lowers the chain. "That's all," he taps Harper on the shoulder, watches Benchere settle his feet on the sand. For his troubles the driver receives an orange which he takes with him back on the bus.

ROSE OBSERVES THE action below, has the binoculars trained. He calls Benchere's ride on the center post, "A circus act."

"It's elevating."

"Uplifting for sure." When the bus reaches camp Rose shifts his view. "How many now?"

"Let's see," Stern finds the clipboard and flips through the pages, checks their list. "Added to the others, almost forty."

"That's quite the gathering."

"Nearly an army."

"Or a platoon."

"At least."

Rose says, "Whatever it is, I don't think they're tourists."

"Could be anything."

"With all these folks."

"All of them finding their way."

"Here they are."

"Here, yes."

"Welcome to Wonderland," Stern says.

IO.

ON WEDNESDAY TWELVE MORE PEOPLE ARRIVE IN THE desert. Included in the newest group is a genealogist, a professor of semantics, two pipefitters from Jersey, a financial advisor, an ex-ballplayer, ex-senator and ex-minister from the Church of the Holy Wreath. Five are women and seven are men. They come by way of hired drivers and guides, with nylon sleeping bags, some with tents and others without. Seekers and wanderers, secularists and spiritualists, curious and eager, they arrive early and late, ask to be allowed to stay, acclimate themselves as quickly as possible to the rhythms of the camp.

More tents are pitched, the grounds expanding west and south. Adjustments are made. Everyone is active, eager to speak with Benchere, to work as assigned and learn more about the project. The extra supplies Harper brought and planned to sell in village shops are needed now in camp, kept onsite to feed the overrun. Once a week Harper flies to Maun and picks up more staples. The trips are expensive, the need for revenue to replenish stock officially an issue. "You see how it is, Mike?" Dancy Mund comes to Benchere's tent and insists on discussing the situation.

Benchere stands in front of his tent, sweaty from the day's work. Bare-chested, his belly still round, his tan line cut across his biceps and base of his neck, his skin covered with the sand and grime from the afternoon's labor. Mund, in contrast, has done no work. He arrives in beige cotton slacks and a blue silk shirt, his skin and clothes crisp and clean. Benchere rubs at his underarms with his soiled shirt. The current size of the camp is a problem, he concedes. In response, he has formed a committee, has chosen Harper and Naveed, Deyna and Zooie to handle all related issues so he can concentrate on building his sculpture.

Those in camp agree to follow what the committee dictates as long as Benchere remains in charge. *This is your project,* they say. *We have shown up solely because you are here.* They are willing to accept what rules the committee imposes if Benchere acknowledges that governing the group is ultimately his responsibility. *As a community,* they say of Benchere's rule, *we are the beneficiaries of your authority. Your position creates an obligation toward those who rely on you.* That Benchere never expected to take on this role or have so many people in camp is irrelevant. *You are Benchere,* the others remind him, as if somehow he might have forgotten.

To put them at ease Benchere agrees to remain in control. He talks with Kyle on Skype, draws from his expertise as a city planner. Mund envies those in authority, comes to Benchere with additional thoughts on what needs to be done. "A group this size can't exist on your generosity. If supplies are bought and distributed then people must pay. No free lunch, Mike. Everyone needs to feed the system," he says this again outside Benchere's tent.

Despite a deep annoyance with Mund, the practicality of his claim is impossible to dismiss. Supplies are at a premium. Harper is doing endless runs. Those already in camp are expected now to contribute funds. When new people arrive they are issued a surcharge. Benchere explains the situation, lets those who have come unannounced know they are welcome to stay but can't be fed and sheltered without buying in. Everyone understands and pays what is required. Those who can't afford the costs to remain linger for a day or two and then disappear.

Mund dabs at his face with a silk cloth and says to Benchere, "I've been thinking more, Mike, about our situation. If we're smart about this, there's a profit to be made from managing a group this size." Beyond the day-to-day, Mund proposes a plan where he is put in charge of collecting payments and expanding the organization of the group. "As someone with experience in these matters," Mund says, "I know how to allocate revenue and distribute it back into the business."

Benchere takes his soiled shirt and replaces it with a fresh one. Decisively, as is the only way to deal with Mund, he says, "There is no business, Dan. We're just a bunch of folks making a sculpture."

"Well I don't know," Mund thinks otherwise. "Most communities have gotten their start on less than this."

"But there is no start," Benchere rubs at his hair with his fingertips, gives his scalp a vigorous massage. "And we're not a community."

"The others think."

"It's just a lazy use of the word," these exchanges with Mund have a draining effect. Benchere has taken to narrowing the scope of his replies, issuing the same comments over and over in the hope of making them stick. He repeats now, "No community. As soon as we finish, everyone leaves."

"Yes, well, about that," Mund continues to have something else in mind, presents once more his proposal to develop the area. As the pitch is old, Benchere turns his back, enters his tent and zips the flap.

BY THE END of the week there are sixty-seven people in camp. Three days later there are seventy-two. Are eighty-five. Are ninety-four.

ZOOIE'S TENT IS set in front of Daimon's. Daimon's tent is next to Harper's, two tents down from Benchere. All the other tents and huts and shelters in camp are arranged nearby. The immediacy creates a cluster. A fishbowl effect. Privacy is out of the question. Zooie and Daimon raise the flaps on their adjacent tents from the inside, remove the stakes and tie the ropes together. Two posts are added to make a navigable passageway between.

Harper kids Benchere about the arrangement. "Whatever happened to good old-fashioned sneaking around?"

Zooie leaves her guitar in its case when not playing, has an extra humidifier to deal with the dryness. The guitar is inside the tent now. Daimon undresses, crawls into their sleeping bags zipped together. Zooie rolls closer, embraced and embraces. Beneath the mosquito netting, beneath a moon outside that glows above the sand, they talk. Every story now is fair game. Daimon explains the scar on his chin, talks of history, of past affairs, of projects completed and others planned. He runs through childhood incidents and familial tales.

In turn, Zooie confides. The cram jam of memory runs from then until now. She talks of events large and small, experiments constructive and otherwise. She tells stories about Rayne, about Kyle and Benchere, confides as to the not-quite-faded lettering scratched into her wrist.

Daimon holds her. Stretched out together they sleep. Their nearness feels natural in a way neither has quite experienced before. When they wake there's a second when separating is hard. Daimon opens the netting, pulls on his shorts and pushes his head outside the tent to inspect the day. Across the grounds, near the field where the sculpture is being assembled, Benchere stands with Deyna and Harper and five new people who weren't there the night before.

TODAY BENCHERE PLANS to weld the south armature to the far post and center spine. Half the people in camp have come to watch. Benchere passes through them, takes in the progress of his sculpture. He thinks of Marti, thinks of the work at hand, thinks of what he would be doing if he hadn't come to the desert; how the familiar made manifest what was no longer there.

He quickens his pace, embraces the benefit of losing himself in the moment. Each day reporters come and go. New articles present Benchere in ways that make him a popular target destination. They quote his mantra on creating art for art's sake and influencing each individual individually. Others write of Benchere's days as an activist running with Brian Haw, Jody Williams and Chokwe Lumumba. His history attracts debate, causes folks to wonder what he is really doing in Africa.

In South Sudan, Salva Kiir and Riek Machar attempt to keep their new country united as al-Bashir sends more soldiers and air attacks across Abyei and the Nuba Mountains. In South Africa, Libya and the Congo, Zimbabwe, Mozambique and Zaire, Angola and Chad, all the sands of the desert sweep across the same planes, while in his tent late at night Benchere sits and listens closely for the lion's roar. He closes his eyes and remembers what Marti said about the root of all things and the reason we're here. Desert winds create their own chaos, send Benchere forward and back, forward and back.

HARPER MANS THE crane, has mastered the levers. He lifts the armature overhead while Benchere walks to the south end of the field, fixes the safety belt to his waist and climbs the scaffolding built around the beam. A pulley system is used to deliver the clamps and welding equipment. The armature itself is huge, measuring more than 100 feet from point to point. Covered with the detailed sheets, the arm is curved in the middle and angled at 30 degrees.

As Benchere welds, Deyna and Zooie work with Naveed and Julie, the BAA students, Linda and the Iowa three to prepare the center beam for where the arm will attach. Scaffolding is built here, too. Pulleys are used for raising the joist clamps. The clamps are painted orange for no particular reason, each large enough to secure the armature firmly to the center post. Once the clamps are lifted, Deyna ties off the rope, mounts the scaffold with Naveed and sets the lock in place. Zooie comes up the opposite side to help. Warm winds circle through the angles and curves of the beam as Daimon stands below and films.

Around noon Benchere finishes the south side, moves to the center beam and climbs up. Welding the armature to the spine requires an extra length of hose running from the oxygen and acetylene tanks. A series of intertwining ropes are employed as a safety harness to support Benchere while he works. The sun has started its slow shift west as Benchere tends the weld. Deyna and Zooie wait at the base of the beam, make sure the oxygen tank and other equipment are operating smoothly.

Halfway through the wind picks up and tangles the hose. The armature turns inside the clamp, causing it to slip away from the center. Benchere curses, attempts to pull the arm closer but the lock is angled underneath and at a position he can't get to without dropping the rod. Deyna notices and re-climbs the scaffolding. More fluid in her ascent than Benchere, she is able to move along the wooden planks with an agility bordering on grace. One rung down, she untangles the hose, brings a rope through the pulley, shifts the armature back as it needs to be inside the clamp and resets the lock.

Benchere leans in and applies the rod. His mask fogs from the heat. Zooie uses a second pulley to send a face shield up to Deyna who covers her head as Benchere starts to weld. Jazz lays in the shade beside the sculpture, has learned to reserve his energy until evening. Benchere works the seam, seals the metals as a shower of sparks washes over Deyna beneath.

Once the welding is complete, Benchere shuts off the rod. He relaxes his shoulders, lifts his shield and inspects his handiwork. The sun sits behind Deyna as she removes her mask. Benchere looks her way but can't quite see through the glare of the sun. Back when he first left L/L, Benchere had Marti to help with the welds. Together they wore masks while setting the bronze, brass and copper tubes of *Want, Spread, Heart.* For a second now he's confused. He stares down until slowly he realizes. Clumsy, he nearly burns his leg on the heated rod. He leaves the equipment, pulls off his gloves, makes his way down the scaffold in silence. Finding Jazz, he walks from the far side of the field back toward his tent.

HARPER COMES FROM his tent the next morning and walks toward his Maule. Those in camp are used to his flying off. Rather than head north toward Maun however, he goes south, past Tshane and closer to Pomfret. With him are goods he's managed not to surrender: two crates of Captain Crunch, half a dozen packages of dried fruits, six boxes of cigarettes, assorted chips and nuts. He lands 100 yards outside of Cheo, a village dot on the map with a single store, a few dozen hutches and one dirt path for a road. The ground is a sun-baked hard dry sand, grass tufts, some thorn scrub and hutches.

People stop what they're doing. Children hurry toward the plane while mothers call out with caution. The store is no more than a wood shed, the shelves a series of planks set out on crates, lined with trinkets and random staples, bins of grain and seed. The village itself appears to exist for no clear reason. Harper suspects there must have been water nearby once, in some ravine or tributary. The only water now sits in a single trough shaded by a canopy. The color of the water is grey-green. Insects buzz just above the surface.

Harper goes into the shop and speaks with the owner. The cost of fuel for his flight makes turning a profit off his limited supplies unlikely, but Harper is stubborn and insists he can still earn a dollar. When he comes out of the shop the sunlight blinds him briefly. He puts his glasses back on, returns to the plane where several of the older boys are waiting to help unload the crates. Sand and dust swirls. The smaller children are coated in it. Without knowing what's in the boxes, the boys race toward the store. The owner is a heavyset woman in a sleeveless orange cotton dress. She has not come with the others into the field, but stands in the doorway by her shop, imperial in her posture.

The boys deliver the crates of cereal, chips and cigarettes and dry fruits to the hut. Two of the smaller children hold on to the side of Harper's shorts as he walks. He notices their bare feet, the cracks in their skin, and thinks of the bet he made with Benchere. *Easy money*, Harper swears again he's only here to make a profit, is no soft touch and has nothing but pecuniary interests in mind. He shakes hands with the owner of the store, tucks his cash away, waves over his shoulder before flying off.

Halfway to camp he adjusts his navigation, curses differently then groans, gives himself the sort of *yeah yeah* he has coming. He veers east, goes to Pomfret where he purchases as many gallons of water as his Maule will carry. This time when he lands in the field outside the village everyone hurries toward the plane. Harper says *Hallo* and has them unload the water. He leaves as soon as they are done, heads north again. His wallet is empty from the purchase. He will not tell Benchere.

II.

ROSE SITS, BINOCULARS IN HAND, WATCHING BELOW.
Stern is behind, doing deep knee bends and a few pushups to get
the blood flowing. He says as he finishes a set, "Damn hot."

"It's the climate."

"Comes with the territory."

"Pre-conditioned."

"Longitudinally speaking." Stern stops and looks down the
hill, says to Rose in relation to the heat, "A crowd like that creates
friction."

"Can't help."

"All pressed in."

"Shoulder to shoulder."

"It seems the seams are near to busting."

"One might say."

"I just did."

"The way it goes."

"It does go."

Rose holds the binoculars steady, stares directly into camp
and croons, "Every picture tells a story."

"Don't it?"

ZOOIE FINDS DEYNA out beneath the southern beam of the
sculpture. She is sitting in the shade, reading *The Essential Ellen
Willis* and drinking filtered water from a tin cup. Zooie has her
guitar. Deyna faces the hills, her back against the beam. A hun-

dred yards in front of where Zooie sits is a small patch of acacia. The music Zooie plays is faint at first, a gentle picking that moves inside the breeze. Deyna almost doesn't notice, so perfectly is the music knitted to the other desert sounds, but then Zooie's playing takes over, becomes more assertive. All other sounds slide into the background, provide a supportive refrain while Zooie's playing rises above the desert and carries the moment. Deyna smiles and goes on with her reading.

THERE ARE NOW 108 people in camp. Tents and shelters for the main group extend 200 yards back. Additional trenches have been dug, a second area cleared for cooking and washing. Given the size of the group, keeping everyone satisfied is its own chore. Those who fail to exhibit specific skills for working on the sculpture are left to perform mundane tasks: taking care of the trash and food, washing clothes and cleaning tools, policing the general area.

Throughout the day, people assemble idly and discuss the weather, politics and sports. Books are shared, ideas and meditations. Theories are invented as to why Benchere is here. They talk of Marti's trips to Africa, gossip about Benchere's days demonstrating on behalf of Oliver Tambo, Pieter Wilem Botha, George Bizos and the Groote Schuur Minute. Bored, they stare at the sculpture, squabble and raise complaints, want to know, *When is something going to happen?*

Supplies are brought in now by both plane and truck; bags of wheat and oats, canned beans, fruits and water. The trash is burned or buried to reduce the risk of attracting desert beasts. Papers and bloggers post new stories suggesting Benchere is building a permanent settlement in the Kalahari; a collaborative colony to further commemorate his sculpture. Benchere denies the claim, accuses Mund of planting misinformation.

Dancy wears crisply pleated Bermuda shorts, deep blue, with a paisley shirt and open-toed sandals. He comes again to Benchere's tent, stands off his shoulder, too short to hover, cramping the space just the same. For ten days now he's pitched his plan to commercialize the area. His appeal includes power points, promises and projections. Benchere rejects all. Tonight Mund tries a different strategy, attempts to gain support by advocating the needs of the group.

"The way I see things, Mike, people are restless because they feel undervalued. No effort's been made to address internal concerns. A group this size needs to operate by consensus. Permanent or not, size matters." Mund laughs at this, comes close to giving Benchere an elbow then thinks better, leans to his right and asserts, "Your committee worked well when we were small, but the responsibilities are too important now to appoint positions ad hoc. What we need is a general election with committee spots decided by a majority vote."

Benchere moves to the basin outside his tent where he washes his face. He uses a brown towel turned stiff by the sun to dry off. Mund's appeal for leverage camouflaged as a grassroots movement rankles. The idea to wrestle control of the project by disguising the coup as a call for democracy causes Benchere to tell Mund, "Be careful what you wish for, Dan. A vote could send you packing."

A group gathers near the tent, lined up like a supporting chorus. They listen to the conversation, echo Mund's sentiment and argue for representation. "Now that there are so many of us we should have a say."

Benchere scoffs, "A say in what?"

"A say in how we get on."

"How do you get on?" Benchere can't quite believe. "Your food and protection's provided, your supplies flown in."

"All of which we pay for."

"Sure you do. Why shouldn't you? I'm not your dad."

Here again the others insist, "We should have a voice in how our money's spent and the way we're governed."

"What govern?" Benchere finds the whole suggestion absurd. "We're building a sculpture not forming a state. I've agreed to feed you while you're here. If you're unhappy let me know and I'll return your cash and you can take off."

Mund's features are porcelain, his eyebrows sharp lines groomed so that when he creases his forehead and replies his brow appears as two deep slits. "Now Mike," he says and lifts his shoulders, tries to calm the tide, attempts to answer for the others. "We appreciate what you've done. Truly we do. You've handled everything like a prince. All we're asking for is more input into how our money's allocated."

"It's allocated to keep you from starving."

"But it's unfair treating everyone the same," the group is determined to press the point. "Your way is collectivism. It's communism. We pay in and the committee controls all disbursement."

"That's right. The committee's in charge of feeding you and buying supplies." He's had enough. His volume draws more people to the tent, including Harper and Linda and Deyna. The chorus continues to chirp about injustice while Benchere shouts over them, "You all pay the same and you all get the same. How is that unfair?"

"It's unfair because we're not all the same and we all don't want the same."

"Hell," by this point Benchere has started to walk away. He heads in the direction of the common area for something to eat. Mund hurries after him as do the others. Jazz cuts through the crowd, while still more people follow. "Pooling funds to purchase supplies for mass distribution is socialism," those in dissent have their lines rehearsed. References are made to the state of nature and state of man, social contracts, Rousseau and Locke, the Han Dynasty, the Ottoman State and the authoritarian transition. As for the camp itself, they say, "This is not how to run a free community."

Benchere in full stride replies, "I'll keep that in mind should I ever want to run one."

Mund heaves himself forward, attempts to keep up, calls for Benchere to "Wait," and begins discussing a plan for improved economic policy.

"Christ," Benchere makes a quick motion with his hand. The sun is just over the top of the tents. Those assigned to prepare dinner have a fire going, are cooking potatoes, toast and rice and strips of dried beef. Everyone stops as Benchere does. Some in the rear collide with the person in front as Benchere turns and says, "The only economic policy at play here, Dan, is a pay-to-stay system. If you want to eat, you pay your share."

"Of course. But what if we expand the concept a bit?" Mund goes, "What if we improve the way we do business?"

"We don't do business, Dan."

"Which is my point. What if we could buy and trade among ourselves?"

"Buy and trade what? Your dinners and shoelaces?"

"For starters."

"Bah," Benchere grabs up a piece of toast and bites through the crust, waves the uneaten half through the air. "You're talking through your hat," he breaks off a piece of toast and gives it to Jazz. "Everyone's needs are taken care of."

"But you're forgetting the free market system," Mund says.

"The free market has no application here," Benchere eats the rest of the toast. "If you want freedom, go fend for yourself."

"Now Mike," Mund laughs, less comfortably this time. "You know that isn't what we mean."

"No? What do you mean, Dan? A minute ago you were angling to rally the vote. Now you want to replace democracy with capitalism."

"Not replace, Mike," Mund leans off his bad leg. "What I'm saying, what we're saying is if you have capitalism you will have democracy. The market is the great equalizer. Allowing people to sell and trade their goods and services and the land they occupy in the secondary market will give everyone a sense of ownership and belonging."

"Wait now." Benchere makes Mund stop. "Did you say land?"

"Where the tents are. The plots we occupy."

"But you don't own the land there, Dan. I provide you with the space. You can't sell what's not yours."

"Alright," Mund rephrases his suggestion. "Let's call it a transfer of the lease then. For profit."

Benchere sends both his arms skyward, his exasperation on high alert. "What lease? You want to transfer property I never charged you a nickel for and get paid in turn? That's a sweet deal."

"Your placement of the tents is arbitrary," Mund tries this. "You've handed out plots as people arrived. Trading our positions would allow us to feel we have a more vested interest in the community."

"But we're not a community, Dan," Benchere refuses to consider, marches over to the beef. *All this chatter*, he gives a look at the others, reminds them, "You don't have a vested interest. You're transient. You're barely guests. You can't sell what I've let you borrow."

Mund corrects again, "Not sell. Transfer."

"For a fee," Benchere looks at Harper, looks at Deyna and Zooie, looks at Daimon holding the camera and getting all of this down. At the core of what Mund is saying, Benchere knows, is a ploy to gain further cooperation from the group. Once achieved, Mund will attempt to put a quorum together, demand a vote and maximize his newfound majority to push through plans to develop the area. Benchere lays all this out, leaves everything exposed as he charges Mund with gamesmanship and maneuvering the group toward mutiny.

Mund shuffles his feet. His sandals are soft leather, impractical for the desert. He stares at Daimon filming. Benchere moves closer to the dinner fire, has a sudden idea and says, "You know, Dan, if it's the free market you're after, we'll have to make some changes. In a real market economy capitalism is all about efficiency. I'll have to pay people for their labor and let those of you who are inessential to my project go. That's the way a free market works. Dog eat cat, right? If you want this let me know," Benchere gives the others a stare. "I'll get rid of almost all of you then, trim the fat and reduce the cost of running the grounds."

Mund falls silent. Jazz comes over and sniffs his shoes. The others whisper among themselves. Deyna watches Benchere as Mund continues to calculate his response. He smiles cautiously and says, "Ok, Mike. Point made. No reason to go to extremes. For now let's do this," he changes his demands for a second time, suggests setting up the market only for supplies. "Forget about the land and everything else. We're good with that. Let's start with dinners and personal possessions."

Benchere weighs the retreat, considers the worst that can happen, thinks of what Rousseau wrote about those in positions of power who aren't quite smart enough to apply their *Might as Right* effectively and lose their authority. He looks at Mund, looks at the others. Having prevailed, he examines the course of small victories, the consequence of extending Mund and the others a minor taste of what they want. *Hell*, Benchere raises his hand, measures an inch between his fingers and presents the group his offering.

KYLE PARKS AND waits for Cloie outside the Taubman Center. He has the windows down, the radio off. The distance from the curb to the front steps of Taubman is approximately 100 feet. Groups of students walk past. Cloie comes and kisses Kyle as she gets in the car. In the back seat are books on Africa: Laurens van der Post's *The Lost World of the Kalahari*, Rupert Isaacson's *The Healing Land*, two works by Mark and Delia Owens, and Samuel Huntington's *Political Order in Changing Societies*.

Cloie turns the radio on, finds WNRU and Miguel in midsong. Yesterday she finished reading Bernd Heine's treatise on the two thousand languages of Africa. Within the four major dialectical groups – Afro-Asiatic, Khoisan, Niger-Congo, and Nilo-Saharan – as well as the Austronesian and Indo-European subsets, there are hundreds of etymological variations. Cloie lists for Kyle some she can remember: Hausa, Swahili, Yoruba, Dahalo, Shabo and Laal. She thinks of how, 10,000 years ago, languages evolved out of isolation, as tribes living no more than a mile apart created territorial boundaries. "Today, with everything overlapping, there's no reason for all these dialects, and still people use them as a source of separation. It's sad, really," Cloie says. "Language is supposed to bring people closer together, but the variations are divisive. Everyone talks but no one knows what the other is saying."

"Ha," the statement is perfectly Cloie. Kyle values her talent for synthesizing things down to their most human root. Earlier that morning Kyle Skyped with Benchere, discussed similar themes. Kyle talks with Cloie now about Benchere's situation in the desert and Mund's latest effort to overhaul the economic construct of the camp. Despite Mund's chatter, Kyle is convinced something positive is evolving in the Kalahari. "You have more than a hundred people coming together and learning to live collectively and what is more impressive than that?"

He envies Benchere his experience, wonders if there isn't a way of applying the lessons learned in the Kalahari to the south side, and what if they could take the best parts of the desert and work them in here? "What if we weren't building sixteen separate row houses but an interdependent co-op where people came together communally for a united benefit? Suppose we re-defined urban renewal by creating a cooperative on Broad Street, and from there we took the model and expanded out?"

He says all this excitedly, brings the car down Manning Street, reaches over with his right hand as he drives and touches Cloie's arm, her shoulder and leg. Cloie laughs and slaps, tells Kyle to wait until they get home. "Cooperate," she says and he agrees.

ZOOIE FINDS BENCHERE early the next morning. The sun is hill-high, already yellow-white. Together they walk with Harper, Daimon and Linda to the Maule, climb in and fly east. An hour later they land sixty miles west of Serowe. Out in the flats, the water wells Marti first constructed and returned to update over the years continue to operate. The wells as modified are solar. The tubular pumps work their way 100 feet beneath the sands. An incongruous landscape, devoid of rivers or spring-fed lakes, yet one of the world's largest freshwater deposits lies just beneath the desert, in the basin of what was once the Makgadikgadi.

Several years ago, Debswana Mining Company drilled holes and installed casings throughout the area as part of their deal to gain the rights to diamond explorations. Many of those same holes are used now to retrieve the water supplied to nearby villages. Benchere stands by one of the wells. Its teepee posts are fifteen feet high. The pump emits a hum. A humid scent rises from the hole. The site itself is solitary. Zooie treats their visit as a reunion, is glad they've come; has photographs of Marti at this same spot.

Linda smokes with Harper. She calls the miles of water beneath the desert a cruel tease. "Like me, baby," she pokes at Harper's side. In her sober state she has developed a different level of awareness. She waves Daimon over, tells him to stop filming, puts a hand to his lens and reminds him why Zooie wants him here.

Benchere sets his fingers around the first metal post. He can sense the vibration through the ground, the churning, churning, churning of the well as part of its own unbroken cycle. Today marks the first time in weeks Benchere hasn't worked on his sculpture. The brief respite is nicely timed, the visit to the wells overdue. With all else that is going on, coming here is palliative.

The post inside his grip is warm. For a moment there is comfort. Benchere closes his eyes. The physical proximity helps him to remember. It also produces urgency. As much as he feels Marti there, he experiences the endless draw forward. The hum at the well is constant. The vibration alive. He remembers all and at the same time thinks, *I am here.*

Zooie stands beside Benchere, takes his hand.

12.

"WHAT NOW?"
"What?"
"Now."

ONE HUNDRED YARDS east of the main camp, a second group begins to gather. These are not Americans or Europeans but Africana who have learned about the sculpture through the handlers at the docks, the clerks in Maun, in the markets, on the buses and trucks transporting goods to the parks and reserves, out into the desert where Hereros and Wayeyi, Barolong and Basubiya, San and Shona carry Benchere's story and spread the word.

They come from west Botswana, Namibia and further south, from Swaziland and Johannesburg, Mpumalanga and north-east from Zimbabwe. Uprooted from their homes, their villages and cities by famine, rebellion, poverty and war, disenfranchised and without jobs, having heard about the sculpture and camp above Tshane, they arrive as pilgrims hoping for refuge, for physical and spiritual asylum. They assemble in silence, set up their own camp a safe distance from the others and sufficiently out of the way.

BENCHERE WORKS ON welding the third and fourth armaments in place. Atop the scaffolding, he applies the heat. In the distance, he can see the new group standing back near the baobab trees, watching him. Unconcerned, he keeps all focus on his sculpture. The Munds are not as accommodating. No sooner does

Benchere finish with the day's weld than Dancy wants to know, "What are these *bergies* doing here?"

Benchere wipes his forehead with the end of his shirt, answers Mund with, "They're Africans in Africa. Where do you want them to be?"

Dancy's hair has been trimmed by Gabriella, is combed neatly and treated with a conditioning gel. The limp he exhibited when first reaching camp has become almost a swagger, his popularity heightened by the creation of a marketplace. Just yesterday he expanded his enterprise to include the sale of labor. A green marker and flat board are used to post information on who is selling what and the current price. Each trade is monitored and the Munds extract a fee. Dancy takes a step forward, says about the Africana, "We have supplies and they have nothing. This is not a good combination. What assurance can you give us there won't be trouble?"

Benchere treats such babble jabber as another straw on the camel's back. He shakes the sweat from his hair, pictures the second group quiet in their assembly, how they first arrived, two men and a child sitting in the distance, near the baobab, in the soft shade as the main group woke. Harmless and half-dressed. Today there are more than thirty women and children, young men and old. How they get by Benchere can't be sure. They seem to have no food or water, though they've made a fire and obviously know the lay of the land. Benchere has not spoken with them and they have not moved closer or sought him out.

He pulls at the front of his t-shirt, the old sweat on his chest sticking as he looks for his towel. "I need to shower," he says, only Mund doesn't care, is already going on again about the gravity of the situation. "These people have come here because they have nothing. Eventually," he says, "they're going to want what we have. How can you know they aren't sizing us up right now?"

"Christ."

"We've paid for the supplies," Dancy's voice rises, his face squeezed tight. "We are here under your watch. You have a responsibility. You need to do something."

Benchere scoffs, "So now it's my camp again." He considers his options, weighs what he sees as his responsibility. "Alright. Alright," he replies and begins to walk in the direction of the common area. Both Dancy and Jazz follow. A path runs between the first series of tents back to the main communal area where meals are prepared and served. Benchere grabs an empty crate from beneath the first serving table, drops in a loaf of bread and three freshly baked potatoes before continuing on.

At the storage unit he unlocks the door and adds a gallon of water, some dried beef – *biltong* – and a bag of flour to the crate. He heads next to the garden where the fruits and vegetables are kept above and in the ground. He removes oranges and an onion, radishes and carrots. Jazz trots alongside. Benchere sets the crate down, pulls a few loose bills from his pocket, $27 in total which he stuffs into Dancy's front pocket. "Cash and carry," he says, and lifting the crate again, proceeds to cover the distance between the two camps.

On his bad leg Dancy can't keep up. Others now trail behind. Some twenty yards from the new group Benchere is met by three people, a woman and two men who've come to greet him. Benchere sets the crate down, wipes his brow with the rag in his pocket, dries his fingers and extends his hand. The reception cordial. Benchere laughs. The sound echoes above the desert. Deyna and Zooie stand together with the sun at their backs. Benchere lifts the crate and hands it forward, bows at the hips, laughs again, loud enough for the sound to travel and everyone to hear.

ROSE STUDIES THE scene below, says to Stern, "Apparently what we have now is urban sprawl."

"Endless developments."

"A constancy."

"There is that."

"That's for sure."

THE AFRICANA BUILD a fire in the evening and prepare their foods. Dancy remains uneasy. He has organized a patrol in order to maintain the integrity of the border between the two camps. Six men in rotation now monitor the Africans' activity. Benchere finds the enterprise ridiculous, whistles *The Colonel Bogey March* as the patrol practices its maneuvers.

EVERYONE GATHERS IN the common area at dinner where they argue heatedly about the Africans. Mund and his supporters insist Benchere has gone too far, that assisting the bushmen has created a dangerous precedent. Others find the sharing of provisions morally exact. The horse trainer and the ex-senator from Sioux Falls see Benchere's enterprise as neither virtuous nor threatening but practical; like soup kitchens and shelters keep those in need from rising in revolt. Meanwhile Deyna and Zooie, Linda and the BAA students, Daimon and two of the Iowa three believe Benchere has not gone far enough, that he should invite the second group to merge with the first and create one unified camp.

Benchere lets the others have their say. His own position clear, when pressed to clarify how he views the main group managing the Africana, he says only, "I don't see us managing them at all."

He looks at Deyna, recalls what she said before, how every action has consequence and things are bound to happen in the desert that he can't foresee. *No doubt.* Beyond those events involving the camp, he thinks of things more personal, how surprised and confused he was the other day when Deyna removed her mask as he finished welding. He blamed the mistake on a momentary lapse, a blurring of then and now, and yet it happened again at the wells, while resting his hand on the side of one of the posts; the pulse through his fingers so insistent and alive that he couldn't help but give into the urge, and there again was Deyna. The intrusion upset him, made him angry, as he released his grip and looked about to see if anyone else had noticed.

After dinner, Benchere walks with Harper and Deyna and Jazz out toward the hills. It is habit in the evening now for

Benchere and Deyna to find time alone and talk but this evening he is more acutely conscious of her and invites Harper along. The conversation is still about the Africana though soon segues into related topics. Harper says of Mund's reaction to the Africans, "People never cease to amaze." He tells of getting into an argument with a man back in Providence, on West Exchange, after he had given a homeless woman a dollar. "The bastard accused me of supporting a con, said most beggars were either secretly well off or flat out lazy criminals who would just as soon stab us in the eye and steal our wallets as get a job." Harper's response was to curse the man with a quick *fuck off friend*, while labeling his insights as sloppy fictions and saying, "The only thing criminal is not helping people down on their luck. Assholes like that want to go all Darwinian and let defenseless folks die, but that sort of bullshit just exposes the underside."

Benchere jokes with Harper, says, "Soft as soup, what did I tell you?" He has a story of his own, describes the time soon after he left L/L and was restarting his career as an artist. "I was working out of a studio which was actually an old warehouse converted into divided areas where a half dozen other artists rented space. We were a block away from Hartford Park and the housing projects. Every day I saw a man with a small brown dog set up a table and a stool and work with cheap copper wire and pinch-nose pliers to make bracelets and miniature figurines. It was a rough neighborhood and Marti and I had spent a lot of time meeting with civic groups to try and mend relations between the people in the projects and the police. Seeing the man each day took the edge off the neighborhood for me, created an almost sanguine effect."

The other artists in the building did not agree. Benchere explains, "As we were not allowed to sell our art inside or out on the street, the others objected to the man getting special treatment. These were folks who claimed to be serious artists, and each complained that the man and his little dog were cheapening their effort to make great art. It was ridiculous and petty," Benchere says. "It was hard to believe, but time and again the others would call the cops on the man, would walk outside and deliberately knock over his table, would kick his dog, would stomp on the little things he made. I got into it hot and hard, verbally and physically, yes. I threatened to buy the fucking building and throw them all out, told them if anything happened to the man or his dog I would hold them responsible. I brought the man supplies, better wire and metals and tools. I tried to get him to come inside and work with me, offered him a job but he didn't want to leave the street.

"The cops came and hassled him, said he couldn't sell his stuff without a license, that he couldn't create his little wire pieces in a public space. He would disappear for half a day then come back. The cops took his dog, said he needed a license there, too. I went downtown and bailed the pooch out. The hassle continued until others in the housing project noticed and came to the man's defense."

Benchere recounts the artists looking down from their studio windows and cheering as riot police were called in to confront those trying to protect the man. "Everything got crazy fast. There was shouting and then the cops turned physical and made arrests and the newspapers misreported what happened, accused the protesters of inciting violence. It was nuts, and yet here's the perfect ending.

"I came down, and let's just say I got involved in the protest, and wound up arrested. The news found out I was there, and after Marti bailed me out, I made a statement, described the man as a great artist, a street legend, and called out the assholes in their studios as jealous turds, called out the cops for overreacting, spoke of the city's need to embrace the man as a unique local talent even though his wire works were little more than trinkets. All this noise got the media's attention. Galleries came calling, took an interest, began to sell the man's art. As fast as he could make it, they pitched and sold his stuff at high-end prices, until the man was firmly established and well enough off to move to Barrington with his little dog."

"Ha now," Harper knows the story, is amused each time.

"You have to give the world credit," he says, "for sometimes getting it right."

Deyna is walking between the two, takes in both stories. She thinks again about the Africans, considers the way things turn on all that came before, then teases and calls both Benchere and Harper inveterate do-gooders, laughs at this and offers them a tale of her own. "One of the first field studies I joined was in Puerto Rico, where we were gathering data on peasant communities and looking at the impact of changes in the outside world on provincial cultures. I was still a grad student and my mentor at the time was Peter Whitle. As I was young and Peter was highly accomplished in my chosen field, as he was almost handsome and had a significant influence over my career, I developed a certain attachment toward him. In the academic setting Peter was charismatic and I expected the same away from school.

"What I found instead was that Peter cared little for the people we were living with and studying. There were six of us as part of the team and we had rented a small cottage. Each day we would observe and gather data and study how the poor in these outland areas survived. After a week or so, when people began to understand who we were and where we were from, a small group came to gather outside our cottage."

"Like the Africans," Harper notes, to which Deyna says, "Yes, but with a slight difference. The Africans have not yet asked us for anything and it's possible they never will, despite what we may offer. The *jibaro* in the *barrio* where we were in Puerto Rico came to us eagerly, not as beggars but with requests. They offered their services, wanted to sell us vegetables, labor, tours, protection, whatever we might need.

"I spoke to Peter with the hope that he would be receptive to doing something for these people but he refused. Any involvement we had with the peasants would skew our research, he said. In a vacuum this was true. We couldn't influence our study, I understood. But we could accomplish both. I argued that Eric Wolf's theory defined all cultures as dynamic and every community changed because of outside influence. Peter reminded me that we were not a culture or a city whose economic and social construct impacted life in the *barrio* through a natural process, but rather we were six scientists and whatever aid we offered the people would be artificial and short-lived.

"Again, I understood, but complained to Peter that he was being too rigid. I reminded him of the work Paul Farmer was doing, how it was possible to study cultural phenomena and still bring things like medicines and clinics and schools to a community. Peter didn't want to hear. As far as he was concerned, the people we were researching were cold subjects, like fossil bones and pottery chips discovered in the ground. When he left the cottage in the morning and returned at night, he would push through the group that was gathered with an arrogance that was both deliberate and cruel."

Deyna stops for a moment, reaches for Benchere's elbow to balance against as she lifts one leg and removes a small stone which had gotten inside the top of her boot. "One night a woman from the group knocked on our door," Deyna resumes. "She had a small boy with her, sick with fever, his skin a wan yellow and his eyes halfway closed. She begged us for help. Peter in the doorway stood imperiously and sad no. His rejection had nothing to do with our study, I realized absolutely then. He simply wanted nothing to do with these people. *Vete, vete,* he said and tried to close the door.

"I can't say what happened first, whether the others in the group in front of Peter began to close in on us, or if I was already pushing past, the keys to our jeep in hand, and leading the woman with the boy away. I suppose it doesn't matter. I got the child to the hospital. I stayed the night. When I came back the next morning, Peter had my bags packed by the door."

"Fucker," Harper says.

"Assholes are everywhere," Benchere now.

"What are you going to do?"

"Shit happens."

"Don't it."

"I've been telling you," Deyna still between the two, leans closer to Benchere who feels her there and, suddenly reminded of where they are and all that has happened, he slows his pace, turns and looks back across the field and toward the fire from the new group's camp.

IN THE MORNING, Benchere heads out to his sculpture and works on welding the first copper moon. A harness is connected to a wire pulley which Deyna and Zooie and the Iowa three use to raise Benchere skyward. Harper mans the crane, holds the moon steady while Jazz barks below. Deyna engages the safety locks, checks along the inner beam, uses a different winch to get the second lock to click in.

The hose passing from the welding tank snakes up through the center of the sculpture. Benchere clamps the first quarter-moon in place. He lights the torch, applies the heat and welds the metals together. Tomorrow he will attach the second moon to the east side of the beam. When both halves are complete the moons will form a celestial head. Benchere adjusts his hold. His gloves are sweat stained, his face shield lowered, his arms bare and unprotected in a sleeveless blue t-shirt.

As he works, he catches Deyna once, then twice, there beneath him. He shifts his shoulders, resettles his gaze, concentrates on the weld and looks for the work to distract him. Art is this. At times he asks no more of it. When Deyna appears again he doubles down and fills his head with Marti. He thinks of her involvement with Engineers for Humanity, the Rhode Island Urban League and RICADV, the many support groups in Providence, the time she organized a teaching forum for single mothers, connecting them with programs for daycare, healthcare, job fairs, educational opportunities all under one roof.

He thinks of what was and all he misses now, recalls how he reacted after Marti's cancer returned. Once the tests and prognosis were in, after Benchere had wept and wailed and set off on a new course of reading and research, making phone calls and chasing down new experimental treatments, he went into his studio and lost himself in his art, banging on the metals for a fresh sculpted work. When Marti came to find him, Benchere buried his head and insisted he had to finish the piece. She gave him the day, and then another and another after that, until the time when she returned to the studio, she found him hammering still on the same raw sheet. Gently she approached him, gave him no warning, took his hand from the hammer knob and set it on her cheek, told him what he knew already but didn't want to hear.

The rope in Deyna's gloved hands runs taut. The winches are locked but she keeps the pull in place just the same. Guarded, Benchere stares past Deyna, finds the base of the foundation posts and calculates how deeply beneath the girders are buried.

For nearly an hour, Deyna eyes the ropes while Benchere runs the rod in steady strokes along the seam of the metals. He ignores the sparks against his skin, maneuvers the heat from the rod to set the vein. Leaning in, he commits himself to the moment, so much so that when Mindy and Heidi come and shout up at him, announcing what they have found, he doesn't quite hear. Only after they insist and insist again does Benchere remove his mask and turn off the rod. *What now?* High up on his sculpture, he has them repeat what they are saying, pauses to consider as they dance below and sing like copper sunbirds there in the desert.

13.

ROSE SHOWS STERN, TURNS THE COMPUTER AROUND.
"Photographs and everything," he says.
  "Do you think it does justice?" Stern asks.
  "Justice?" Rose again.
  "Ha," says Stern. "Yeah."

IN ZIMBABWE, IN the city of Mutare, in the middle of a peaceful rally by supporters of the MDC – the Movement for Democratic Change – Zimbabwe's president, Robert Mugabe, orders his soldiers to open fire on the crowd. The carnage is swift. Through a spokesperson, Mugabe denies any wrongdoing, accuses the demonstrators of being insurgents intent on overthrowing a freely elected government. When the streets clear, a stone and wire sculpture some nine feet high is left behind. Fleeing, the men and women responsible for the sculpture are heard to chant, *Vryheid! Vryheid! Ben-cheer, Ben-cheer. Ben-cheer!* while soldiers on foot and in jeeps give chase.

BENCHERE'S STUDENTS ARE giddy with the news from Mutare. By the fire now, Linda sits to Benchere's left. Mindy and Heidi cannot sit at all. "You had us going," they say to Benchere, laughing at the way he once claimed art should never be used to support a cause. "Things are different outside the classroom, aren't they, Professor? We see now what you had planned from the start."

To this Benchere refuses to reply, gives his students their moment and leaves it at that.

Linda wears a teal colored sweatshirt and black jeans. Harper sips his whiskey. Naveed and Julie share a crate. Mund is off on the far side of camp meeting with his supporters. Gabriella comes alone to the fire. In Valentino slacks and a thin wool sweater, her shoes are Dolce & Gabbana pumps, the pointed heels piercing the surface of the sand. As a woman of some height, Gabriella has learned to slouch in a way that appears almost natural when walking with Dancy. Without him, she straightens, becomes statuesque, inhabits her space fully.

Mindy stands beside the stack of wood. Heidi and Doran find room on the ground with the other students. Deyna sits in one of the folding chairs. The Africana remain in their camp, surrounding a fire of their own. Eager to discuss what they believe should happen next, the BAA students talk about Zimbabwe, about *Dada*, Jenny Holzer, Alfredo Jaar, An-My Lê, and I.M. Bogad, Joeseph Delappe, Coco Fusco, Aaron Gach and Hans Hoacke, Eve Mosher and Dread Scott. All believe in art as a form of social activism, while Mindy and the others are convinced the sculpture in Mutare is a powerful force, influenced by the integrity of Benchere's Kalahari project, which serves as a symbol for other movements to rally around.

Gabriella ignores the students, addresses only Benchere. Standing with the fire behind her, she is lit in a red-yellow glow. Calm as a cobra, she grins and tells Benchere, "I think your sculpture is turning out just beautifully, Mike. It's too bad what's happened in Mutare. These *jinais* should not be connecting your name to theirs."

Mindy is several inches shorter than Gabriella, is built along Germanic lines, with thick legs and flat shoulders, her hair cut above her ears. Reactive, she issues her own salvo against Gabriella, calls her uninformed and says, "The whole purpose of our being in the desert is to inspire demonstrations like the one in Mutare."

"Now dear," Gabriella yawns through three fingers. "The government in Zimbabwe was freely elected. Forming mobs to riot in the street won't change that."

"What mob? What riot?" Mindy swings her arms behind her like a diver about to launch. "It was a peaceful demonstration."

"If it was peaceful dear, the soldiers would not have been forced to defend themselves."

"What?"

"Defend."

"Jesus."

Gabriella runs her thumb under the nail of her index finger. She has a steelier demeanor than her husband. Where Dancy tries to cajole, Gabriella makes no such effort. She looks again toward Benchere and says, "The mobocracy in Mutare misappropriated your name and your sculpture's image to create a blitzkrieg."

"A blitzkrieg?"

"Did she say?" Harper nearly spits his whiskey.

Mindy raises her shoulders, which have acquired a layer of muscle from the work she performs in the desert. She takes two quick steps toward Gabriella and snaps, "No one misappropriated a thing. Building the sculpture here is meant to show that anything is possible."

Gabriella looks between the students and says, "Including the killings, dears?"

"But that was the soldiers."

"Fending off insurgents who started the attack," Gabriella says smugly. "And here is poor Michael, caught in the middle."

"Who's caught?"

"What is your problem?"

Mindy jumps. "You don't get it do you?"

"Tell her, Professor," Cherry shouts.

"Tell her."

Mindy lists the names of other artists, Lynn Chadwick, Norman Carlberg and Susan Crile, Willie Bester and Jane Alexander in South Africa. "Everyone in Mutare understands why Benchere came to the Kalahari," she says.

"The only way the world gets changed is when people who suffer and know about suffering confront those in power with the truth." Heidi quotes Gandhi, then says, "Art is truth."

"Art shines a light."

"Art is the light."

"Art is freedom."

"Art is peace."

"And change."

"Art is possibility."

"Art is faith." Mindy flicks all ten of her fingers in the air like stars and yells, "*Amandla!*"

"*Awethu!*"

"Power to the people."

"*Uhuru!*"

Linda cheers the students on with her own chant of *Awethu! Awethu! Uhuru!* though caught up in the moment, she isn't quite sure what it means.

LATER, AFTER THE others have gone, Benchere and Deyna stay by the fire. He moves his chair so that he's facing her, a crate between them. His green sweater has several loose threads along the sleeves. Daimon's brown safari hat is worn at the back of Benchere's head. The whiskey bottle is to the left of his chair, drained once and refilled now with sand.

Deyna has her Carhartt sandstone jacket on, halfway zipped. Her hair is recently trimmed, exposes more of her face. She moves the collar of her coat away from her neck, puts her feet up on the crate. Jazz lays nearer the fire. From a distance, the top of the sculpture appears to rise above the hills. Deyna points out toward the field, flicks her foot so that it taps against Benchere's ankle and says in reference to Mutare, "Look what you've done."

Benchere denies the connection. "It's a stretch at best and has nothing to do with me."

"They chanted your name."

"They're confused."

"Your students think otherwise."

"My students think a lot of things. They're young," Benchere reminds. "They make mistakes."

"And you?"

"Sure, but not on this."

"You don't feel what happened in Mutare is a good thing?"

"I don't think the demonstrators should have put me in the middle of their boil."

"So you agree with Gabriella?"

"Hold on," Benchere rubs at his chin, removes his hat, pushes his hair around and plops the hat back down. "Listen," he attempts to distinguish, calls Gabby a self-absorbed clam. "While I'm warm and fuzzy and not without sympathy. I never called the demonstrators a mob and I don't blame them for what happened."

"But?"

"But that doesn't give them the right to drag me into their mess. It's wrongheaded. If I want to get involved on my own, fine. If I want to march in the streets and throw eggs at the castle, that's good for me, but don't go using my name and my art without permission." Benchere stretches his back, shifts his feet on the crate and says of his sculpture, "That's not what this is for."

"What is it for then?"

Benchere frowns, states for the record, "Art is open to interpretation, but that interpretation is personal. People are free to interpret my art any way they like. But people can't use my art to assert their own shit and pretend that their assertion comes from me. You can't hoof-tie art and drag it around in a gunnysack, yanking it out in order to tell people what to think or not think."

"No one's doing that."

"Sure they are. That's exactly what they did." Benchere flicks Jazz's ear. In the distance, Rose listens through the Lithium powered Electromax EPM parabolic microphone hidden inside a tiny casing that looks like a rock. Last week Stern snuck down in the dark, used a Marksman 3040 slingshot to shoot the mic against the side of Benchere's tent. The fire now is too far away for much to be heard though Rose keeps his ear trained just the same.

The wind at night sends sand into the fire, which causes the flames to sizzle and shift. Deyna tugs at the zipper on the front of her jacket. She studies Benchere's face, the round underside of his chin, his whiskered clef, his eyes keen, softer than others tend to see; mischievous even when he howls. His hair beneath his hat is wild, his green sweater ancient, the cuffs loose and collar frayed. Disheveled, his appearance is endearing. Deyna thinks of the story he told before, about the man making trinkets on the street. She switches the direction of their conversation just slightly, references the group of Africana and says, "These folks are here because of you."

"Are they now?" Benchere doesn't care to admit.

"This is a good thing," Deyna says, but much as Mutare Benchere denies, says of the new group, "They don't know me from butter. They're here because they heard this might be a safe place to stay."

"Of course they did. And why is that?" Deyna gives her voice a soft accounting. She speaks of social evolutionism, of consequence and setting things in motion. "Being here is not a static condition," she tugs her jacket sleeves down over her hands, places Benchere in the center of both the new group and the 100-plus people in the main camp. "This may not be what you expected," she tells him, "but that doesn't mean what's happening isn't notable."

"Notable you say? Ha. What sort of word?" Benchere rubs at his chin and goes, "Believe me, I've noticed. These new folks," he says of the Africana, "it's all fine by me, but the rest has worn thin. All this chatter clash is not what I came here for. What's important is this," he points out to his sculpture. "Everything else is annoyance."

"Really Michael?" After so many weeks, Deyna has a way of addressing Benchere which is both scolding and amused. She gives him a telling look, intentionally open to interpretation as she says, "You can't go around treating the world as an irritant just because it gets in the way of your art."

"Who says I do?" Benchere remains defensive. "I didn't come here to be caretaker to a bunch of mealy knockers. I'm tolerant enough but all of this isn't real." He waves his hand this time in the direction of the two camps and says, "It's just temporary."

"Everything's temporary." Deyna extends her argument outward, calculates again how far she wants to go before saying, "It's what makes each moment meaningful."

As best he can, Benchere ignores. Deyna talks about her own work, how when examining pieces from a dig, a bit of pottery or the handle from a tool, "It's never the artifact I care about, never the temporary status of the social order from where the piece came, but that someone made it and that it was part of a life."

"That's all fine," Benchere sets his heels in the sand on the sides of the crate, "but there's a huge difference between examining things after the fact and being stuck in the middle. I'm here to make a sculpture," he repeats. "What happens around me is irrelevant."

"People are not irrelevant, Michael." Deyna gives him this in quick return. She knows his bark is just that, has seen him carry the food to the Africana, and more before, understands him well enough and all he's trying to tell her.

Jazz comes and inspects the stick Benchere has picked up from the pile. He bites at the end, pulls against the grip. Benchere looks again toward his sculpture and then at Deyna watching him. Her features are classic, the angles and expressions found in paintings by Morisot or the sculptures of Leo Mol. He pictures Mol's *Anne*, the bronze casting of a woman seated naked, inscrutable in her posture, meditative, her thoughts distant, her strength and intelligence clear. Her wave of thick hair is moved back as a singular action, revealing only what she wishes to show of her face.

In contrast, Benchere thinks of Marti, sees *Aphrodite* by Saint Clair Cemin. The goddess sculpted in copper, honed in primitive form, the maternal figure, indomitable, hieratical, with rounded hips balanced and affectively forged. Beautiful, both ancient and immediate, Benchere can hear her calling, *Here I am. Before and after me there is no more.*

One by one the lanterns around camp flicker off. Mund's patrol passes twice. The breeze through the menagerie of tents moves the fabrics ever so slightly, and yet by the sheer number in camp the sound is like that of a collective thrashing. Deyna wipes sand from her jeans, starts over, her voice like Marti's, full of chafe and amusement. "You're not fooling me," she says. "If you have sympathy for the demonstrators, why should it matter how they use you?"

"Back to that again."

"That, yes. It's really something what's happened."

"It's a freak occurrence is all." Benchere reaches for the whiskey bottle, heavy with the sand. He shifts about, looks for a way to make things clearer. "Whether I feel for the folks in Mutare or not is irrelevant," he answers. "My personal politics are just that. My beliefs are mine and my art is something different." He leans forward as if to stand, is used to asserting his height as leverage. No sooner does he do so, however, than he sits back down again, does not wish to tower over Deyna, prefers to look directly at her. "What I'm trying to tell you," he says, "is that art is not some thump drum billy club stick. When I make a sculpture, I'm not trying to tell anyone what they should see. That decision is up to them. Even if I feel for them, and I do," Benchere continues, sincerely so and for the first time here with a hint of the conflict in his judgment. "It's not ok for any group to force feed their interpretation of my sculpture onto the masses and then use my name and my art to support their agenda. This is bullshit," he gives animation, bobs his head and stomps the sand. "What if Mugabe did this?" he argues. "What if Mugabe used my name and my sculpture's image to support his politics? Would you say he had a right, too?"

"That's different," Deyna replies.

"How so?"

"Because you don't support Mugabe." She says again, "You support the demonstrators."

"That herring's red," Benchere pours the sand from the whiskey bottle, lets it gather between his boots. "This isn't about me. It's about art," he jabs the air with both index fingers extended.

Deyna tries again, says of Benchere's main complaint, "It's all well and fine to describe art as belonging independently to each individual, but when you have exactly that," she says of Mutare, "when hundreds of individuals have the same view and come together to reinforce their interpretation of your sculpture, how is that a problem?"

"It's a problem because that's not what happened. Individuals did not come freely to their opinion of my sculpture. The demonstrators created a convenient perception of what they wanted my sculpture to mean and demanded everyone else think the same." Benchere reaches for another stick and pokes it in the fire, goes on again about the progressive modernists, Jean-Paul Laurens, Edouard Manet and others producing social billboards, how once a painting or a sculpture is used as an instrument to further a specific cause it's no longer art.

He shows the stick now burning, chants the rally cry of Theophile Gautier, "*L'art pour l'art!*" then tosses the stick onto the fire, quotes James Abbott McNeill Whistler, who wrote: "Art should be independent of all claptrap, should stand alone, and appeal to the artistic sense of the eye and ear, without confounding this with emotions entirely foreign to it." In his own words Benchere says, "Art is no backyard totem. You don't use art to sell laundry soap and you damn well don't use it as a pistol prop in some African rebellion."

The light of the fire is bright enough still to create shadows. Deyna follows across Benchere's face, from the half-lit to the half-shaded. Rather than argue further the surface points of his contention, the academic observations and distinctions made, she looks for the root and asks him then, "If art is meant to move each individual separately without ever dictating what they see, and groups and gatherings are not supposed to impose their interpretation either, the implication is still that art is there to move people toward something."

"It's true."

"And what is that thing?"

"This," Benchere says and slaps his chest then throws out his arms with such force as to surprise himself. He gives Deyna a look, different from before. *I know, I know,* he almost says. If setting up in the desert and refusing to invest in anything other than mounting steel upon steel three hundred feet high appears as a fully effected form of escape, if his ambition seems an effort to create further distance, as he denies any connection between himself and the demonstrators in Mutare, between himself and the people who have come to the Kalahari because of him, between himself and anyone with him now, there is nonetheless the sincerity of his outburst, the way he howled *This!* and exposed absolutely the clarity of his purpose and appreciation for life.

Deyna stares back at Benchere. There is something perfect in his response. *This!* The thumping of his chest makes her happy, makes her think despite all of Benchere's other declarations that he is still determined and fighting through. This is what she wants for him, more than the connection his BAA students see for his sculpture, more than the link between the world and his art. And still, she knows, there are other nights when Benchere is moored differently, and weighted with the past, is able to speak of nothing but Marti.

Here is another truth: *What was, is.* It's foolish of her to push at ghosts. She has an advanced degree in the study of things dead and gone and what consequence the past has on the present. To deny is a mistake, and yet it was Benchere who howled, Benchere who slapped his chest and told her, and what is she to do now? Her training as a scientist makes it her job to resolve what initially appears lost; the chase of things buried deeply. It's her belief that where she digs something will be found. That she can never be completely sure what that something will be lends mystery to her application and forces her to rely more than she otherwise would on the unempirical state of faith.

A twig cracks in the fire. Deyna watches the sparks rise then settle. She places her feet back on the crate. The sounds out in the desert include the occasional animal roar, which causes Jazz to lift his head. Deyna's hair has been cut in response to the heat. A convenience, and still it flatters her, complements her eyes and cheeks. Benchere notices, though has yet to comment, his restraint strictly imposed; even if he wanted he has no idea what to tell her.

The sculpture stands outsized, creates shapes upon shapes in the dark. The sky is a vast charcoal pane dotted by starlight. Benchere looks up, spots Leo Major flipped over and lying on its back. Jazz has settled again to the left of Benchere's chair. The cries in the distance grow louder. Benchere dismisses the jackals, says, "It's nothing." He tries to downplay his earlier chest thump, sends his hand out sweeping once more, takes in the expanse and says, "What I meant by *this* is everything. I mean, what is now is this. Here. When I finish here it will be something different." The claim is confessional, exposes more than intended. He tries again, a clumsy Benchere, he hasn't performed this poorly in a long time. He starts over, stutters and stumbles and struggles again.

Deyna finds a sweetness in Benchere's frustration. He begins anew, falters then and stops himself once more, points this time, does not even realize he's about to do so until he asks, "Did you cut your hair?"

A scarabaeidae beetle, grey against the sands, digs upwards, draws Jazz's attention. Deyna turns back to the fire, feels the heat like a blush against Benchere's question.

Benchere moves his hat forward then lifts his head again, finds Ophiuchus there besides the Milky Way. He tries not to think, focuses instead on the sky and the array of stars containing their own eager majesty. He pictures *Avenue de Clichy in the Evening* by Anquetin and van Gogh's *Starry Night* trilogy, imagines the forming of the constellations, the chaos before and after the first universal explosion.

"There's a quote from Goya," he tells Deyna. "Marti liked him. We have a Goya painting. A print. I have it now." He pauses for a second then recites the quote: "Fantasy abandoned by reason produces impossible monsters; united with it, she is the mother of the arts and origin of marvels."

"I like that," Deyna says.

"The stars are a fantasy," Benchere tells her. "But there's a reason they're here."

Deyna smiles. The beetle Jazz has been hunting burrows beneath her chair as she weighs her reply, hesitates then goes ahead and says, "I think Goya's right. At some point you have to make sense of your fantasies, but I think the opposite is also true. Reason without fantasy is like art without imagination. It's a sterile fish."

The twitching that is Benchere's finger dance stops. *Did you just say ... ?* He brings his head forward, lowers his arms for balance and grabs the bottom of his chair. "A sterile fish is it?" He starts to laugh but the sound he makes comes out more as a struck calf's moo. He releases his grip and rubs hard at his chin. Ophiuchus shines. The height of Benchere's sculpture casts the moon heads into the stars. The armatures crooked and the thick trunked beams below give the piece human form, appears as Phaethon on the verge of bursting skyward in an effort to gather up what is there.

Across the way, the glow from the Africana's fire burns orange. Coals made from charring down acacia wood are set inside a shallow pit. Zooie sleeps with Daimon, Julie now with Naveed. Linda sits and talks with Harper, has struck up a friendship, while the BAA students have adopted the Iowa three. The rows of tents stretch past where Benchere can see in the dark. The Munds have moved just east of their original spot, inviting all of their followers to join them. Benchere looks off again, then back at Deyna. He recalls the first afternoon they met, how he asked her with some confusion, *Who are you?* Confused again, he pushes away from his chair and stands.

Jazz runs once around the fire and stops. Whereas in Tiverton he would race through the house each night in search of Marti, in the Kalahari, with no point of reference, he has abandoned this. It's understandable, Benchere thinks. Everything in the desert is different. He brushes his hands across the front of his jeans, gives another long look at his sculpture out beneath the stars, then turns to Deyna and says goodnight.

LINDA SITS ON Harper's cot, the mosquito netting rolled behind her, a Lucky Strike in her left hand. Harper has brought the cigarettes from Pomfret, smuggled through without their tariff stamps. Linda has gone with him twice, likes to fly in the Maule, jokes about gaining a new appreciation for the cockpit. Theirs is a harmless banter, what passes as physical between them is mostly sport. Harper cracks, "Come on, I'm old enough to be your brother."

Benchere comes into the tent and sits on a spare wooden crate. Linda launches smoke rings off her tongue. The circles dissolve slowly, like miniature clouds. Earlier, Harper had worked on one of the generators, cleaning out the base skid, the reduction gear and air inlet, replacing the oil cooler with the spare he was wise enough to bring along. The motor charged gives a general hum to the air. Linda hands Benchere water, says, "What's the worry there, captain?"

"Nothing. I'm good."

"You look a little flustered."

"It's nothing," Benchere says again.

"Nightcap?" Harper offers. Benchere considers then says no.

Linda mentions the news from Mutare. "Some day, huh?"

"Someday, Darling," Harper winks and Linda scolds. "You keep that wish, sailor."

Benchere rubs the back of his neck. Whatever impulse had him coming to talk, he changes his mind now. Linda leans over and drops her cigarette into the tin can. Harper keeps an eye on Benchere. He reaches into the can and fishes around for the butt, straightens what smolders and puffs it back to life. Untying his boots, he removes the left one first, pulls down his sock and shows his pterodactyl toes. His nails have yellowed and his heel is calloused. "So," he, too, senses in Benchere's mood an agitation. "What's up?"

"Nothing's up," Benchere wishes he hadn't come.

Harper puffs twice more, drops the butt back into the can. "Where's Deyna?" he asks.

"I don't know. Why should I know?"

"Weren't you hanging out by the fire?"

"It's late. I left."

"I see," Harper looks now at Linda who takes the cue and says, "I like her."

"Who?"

"Deyna."

Harper undoes his second boot. Benchere on the crate forms a Buddha shape. His face is clenched, defensive. Harper drops his boot, stretches his legs out from the chair, sets his heels atop the tarp. "I like her, too," he says.

Benchere rises, his body stiff and not as easy to unfold as it once was. "I'm going to go," he says.

"What?" Linda calls. "But you just got here."

"I'm tired," Benchere stands hunched inside the tent. "I just came to say goodnight."

Harper shakes his head, has seen enough in the last few weeks to know, is more than guessing as he says, "Listen, you're human."

"Am I now? Thanks for that."

"You know what I'm saying."

"Do I?"

"Quit being so hard on yourself."

"I'm not hard."

"Oh, brother," Linda laughs.

"Give yourself a break," Harper goes for broke, becomes serious and says, "This is where you are now."

"Goddamn it, Harper," Benchere grabs at one of Harper's loose boots and throws it at him. "Don't start."

"If you like this woman."

"Fuck."

"Well, I would not have put it so crudely, but yes."

BACK IN HIS tent, Benchere drops into his chair. He finds his lantern and turns it to low. The air inside is a mix of kerosene, fresh *biltong* and old socks. A photograph of Marti, unframed, is taped to the far side flap. A pair of blue cargo shorts, a grey backpack, brown BU sweatshirt, three books and several t-shirts lay scattered about. Benchere unties his boots and kicks them into a corner. The lantern draws his shadow across the floor. The mosquito netting around the cot has changed color from a once fresh white to a more jaundiced shade of near yellow. Benchere listens to the wind at play, pictures Deyna by the fire still and groans, "Aaargh."

"What's that?" Stern can almost hear through the headphones Rose is holding.

Rose adjusts the volume on the Electromax mic.

Jazz settles on the tarp near the cot. Benchere pulls off his sweater, lifts his t-shirt and wipes his face. He thinks of what Harper said and curses. Whatever feelings he's having for Deyna, he swears they are sentimental at best. Circumstantial nonsense he calls them, not real affection, the attraction impersonal and reflexive. A spasm. Like staring at a bolt of lightning, the flash draws the eye but doesn't last.

He folds his hands and swears again, "Fuck."

"What?" says Stern.

"Bah," Benchere drags his bare feet over the tarp. *I will not think,* he tells himself, tries to read but can't. He lies down, gets up, calculates the time and considers skyping with Kyle. He recalls the story Deyna told last night, what she said after Harper and he presented their tales, how she called them inveterate do-gooders and how funny this was really. Sure, maybe, in those three instances when everything was clear they had made the right choice and reacted in a way that was *good*, but those sorts of decisions, Benchere thinks now, are easy. Saving sick children and the homeless and helpless and what is that? What's hard, Benchere knew, is doing right in the day-to-day, in knowing what to do and how to get on. Here is where he tended to fail, was gruff and loud and impatient. Terse with his students and tough on the fools he refused to suffer even when he understood a little kindness would have been better. He trusts his instincts only with his art, and with his love for Marti and his children, for Harper and Jazz in a different way and what else? *What else now?* Therein lies the question.

He remembers what he said to Deyna about influence, considers the irony, how influence is always the first sign, a symptom as it were, and where it all starts. In Deyna, there seems a sense of this now, the influence she has even against his resistance. He remembers with Marti, a related story, back before Zooie was born, a year or so after Kyle, he and Marti went to Cancun. On their second day they hired a sitter for Kyle and took a snorkeling trip. The brochure at the hotel sold them on warm clear waters in the Gulf and a five-star ship to charter them out. Professional divers were to watch over them, but when they got to the boat they found it was nothing more than an ancient Wreck Valley fishing tub operated by an old man and his daughter.

The day was overcast and the waters pitchy. Neither the old man nor the girl spoke much English and Benchere's Spanish was rusty. There were seven other people on board, all tourists eager for adventure. The further they went out the rougher the waters became. The shore disappeared and the horizon ran flat against the sky. When the boat finally stopped and anchored, everyone was handed flippers, masks and a snorkel. The waves by then were large enough to rock the boat several feet high. What instructions they were given involved little more than a pantomime of how to fall backwards over the side.

Marti was the first in the water. Benchere soon followed. The power of the waves tossed them about, made snorkeling impossible as no sooner did they put their faces down than a wave would come and fill their air tubes. The water itself was green, much too thick to see through. They were given pellets to feed the fish but the schools came darting from out of the murk, all but invisible, frightening as they nipped and actually bit at Benchere's fingers and Marti's legs until all the food was dropped.

Hoping to make the best, Benchere dove with Marti between the waves. As she scooted below the surface, Benchere rose and fell, attempted on his own to have a look around, but the waters were disorienting and moved him off his mark. Each time he came up he found that he had drifted further and further from Marti and the boat.

The old captain sat on deck, watching his passengers with no particular interest. The waves grew higher and moved Benchere backward like a bloated piece of fruit. In no time he was some 40 yards away from the others. He tried to swim, but no matter how hard he pulled and kicked the waves were unremitting and prevented him from closing the gap.

As Benchere struggled, he yanked off his mask and tossed it. The water sprayed into his mouth and choked him. Exhausted, he began to panic, realized he could actually drown and neither the old man nor his daughter would save him. Marti started swimming toward him only Benchere yelled, "Stop. Go to the boat."

"Roll on your back," Marti shouted.

When Benchere tried this the waves took him for a fat piece of wood and continued moving him off. The others by then had returned to the boat. Marti attempted to get the old captain to help, yelled and signaled their distress, but the captain did nothing more than sit and watch.

There was Benchere then, laboring, kicking and flailing, screaming out for Marti to head to the ship, telling her that he loved her and Kyle, splashing and bobbing while his every effort to swim proved futile. Engulfed in the gulf, in wave after wave, he was sure at any minute he'd go under for good and be eaten by a shark.

The seriousness of the situation caused Marti to rethink her effort, and rather than continue her shout, she started to laugh.

What the ... ?

Immediately her amusement calmed him. "Come on, Shamu," she said, and did he really want to be one of those silly Americans who wound up dying on vacation? If he was going to die he at least should have considered a jet ski or zip lining or parasailing accident. The sort of drowning he was doing, Marti said, was embarrassing and been done to death, she joked then laughed again.

By the time she reached Benchere, he was laughing as well, sputtering and spitting out water and saying damn it to hell and then he was swimming somehow, he didn't know by what power but together they were moving through the water back toward the boat, up the chain ladder and onto the deck.

Sitting in his chair, inside his tent, Benchere recalls. He thinks of Deyna next, sees her as she was the afternoon he first carried supplies to the new group. The heft of the load had centered in Benchere's arms and the low end of his spine. When the Munds and some of the others complained about his giving away the food, Deyna challenged their protest by accusing them of cupidity while asking, "What is it you're afraid of exactly?"

What is it ... ?

The question resonated then and now. Benchere straightens and stands. His head presses against the roof. He bends again, goes and lies on his cot. "Enough," he mutters.

"What?" asks Stern.

"You heard him," says Rose.

Benchere takes a deep breath and then another, heaves his chest as if swimming still in deep waters and going under. He breathes harder and harder until his ribs begin to ache, and exhausted, he gives way and drifts off to sleep. Surrounded by the yellowed mesh netting, he dreams of Tiverton, is home, only instead of being alone the house is filled with dozens of people and the floors are covered with sand. Benchere looks for Marti but she's not there. Deyna is in the den. When Benchere walks out to the garden Deyna is there as well. He stays in the dream, doesn't wake when the zipper on his tent is tugged down and Jazz gets up to see who it is.

It takes a minute for the voice to reach him, the whispering of his name closer now until slowly he stirs, thinks one thing and then another against the almost familiar sound.

14.

KYLE WAKES FROM A DREAM AND REACHES FOR CLOIE.
"Baby?" he says and rolls closer, does all he can to make sure she's
there.

DEYNA IS SLEEPING when Benchere wakes. He finds her curled
against him, breathing gently, her cheek half on his chest, his right
arm wrapped around and keeping her close on the cot. He gives
himself a minute to take everything in, can feel the rise and fall of
her, the heat off her skin. He considers what to do next, tells himself what happened last night was an ambush and hardly fair.
Rather than wake her and send her off, he lies quietly for a minute
more, takes in her scent, then slides away, gets up slowly and
dresses.

Sitting again in his chair, he faces the cot. The scene
reminds him of days toward the end with Marti, how he used to sit
by her bed and wait for her to stir. He looks at Deyna, recognizes
the distinction, remembers something he read once, how all that is
ends and all that ends begins again. The statement is the universe
in summary. *Even you can't break the cycle, Michael.*

"Bullshit," Benchere whispers, and "Bullshit," again.

MINDY TURNS ON her computer and reads about the demonstration in Kampala, Uganda, where 6,000 people marched in
protest against President Yoweri Museveni. At one point, a sculpture similar to the piece in Mutare appeared in front of the Ugan-

dan capital building. As the demonstrators ran from the soldiers sent in to disperse the crowd, thousands of voices shouted the name of opposition leader Kizza Besigye and the American Michael Benchere.

In Somalia's Kismayu National Park, wood from tables and chairs was collected and cast together with wires and bits of ribbons, creating yet another totemic sculpture. The work was assembled to protest the removal of Prime Minister Mohamed Abdullahi Mohamed whose populist appeal unnerved the ruling elite. Here, too, the streets filled with the chanting of *Amandla! Awethu!* and *Ben-cheer, Ben-cheer, Ben-cheer!*

A jubilant Mindy shuts down the computer, hurries off to tell the others.

THAT AFTERNOON BENCHERE finishes welding the second quarter moon to the top of the sculpture. In the distance those from the new group gather to watch. Their fascination with the sculpture has taken on a spiritual significance, their interest in Benchere amplified ever since he carried the first crate of fruits and bread across the desert.

The Munds' interest in the Africans remains something less than reverential. Their concern now is whether these new developments, including what's happened in Mutare, Somalia and Uganda, will affect their plan to develop the area. Benchere declares there is no plan, but Dancy persists, gives fair warning, "We're in this for the long haul, Michael."

The BAA students want nothing to do with the Munds, and yet, following the events in Mutare, in Kismayu National Park and Kampala, they also wish to remain in the desert once Benchere's sculpture is complete. "We have some thoughts," they say, different from the Munds, they want to establish a permanent community. "An intentional cooperative, like Morningstar and Wheeler's Ranch," Mindy explains.

"A communion."

"Transcendental."

"A sister campus for the BAA."

Heidi describes, "Something mesmeric."

"If art is supposed to drive the movement," Mindy adds, "we need a Mecca."

"Do we?" Benchere is not persuaded. "What Mecca? What movement?" He refuses to consider, tells his students and the Munds the same. "Everyone leaves as soon as we are through."

At 300 feet, Benchere balances inside his basket. Below him, Zooie and Deyna, Julie and Naveed and the Iowa three work to keep the welding hose untangled and the ropes to the basket secure. Benchere concentrates on the task at hand. He does not think about Mutare, does not want to think about Uganda or Somalia, about Marti or Deyna, about the Munds or his students, the new group, or those in the main camp now squabbling like children. Atop his sculpture, he wants to think only about his art.

He sets his hands firm around the torch, focuses on sealing the weld beneath the moon. Deyna checks the tension in the ropes. Despite all efforts otherwise, Benchere feels the tug. Through sparks, behind his shield, he is tempted twice to stop and call down, *Hey Deyna!* and demand she apologize for last night. He wants to believe her coming to his tent did not really happen, though her scent is still on his skin, the sense of her proximity too specific to be imagined. The details of her touch, her sounds and movements are part of him now, as indelible as history; it makes no difference if he doesn't want her there.

DAIMON COMES TO Benchere's tent after dinner. He wears his driest t-shirt and nearly clean brown shorts. The film he's been hired to produce has some two hundred hours of footage already recorded. With much work left to edit the pieces into one coherent film, Daimon would still like to add shots of Benchere alone; an interview or dialogue where Benchere has a chance to speak into the camera. Tonight however, Daimon hasn't brought his camera, has come to talk of something else.

Benchere has retreated from the common area, is staying

clear of Deyna and the others this evening. His absence is noted. Daimon sits on the edge of Benchere's footlocker. Jazz comes over and receives a rub of his side. Being in close proximity all these many weeks, as these sort of projects create their own intimacy, Benchere has gotten to know Daimon better, has conceded a certain liking, finds him relentless and fully professional, a good egg as Marti would say, and especially kind to Zooie. Daimon, in turn, has watched Benchere at work and with the others, has witnessed his reaction to the Africans, to the Munds, to the growing numbers in camp, and the new sculptures appearing in different countries. Rather than mention any of this, Daimon talks with Benchere about things more personal, discusses here his earlier travels.

"When I was working on my film of Gao Zhisheng," Daimon says, "I went to China, and after several weeks' delay, I was finally able to see him in Shaya Prison. The prison is located in the Aksu region of Xinjiang Uygur, a very remote area, and getting there I had to drive on narrow roads through the mountains, where one false turn would have dropped my jeep a hundred feet or more. The room in which I was able to meet with Gao Zhisheng was grey and cold, the two chairs we were allowed to sit on made of blackened metal. A soldier was present the entire time. I was not allowed to record our visit.

"I came with a long list of questions, was eager to assist in presenting whatever statement Gao Zhisheng wanted to make to the world. Instead, the whole time I was there, the entire time, Gao Zhisheng wanted to talk only about his wife. He told me stories, asked questions of his own. He described their apartment, recalled details regarding the texture of his wife's hair, the movement of her head when she laughed, the way her eyes smiled and the sound of her voice which he said he heard in his prison cell like private choral music. As he spoke, I noticed the bleakness of Gao Zhisheng's constitution lifted and I came away from Shaya with a completely different sense of the man than anticipated. Where I arrived expecting to feel outrage and pity and alarm for his condition, while these concerns still existed, I also left feeling tranquil and almost envious."

Daimon gives Benchere a moment to let the story sink in, says after a minute, "Does that make sense?" and hoping it does, he talks then of Deyna and Zooie.

BENCHERE STAYS INSIDE his tent for much of the evening. Late that night, Heidi rushes in and finds him pacing awkwardly about. Bent at the hips, he turns every three strides, his back rolled and hands fisted. The side of Heidi's face is dotted with gold and brown grains of sand as she tripped while running from the sculpture. She sticks her head inside the flap, calls for Benchere to "Come out, please, now!"

A crowd has gathered in the area just west of the sculpture. Benchere pulls on his boots and hurries with Heidi across the grounds. Four men from Mund's patrol are holding a teenage boy from the new group. The boy is wearing a dusty grey t-shirt and shorts cut from trousers. The men have pistols tucked in their waistbands. The guns are a surprise. Other than Harper's rifle, all weapons are barred from camp. A scratch runs from the side of the boy's neck down to his left shoulder. He has given up squirming. His eyes are nervously wide and confused.

Dancy stands to the right. He has on a pair of black boots laced high, beige pleated slacks and a blue sweater. Excited, he points as Benchere gets close. "You see? We caught him here, in the middle of the night, and with a knife."

Benchere moves toward Dancy, who is clasping an old hunting blade still in its sheath. He takes the knife from Mund and slips it, sheath and all, inside his back pocket. The boy recognizes Benchere, shows a brief flash of relief before Dancy cuts between them and repeats what he said a moment ago. "We caught him armed and breaking into camp."

"Was he now?" Benchere's tone is vexed, his tolerance spent. Not three days ago, after he delivered a new crate of supplies, the Africana left a freshly killed antelope outside Benchere's tent just before dawn. Mund's patrol failed to intercept the conveyance, did not spot the Africans as they came and went, causing Dancy to yip, "Our security has been breached. This is unacceptable. You see how it is with these gate crushers?"

Benchere turns now from Mund and asks one of the men holding the boy, "What happened?"

"He was running."

"Where?"

"Over there," the man uses his elbow to point toward the sculpture.

Benchere glances. "Coming or going?" he asks.

"What's that?"

"Did you catch him running to or from the sculpture?"

"He was running from."

"So when you found him he was what?"

"Standing there."

"By the sculpture?"

"That's right."

"And you chased him and he ran?"

"Something like that."

Benchere looks at Zooie who is there with Daimon. Deyna is standing beside Naveed, near Julie and Mindy and the other students. Benchere turns to Mund again and says, "So let me get this straight. You chased this boy who was doing nothing but looking at the sculpture. You didn't catch him in camp, you didn't find him stealing or breaking into anything."

"He was here," Mund says. "With a knife."

"It's the Kalahari. Everyone in the desert has a knife."

"But he was here."

"He lives here!" Benchere is no longer restrained.

Mund in turn shows his own exasperation. "We caught him outside of where he belongs. He can't be coming into our camp. He has no right to be here. There are boundaries. Legal zones that need to be enforced."

Zooie groans. Mindy, too, fills the darkness of the desert

with her sound. She has on a blue spaghetti-strapped tank top that falls only to her midriff and covers just the center portion of her *The Liver Is the Cock's Comb* tattoo. Others have heard the commotion, wake and come outside. One of the Iowa three has brought a lantern. Harper carries the rifle. Linda is somehow now wearing Harper's boots. Additional supporters of Mund appear as well.

Mindy goes up to the boy and says, "*Hallo.*"

Dancy warns Mindy to stand back. "No fraternizing."

"Christ," Benchere pushes past Mund, goes and asks the boy, "What were you doing here?"

"I came to look." He says, "Sorry sir, but I wanted to be closer."

"To the sculpture?"

"Yes sir."

"Why at night?" Mund does not believe.

"Why at night?" Benchere poses the question in a different voice, gives the boy a chance to explain.

The men tighten their grip on the boy as he tries to raise his arms. Instead of pointing then, he lifts his chin, tips his head far back and gazes skyward. "The stars, sir," he says. "I see them glowing above what you made. I wanted to come closer and see her differently than in the day." He looks at Benchere, does not look at Mund.

Daimon films everything. Benchere stares up now as well, looks back at the boy again. The innocence of the boy's claim moves him. He directs the men to "Let him go."

"Hold on," Dancy arches his shoulders in an attempt to appear more official. "You can't just release him," he squeals, "We caught him here in our camp."

"Christ," Benchere has no further patience. *All this nonsense*, he thinks. *Every day.* First one thing and then another. Is this honestly what comes from gathering together? He recalls something Kyle mentioned the last time they Skyped, a quote from Rousseau's *Social Contract*. In an early section subtitled Of Primitive Societies, Rousseau wrote: "Shared liberty is a consequence of man's nature. Its first law is that of self-preservation … As soon as man attains the age of reason he becomes his own master, because he alone can judge of what will best assure his continued existence."

Benchere considers this in terms of the boy and Mund. He thinks about self-preservation and shared liberty and what it means to each. That every man wants to survive is a given, but the phrase *best assure his continued existence* has an ominous under-tone when applied to Mund. All societies are made up of people in endless conflict over purpose and preservation. Here the boy has come to stare at the sculpture, and here Mund wants to run him off.

Benchere recalls what the boy told him. *The stars, sir. I see them glowing above what you made.* If nothing else is ever said about his sculpture, Benchere thinks, this is good enough. He heaves his chest and takes a quick step away from Mund, toward the four men, where he sets his boots firm in the sand and gets them to "Let go." Immediately the boy dashes from those gathered and heads off into the night.

15.

ROSE AND STERN HAVE WATCHED THE INCIDENT FROM
the hill. "A predicament," Stern calls it the next morning.

Rose describes the squabble as "Internal strife."

"Border skirmishes."

"Growing pains."

"Colonial adjustments."

Rose knows, "It is what it is."

"Always that." Stern takes the binoculars from Rose who
moves to the computer in order to search for incoming news. The
two new sculptures built in Uganda and Somalia have put Stern and
Rose on notice. Rose grumbles as Stern reminds him to "Pay up."

"Who knew?"

"Apparently me."

Rose reaches into the pocket of his shorts and hands Stern a
sweat-damp twenty, suggests another wager. "Double or nothing."

"I don't want to take your money." Stern tucks the twenty
away.

Rose insists, says in reference to Benchere and the sculptures he's inspired, "Let's bet on whether or not he knew."

"Our man?"

"What do you say?"

"I don't think so."

"You don't think so, or you don't think so?"

"I don't think he had a clue."

Rose disagrees, says, "I'll take that bet."

Stern stares down the hill, looks at the latest development as supporters of Mund gather loose bits of wood. "More folly," Stern says.

Rose agrees. "Who builds a fence in the desert?"

"There isn't enough wood from here to Kalkfontein to finish the job."

"Not enough from here to Ghanzi."

Those aligned with Mund's reaction to the Africana, who favor separatism, colonialism, capitalism and imperialism, use sticks and baobab branches to create a visible barricade between themselves and the Africans. "So much trouble and for what?"

Stern says about the fence, "Who do they expect to keep out?"

"Sidewinders."

"Not even."

"They could run the fence a mile in either direction and still the function would fail."

"Everything here is uncontainable," Stern stares through the glasses.

"It goes on and on."

"Like a wild idea."

"Like this," Rose takes the tip of his boot and flicks it through the sand.

KYLE AND CLOIE inspect the progress of the 16 row houses on Broad Street. Demand for the units has exploded ever since Benchere's name was publically connected to the project. Kyle dictates the terms of each sale, markets the units as part of a cooperative. He discusses Benchere and the 108 strangers in Africa creating an inter-reliant collective, tells everyone Broad Street is modeled after Benchere's vision and how South Providence can operate the same.

On tv and radio, in newspapers and blogs, Kyle talks of a community within the community, advocates the power of mutual sustainability, the idea to create even more cooperatives in the area, to establish social and fiscal unity, transforming the south side into a progressive inter-dependent troupe. He preaches the gospel of shared obligation, service and deed, of regenerating the economy by localizing the market, buying and selling produce and goods made in-state. "If a cooperative can work in the Kalahari where resources are limited and the consequence of failure more extreme," Kyle says, "then certainly the same success can be had here."

He does not mention Benchere's troubles with the Munds or his intent to leave the Kalahari shortly, concentrates instead on what has been achieved. Each Broad Street buyer is asked to commit their unit to the whole, is made excited by the prospect. "Think about it," Cloie paints a picture while Kyle drafts the contract and gets everyone to sign.

BENCHERE WAKES TO the sound of men assembling the wood fence. The racket is hard to identify at first. He decides not to look, assumes the worst, then curses and dresses and goes outside, walks toward the fence with Jazz. A flock of weaver birds swarm and he looks up. The blue of the sky seems to extend forever. He thinks of Marti, remembers the summer Kyle turned eight and developed a fascination for kites, how he would go to the park with Marti each evening where they would fly their latest box or dragon. The largest kite they built together was a Rokkako; over five feet tall and six feet across, shaped like a stingray, with Tasmanian oak wooden dowels, handcrafted spars and an orange plastic sail.

For a surprise, late that summer, Marti spent three nights folding multi-colored sheets of crepe paper origami style into hundreds of small butterflies. She then stitched a light cloth pocket to the underside of the Rokkaku and filled it with the foldouts. A thin second string was attached to the top of the pocket and held camouflaged against the main line as Kyle and Marti launched the kite skyward the next night. Benchere and Zooie watched from the side while the kite soared. At its peak, Marti reached above Kyle's hand and lifted the thin string from the main cord, told Kyle to give it a tug.

In a cluster first, and then in separate groupings, each of the paper butterflies floated free and filled the sky in a magnificently colored swarm. Kyle cried out, ran back and forth with the kite in tow, following first this group and then another. Zooie, too, dashed across the park, over the grass and between the trees as all the butterflies in painted streams began to fall.

Benchere remembers this, the swarm and Marti standing in the center of the park, beneath a shower of color, watching her children gather in all that came their way.

GABRIELLA IS OUTSIDE her tent, unfolding her chair to face away from the morning sun. Her hat is a Kangol Dapper straw cloche, her shorts beige Emilio Pucci, her top a green Fendi. Her book for the morning is *Fanny* by Erica Jong. She has a plastic decanter filled with tea. Her chair includes a yellow cloth awning that extends from the back out over her seat providing shade.

Benchere approaches the fence a few feet from where the men are working. Gabriella watches as Benchere sets his hands atop a section of the wood and tests the sturdiness of the construct. A bit of shaking causes the top piece to give way and a portion of the fence collapses. Benchere lets go of the wood and passes through the opening.

Gabriella turns and sits in her chair, adjusts her hat and the awning overhead, opens her book and sips her tea. When Benchere arrives, she says without looking up, "Was that necessary?"

"I thought the fence could use a gate."

"You misunderstand," Gabriella replies. "A gate was never intended."

The sand around the Mund's tent has been raked smooth. Dancy appears from inside. He has on yellow shorts and a pale blue polo shirt, Ralph Lauren, with the collar raised. He, too, is in a disapproving mood, recovering still from last night. After the boy ran off, Benchere had taken Dancy aside. Firmly and with no room for debate, he addressed the issue of the guns. "Get rid of them," Benchere said. "You know the rules."

Mund objected, insisted this was Africa and that the group needed protection. Benchere grew more peeved, told Mund it was only by luck one of his men didn't shoot the boy. "You want to hunt lions, go on a safari," he said. "You want protection, let me know when you spot trouble. Otherwise I want all the guns locked in storage." He turned away, refused to say more, had had enough, only Dancy was stubborn as always and continued to argue about the Africans. Insisting things were unstable and that the guns offered security, he said, "Every man has a right to protect himself. We didn't shoot the boy, but imagine if the situation required."

"Say what?"

"Worst case," Mund conceded. "But what if it wasn't just the boy? What if it was the entire group? What if they get hungry? Or cold? Or just plain want something? How are we to keep them from taking whatever they want if you disarm us?"

Benchere went, "Bah." In no mood for this, he instructed Mund to "Tell your posse the kitchen's closed until they turn in their hardware."

"But you can't," Mund hopped off his bad leg, rocked to the right, angled for a better position and said, "What about this." He offered a compromise, said, "Come on, Mike. Everything's a negotiation," and presented again the idea to construct a hotel. "You help me and I'll help you," he said. "I'll take care of the guns, you work with me to commercialize the grounds."

Benchere didn't bite. "Get rid of the guns or I'll throw you out of camp."

Dancy tries again this morning. Unlike Gabriella, he manages to treat each new encounter as an opportunity and says, "Hey Mike. I thought I heard you. Listen, about yesterday."

Gabriella glares. No subtle gamecock, she refuses to let Dancy start with apology. More blunt than coy, she criticizes Benchere's handling of the incident and tells him, "You do know letting the boy go only means he'll be back?"

"I would hope so, Gabby."

"Ahh, dear," her laugh is disarming, contains decibel jabs, accusing and condemning, mocking and condoling, all rolled together and launched from her chair.

Dancy intervenes, does not want to get off on the wrong foot again, and resetting the exchange, he calls last night a mix-up. "It's our fault," he says. "We're responsible for the area. We've done what you asked with the guns. You can check if you want. It's all good, Mike. But we need boundaries. In order for people to know where they can and can't go, we need to make the borders clear."

These Munds. Benchere ignores their comments and concentrates on the reason he's stopped by. "No fence," he says.

"What's that?"

"No fence."

"None taken, Mike. No offense. You did what you had to do. But now," Mund starts in about the tradition of borders, how all states have a vested interest in securing their boundaries and establishing permanent property lines in order to avoid untoward encounters.

Benchere leans down, puts his nose in front of Dancy's and repeats, "No fence."

"Well, listen Mike." Dancy takes a tougher stance, accuses Benchere of overstepping his authority, says, "Listen now. We did what you asked. We gave you the guns. Now you want our fence down too, and what are you going to give us in turn?"

"I'm giving you the chance to stay here. If you don't like it, leave."

"But we're not going to leave, Mike. No one wants to go. What we want is to work with you and develop the area."

"Not going to happen."

Mund tries again. "You're not thinking, Mike," he says. "A hotel will make us real money. Money matters in the real world. If money doesn't interest you then give it away. You can take every nickel you earn from here and give it to the Africans if you like.

How perfect is that? You think these bushmen are going to care how you got the cash?"

The argument is old fish. Benchere buys none of it. He imagines his sculpture in the center of some Las Vegas-style resort with swimming pools and blackjack tables, his work turned into a decorative lawn ornament. "If I wanted to develop the area in order to raise money," he begins then stops, a new thought having occurred to him. *Ha now!* He paces off again, heads quickly back to his tent where the boy's knife remains beneath his cot, then marches the rest of the way across the expanse to discuss his idea with the Africana.

IT TAKES THREE days before the materials Benchere's ordered to build the storefront for the Africans are delivered. During that time, four additional sculptures appear: one each in Namibia, Chad, Yemen and Egypt. The chant of *Ben-cheer* is recorded and played on the nightly news. Reporters treat the story as a spectacle, converge on the camp, attempt to conduct interviews and gather statements. Political analysts speculate as to the purpose and process and how much of everything Benchere has put in place. The price of Benchere's earlier artwork soars. An endless stream of emails floods his inbox. Twice helicopters fly over with cameras and video lenses visible from below.

Benchere continues to insist these seven sculptures are an anomaly. "I am not behind this," he swears. When his students boast of the project's success and how important it is for them to remain in the desert, he counters their enthusiasm with denial. "Staying is the worst thing you can do," he says. "Whatever is going on, the sculpture doesn't need our company."

The planks of wood for the storefront are carried from the truck over to the trees, near the Africana. Mund watches, incensed as he calls out, "You can't seriously be going into business with these *desert panyas?*"

Without tents, the Africana remain in the thicket of brush and small baobab trees. Several straw and cloth mats are spread out, a cooking area built around a pit. After returning the knife to the boy, Benchere spoke with Kayla Doure, the matriarch of the group. He was offered sorghum porridge and mopane worms already cooked and dried. He tried the worms, which he expected would please Kayla, told her then about his idea and the reason for his visit. An intelligent woman, Kayla understood at once the benefit of what Benchere was offering.

Three men from the second group help Deyna and Daimon, Benchere and Zooie unload the wood. Deyna and Benchere are cordial with one another. They have spoken only casually since the night in Benchere's tent. This sort of avoidance on Benchere's part is disappointing. Deyna had hoped for more, is tempted to say, *Really, Michael?* but hesitates. She imagines how things might have gone had she not come to his tent. Eventually she'd return to Colorado where she and Benchere would exchange collegial emails, talk occasionally on the phone, risk certain confessions, agree to meet after enough months have passed. During one such visit they would stumble through a physical experience and resolve it in time as they are slow to do now.

This or she'd leave and never hear from him again.

Neither prospect is what she wants. At their age, it seems a waste to treat personal feelings like some grievous affliction. Was she wrong to do as she did? Were there other ways to make Benchere speak with her about his feelings? Should she have been more sensitive to his circumstance? But how much more sensitive could she be than offering to love him?

When the truck is empty, Dawid drives off. Benchere works with the Africans, Deyna and Zooie, Naveed and Daimon and the Iowa three to build the store. Together they nail the frame, put up the walls and roof. The sun is a coal-white ash cooked behind a gossamer cloud. In the foreground the sculpture rises. Deyna holds the sidewall steady as Benchere hammers. There is a rhythm to their work established during the making of the sculpture. Benchere notices, sees the way Deyna moves, her gloved hands sliding atop the surface of the wood as he rotates around, secures the wall against the frame. In tandem, their effort is silent. Zooie is on the opposite side of the structure with Daimon and Naveed, spots Benchere glancing at Deyna as she keeps her arms extended, gliding against Benchere's bend and shift.

Yesterday, before dinner, Zooie and Benchere went and sat in the shade of a single baobab tree. The tree was thick trunked, nearly leafless, with branches high up along the base and spreading out wide. Benchere had his back against the tree, his legs straight in front. Zooie sat beside him, stared out at the sculpture and its hooked metals rising. She elbowed Benchere softly and said just as Deyna, "Look what you've done."

"I'm glad you came," Benchere let her know. "You're good company. And a hell of a worker. Relentless is what you are. You have your mother's stamina."

"It comes from dealing with you."

"Ha. Maybe so." A red ant ran up Benchere's arm to his wrist. He flicked the insect off. Zooie turned so she was facing Benchere in profile; her legs folded Indian-style with her knees angled out. Jazz moved to find his own spot of shade beneath the baobab, began digging at the sand with his front paws. Benchere checked to make sure he wasn't chasing a scorpion, felt Zooie place her fingers on his arm. She mentioned the seven sculptures, the arrival of the second group, the BAA students and what trouble the Munds had caused. "It's all good," she said, and then she spoke of Daimon.

If someone had asked her just a few weeks ago what she thought of the world, she said she would have answered in terms of Marti, would have told everyone that she found the universe perfectly horrible and mad. How she came to fall in love when she did, when everything else was still so ridiculously hard, she had no idea.

She pointed once more toward Benchere's sculpture and spoke this time of Deyna, described how everyone noticed the way Benchere was with her; attentive and comfortable, catching himself and retreating, coming forward and backing off. It was impossible not to feel for his resistance. What she wanted was for him to understand, "It's alright to miss mom. And it's alright to be happy. I wouldn't have told you before. I didn't think so myself for a long time, but really, dad, things happen and it's ok."

Benchere listened only because it was Zooie. When she finished he wiped his hands on his shorts and said, "I appreciate, but not everything that happens is ok." The sand ants circled and Jazz gave chase. Benchere told Zooie then about the night Deyna came to his tent, spoke of how he lay in the dark, silent against the sound of his name being called. When Deyna joined him on the cot he remained quiet, hoping even though he knew.

"What did you know, dad?"

"I knew it wasn't her."

On the roof of the storefront now, as Deyna is lighter and able to climb up through the beams, she moves above Benchere on the ladder as he huffs and hoists and slides the wooden sheets into place. Working in concert, Benchere feels the progression, yet tries to disregard as Deyna finishes. He helps her climb down, her legs slipping into the space between his arms and chest. "There then," Benchere backs away, dusts off his shirt and rubs twice at his chin. For a moment he thinks to say more, only to leave things where they started, in the pit of his belly.

Kayla is there, beside Zooie. Both watch Benchere before turning their heads as Jazz barks at the sound of something in the distance. Rose on the hillside shifts his binoculars while Jazz gives chase. *What now?* Benchere studies Jazz, looks up just as three small planes are crossing the horizon, passing over the hills and coming in to land.

16.

ROSE LEANS FROM HIS CHAIR AND HANDS STERN A PIECE
of cheese. "Well now," he says.

"Look here."

"What do you suppose?"

"If I had to guess."

"I'd say it's not tourists."

"Or journalists." Stern flicks sand from his Gouda. Rose has
opened a file for each of the seven additional sculptures, charts the
consequence in the pages of his report. Stern finishes his cheese,
squints down the hill and the planes now landing. "It's hot," he
says of the weather.

Rose wipes the sweat from his head with the underside of
his forearm, looks at Stern and nods, "It is hot."

"How hot it's become today."

LINDA IS WITH Harper on the west side of camp, clearing the
jeep's grill of loose straw and grass which gathers beneath when
driving. If not removed, the grass will clog the engine, collect in
the undercarriage, smolder and burn. Harper takes the spark plug
out, runs a hose into the open cylinder. Linda sits in the driver's
seat, hits the accelerator in order to push the clog free. A flock of
yellow hornbills circles and lands in the ziziphus trees. Two bolder
birds settle atop the jeep. Linda looks up and sees the planes.

Heidi is talking with Mindy over by the supply shed. Julie
and Cherry are checking the meat left to soak overnight in a salt

and vinegar bath. Mund is sending messages on his SL8 Rock Xtreme laptop. Harper closes the hood of the jeep, identifies the planes as Cessna 206s, with Continental IO-520 engines and tri-gears not well suited for the bush. Underpowered but service-able, each plane can carry six passengers, though two of the three planes arrive with just the pilot on board.

Benchere walks with Zooie to where the planes have landed some 100 yards south of his sculpture. A woman in a green dress and flat leather sandals climbs out of the first plane. Long limbed she unfolds through the door, lowers herself the rest of the way with a short leap. Her movements are refined. The green of her dress is dark. A red and orange shoulder sash is set at an angle across her chest, matching the head scarf she wears.

She is followed from the plane by two men in black slacks, white shirts and suit jackets without ties. Each plane has *The Republic of South Sudan* painted along its side in a red Andalus font. The pilots cut their engines, climb down and place wooden blocks in front of the wheels. The emptiness of the final two planes is a puzzle. Even after the pilots close the doors, everyone gathered still expects passengers to come from inside.

The woman's skin is a Babylon-oil dark, smooth with one slight scar just above her right eyebrow. She introduces herself, her voice mannered with the accent of that region. One of the guards carries a package wrapped in tan paper. Inside is a very large *jalabiya*. Ani Risha takes the package and presents it to Benchere.

"Well now," Benchere holds the garment up. "This is quite the thing." He slips the *jalabiya* over his shoulders. The shirt unfurls to just above his ankles. The white material set against his deep tan creates an immediate impression. Benchere turns and lets everyone get a good look at him. The Africana in the distance remain gathered on either side of their new store. Dancy Mund works his way through the crowd, attempts to interpose himself into the greeting, extends his hand and makes his own introduc-tion, inquires as to the purpose of Ani Risha's visit.

A quick study, Ani Risha ignores Dancy, turns back to Benchere and asks if there is a place they might talk.

They walk across the field, away from the planes and toward the sculpture. Jazz follows. The soles of Ani Rishi's shoes are rubber based and slightly ridged. She has a way of moving over the sands which does not disrupt the ground. Benchere's gait is more of a stomp and grind, his boots leaving their mark as he tests the limits of his stride inside his *jalabiya*. As they head off, Ani Risha talks about the desert, tells Benchere about the current conditions in South Sudan, how more than 90 percent of the country relies on firewood and charcoal for fuel, that too many trees are being cut down, the Nubian Desert now without a single oasis, deforestation increasing the risk of turning even more land into desert and yet, "The wars have made it hard for us to develop reliable electricity."

The current conflict with the North, Ani Risha explains, has continued through the South's cessation. "In the Sudan, the North still tries to control what is no longer theirs." She describes 2,000 Northern soldiers entering Abyei and Kadugli along the border where they've slaughtered thousands of Southern loyalists. United Nations workers have abandoned the region, leaving the general population to flee into the Nuba Mountains. Resistance against the North and al-Bashir is cobbled together by teachers and farmers, shop clerks and laborers exposed to, but otherwise untrained in, the methods of war. "Here we have finally negotiated our independence," Ani Risha says, "and we are still fighting as we've done for the last 70 years."

She pauses, gives Benchere a chance to review the information presented. As they pass under the southernmost arm of the sculpture, the wind chimes ring out. Benchere assumes Ani Risha will tell him now the reason for her visit, is surprised when she asks instead, "Have you heard of the Hoodia plant, Mr. Benchere?"

"The Hoodia? No."

"For hundreds of years the Hoodia has been used by the San Bushman as an appetite suppressant. During nomadic treks, the need to eat is inhibited by ingesting the leaves of the plant. The active ingredient in the Hoodia is glycoside which, in 2005, was patented by the South African Council for Scientific and Industrial Research."

"A patent on a plant?"

"On glycoside, yes. It was the San's usage however, which led the CSIR to first investigate the Hoodia. Because of this," Ani explains, "a representative filed a claim on behalf of the Sans asserting that the CSIR was making money off something the Sans had taught them. The Sans now receive a royalty check from Phyto Pharmaceuticals, which markets a diet drug using glycoside."

"You don't say." Benchere has not heard this story before. He asks how this sort of windfall is distributed and who actually sees the proceeds.

"There is a trust," Ani Risha continues. "The money is monitored and claims are systematically processed."

"Well now," Benchere is impressed. "Give South Africa credit. And this sort of fair play is something South Sudan is looking to emulate in its new government?"

For the first time Ani Risha smiles. She has an intelligent if not entirely warm face, her seriousness settled into her features like a steely carved impression. Her tone is officious, not unfriendly though clearly set to task. She walks toward the center beam, examines the details on the surface of the metal. In his *jalabiya*, Benchere is still waiting to hear why Ani Risha has flown out to see him when she asks, "Are you familiar with Salva Kiir?"

"He's your president."

"He is the president of the RSS."

"Is that who you work for?"

"I work for the Republic."

"And Kiir is president of your Republic."

"That's correct." Ani Risha folds her hands together, talks for a time about the Comprehensive Peace Agreement and Kiir's involvement negotiating South Sudan's independence. The latest attack by the North has Kiir more determined to effect peace and democratize the region. "Of course," Ani Risha says, "he has his detractors."

"Don't we all?"

"He's an honest man."

"Even worse."

She allows herself a second smile. They walk from beneath the sculpture, out to where the whole of Benchere's work comes into view. Jazz runs ahead. Rose and Stern stare down from the hill. The group of Africana remains near their storefront and the baobab trees. Benchere has his sunglasses on. He extends his arms to the sides and the cut of his *jalabiya* opens up like a kite. Having been patient, he goes ahead and asks now, "So what's the upshot here, Ani?"

Ani Risha's eyes are russet-brown, both firm and kind, not impervious but something almost generous. She looks at Benchere, unfolds her hands and replies by saying, "Your sculpture is beautiful."

"*Asante.*"

"You should be pleased."

"I am pleased."

"And these other works then," she refers to the seven additional pieces.

Benchere tugs at the front of his *jalabiya*, insists as always, "That has nothing to do with me."

"You're being modest," Ani Risha stops and presumes to scold Benchere with a shake of her finger.

"Modesty has nothing to do with it," Benchere begins to sense himself being set up and feels the need for retreat. All these surprises of late. He stands with his hands tucked inside the sleeves of his *jalabiya* and asks as directly as he can without causing insult, "What is this then? What do you want from me?"

Ani Risha gives the question its due, folds her fingers now in front of her and suggests they consider the possibilities.

BY DINNER, ANI Risha has taken one of the three planes and left with her guards for South Sudan. The other two planes and the pilots remain. Everyone now knows the reason for the visit.

They gather at the evening fire and continue their debate. All the BAA students argue in favor of building a sculpture in Abyei, regard the plan as representing perfectly the *sine qua non* of Benchere's project. Others disagree. They describe what they know of Abyei and the Nuba Mountains, the villages near the border shelled and torched, Nubans, Catholics and Dinkas slaughtered. *And we're to do what now?*

The puppet maker and biochemist, engineer and horticulturist oppose the idea. *We've done what we're supposed to here.*

"Have we?" Mindy believes, " We're members of the movement and need to be involved."

Members of what movement? The others say, *We didn't come here to get killed. We're not rebels. We're not soldiers.*

"Sure we are," Heidi shouts back.

The horse trainer and physical therapist are convinced South Sudan should build its own sculpture. *It does no good if we interfere.*

"But they invited us. There's no interference."

There's an implied imperialism in pushing our way into other people's affairs.

"Who's pushing?" Sam and Cherry chime in now. "They've asked for our help. Where's the imperialism if they want us to come?"

The others roll their eyes, are not comforted by Ani Risha's promise to provide materials and armed protection in Abyei. They accuse the South Sudanese of taking advantage of Benchere's good nature, of wanting a *Benchere* sculpture to use as bait, knowing the destruction of such by al-Bashir will be more newsworthy than having one of their own anonymous works blown up. What better way to gain support for their cause than to dangle Benchere into the conflict?

Benchere sits with his right side to the fire, his drink on his knee. He says nothing, lets the others have at it. His *jalabiya* has been removed and he's wearing his old green sweater and safari slacks. Twice now, while everyone argues, Benchere glances at

Deyna, who sits with her arms folded. Benchere doesn't speak with her, rubs at his chin, shifts his boots on the sand and waits for the fire to burn down.

Mindy presses for answers. Benchere promises a decision on Abyei by morning. "Tomorrow," he says, though he has already made up his mind. When everyone continues to ask, he gets up from the fire and walks back to his tent.

THE GROUND TARP in Benchere's tent has three small tears unmended. Night crawlers, scorpions and desert snakes, puff adders and black mambas, each drawn to camp, look for access, settle inside sleeping bags, in piles of clothes and sacks of wheat. Everyone's warned to check before slipping on a boot or sliding under sheets, but after ten weeks the routine is not applied vigilantly and close calls are common.

Benchere has his lantern turned low. Harper arrives a half hour later, his green knapsack slung over his left shoulder. He is carrying two glasses with shots of scotch. "Nightcap," he calls through the zippered flap, clicks the glasses together and says, "One for the road."

Benchere ignores the comment, calls back, "I'm sleeping."

"No you're not. I can see the light."

"Well praise Jesus."

"Ha. If I unzip the flap right now I'm going to find you in your chair." Harper waits then says, "I'm coming in."

He steps through the opening and hands Benchere his glass. Jazz gets up to greet Harper as he sits on the tarp. "Let's give it another hour," Harper says, his legs bent and arms behind him, his knapsack sliding from his shoulder. "Everyone should be asleep by then."

"I don't know what you're talking about," Benchere drinks the shot, puts the glass beside his chair.

Harper raises his glass though doesn't drink. He estimates the distance to Abyei, the flight route as charted, how far his Maule can go on a single tank and their need to stop and refuel outside Katanga. "Flying at night won't be a problem," he says.

"Not for you because you're not going," Benchere checks his watch, calculates for himself how long he should wait, then goes to the front of his tent and looks outside. The grounds have quieted. Those once at the fire have left. There's a small glow from behind Mund's fence but no sign of the patrol. The pilots sleep near their planes. Benchere returns to his chair, rubs at his chin, realizes he should have anticipated Harper putting two and six together and demanding to come along. He considers wrestling him down, hogtying him somehow, making a mad dash to the planes and waking the pilots.

Harper says, "It's good no one else suspects. Last thing we need is a dozen recruits to watch out for. Better to leave them behind." He advocates sending the two pilots home on their own.

Benchere leans over and reties the laces of his boots. His face is red and there's a pounding in his ears as he cracks, "You don't know what you're talking about."

"Sure. I'm thick as oatmeal." Harper takes his drink and pours it into one of the nearby slits in the tarp. "Clear head," he explains. "I can drink when we get back." He places his palms flat on the ground, talks about the guards waiting for them in Abyei and predicts, "They'll be a couple of kids with fifty-year-old rifles."

"It doesn't matter. I won't need them."

"Right. And your buddy Ani Risha doesn't want al-Bashir to know you're there," Harper taps the side of his head. "How else will your visit be newsworthy if there isn't a little drama? At least with me around you'll know someone has your back while you work." He waits a second then says, "Not that building a sculpture is why you're taking off."

"Don't go there," Benchere warns Harper.

"I could say the same," Harper jokes. "I guess you should be grateful to Ani Risha for giving you this opportunity. All your troubles here, I mean, who wouldn't see flying to South Sudan as an easy out? Better than staying in the Kalahari. Better than getting things resolved. Anywhere but here, right?"

Benchere stands, finds his pack and begins stuffing clean clothes inside. Harper stands as well, says about Marti, not cruelly but with purpose, "You're not cheating on her. You don't have to go."

"Goddamn it, Harp," only the aches in Benchere's body keep him from leaping up and tackling Harper. His head hits against the top of the tent as he rises, and cursing, he bends down again, growls against the inner lining of his chest. "What I'm doing," he snaps then stops, the argument not there. He offers up the only thing he can. "I've had enough."

"Enough is it?"

"That's right."

"Enough what?"

"To last."

"But what does that even mean?"

"It means just that."

"Alright." Harper presses, "And this is what you're going to tell Deyna?"

"There's nothing to tell," Benchere strains not to howl. "We're adults. She understands. It's circumstance is all. Living on top of one another for weeks, working and eating together, things get exaggerated."

"You're full of shit." Harper takes a step closer and asks, "Then you don't?"

"What?"

"Love her?"

"Do I ... ? Christ," Benchere in full confession yells, "I won't!"

"Ha," Harper claps in the shadows of the dim lantern light. "Well now, there you go. That's the first honest thing you've said."

Benchere grabs his pack. Jazz is up and ready to leave the tent. Outside, the wind is still, the night clear. Benchere thinks of how best to reply, but can come up with nothing. He pushes his head through the flap in the tent, checks on the others. The air has cooled. He breathes deeply, exhales slowly. "All of this," he says as if in answer to another question, and coming back inside to face Harper, he grunts, "Hell."

Five minutes later they've awakened the pilots and the three planes take off.

17.

ROSE FOLLOWS THE LIGHT FROM THE PLANES AS THEY disappear overhead. He fishes out his money clip, hands Stern another twenty. "Don't spend it all in one place."

"Not to worry," Stern tucks the bill in his pocket.

Rose sends a message stateside.

"This should be interesting," Stern says.

"I bet."

"Do you?"

"Quit that."

Stern laughs and says to Rose, "Come on now, who knows what's going to happen?"

KYLE ATTEMPTS TO Skype with Benchere. He has read the stories coming out of Egypt, Chad, Namibia and Yemen, has his own stories to tell from South Providence and Broad Street. In gauging the seven-hour time difference, he hopes to catch Benchere soon. With each attempt however, he gets nothing. He tries twice more then leaves a message, goes back to watching the news.

THE SOUND OF the planes brings everyone from their tents. They stumble together in the dark, follow whatever light is shined. Jazz barks from where Benchere has left him. Zooie hears and calls out. The group of Africana wake and watch as well. Deyna walks to where the planes were before, while Mund's group hurries to see what has happened.

Daimon films the scene. Deyna surveys the area. Word of Benchere being gone passes quickly. Deyna answers questions, says "Yes," she is surprised, and "No," he didn't tell her. "Yes," they have enough supplies in camp, and "No," she doesn't expect Benchere to be gone long. As for why he left without them, everyone agrees they were foolish not to expect this before. *What were we thinking?* They turn to Deyna and shake their heads.

Mund circles the group, wearing Briarshun pants and a green windbreaker. He carries a Fenix E21 flashlight, his Doc Marten's tied tightly. Once the situation is evaluated, he hurries back in the direction of the main camp, passes along the footpath through the common area to Benchere's tent and then the supply shed, where he uses the key Benchere left for Naveed to undo the lock.

HARPER LANDS IN Aybei, some sixty miles west of the Nuba Mountains. The recent bombings have transformed the immediate area into a crushed jigsaw shell; the nearest marketplace abandoned, the homes, huts and buildings burned out. Only a handful of people have not yet fled into the hillside and deeper into the mountains. The Ethiopian peacekeeping troops sent into the region are ineffective. Absent a clear directive, they avoid the Northern soldiers, ignore the Maule as it lands.

Ani Risha has arranged for seven men to meet Benchere. Dressed in a mismatch of old shirts and slacks of no uniform color, in tennis shoes and open-toed sandals instead of boots, each man is slim framed and leanly muscled. The rifles they carry are as antiquated as Harper predicted. One of the men introduces himself as Abebe Neen. Sand has settled in Abebe's hair. His eyes are the color of bitumen. His skin is the same dark shade as Ani Risha's, though not as smooth. He has on a green and black faded shirt, brown pants frayed at the cuffs. His belt is twine, his right back pocket missing. "This is all then?" he says as Benchere and Harper come from the Maule.

The two Cessnas have been sent on to Juba. Harper leaves the Maule beside a Timpir tree. Benchere follows Abebe to a jeep where he sits in front. Abebe slides in behind the wheel, hands his rifle to a second man who climbs in back with Harper. A third man is left behind to guard the Maule, while the others follow on foot. The road is rutted from the shelling. Only a few structures remain undamaged. A bus at the side of the road has been torched and the tires removed. The city is built on sands coated with silt and ash. The breeze stirs. Harper takes a dew rag from his pocket and ties it over his nose and mouth. Benchere does the same. The absence of people and livestock makes everything feel part of a violent rapture; the smell less of decay than a swift annihilation.

Harper asks about the bodies, the reported numbers of dead in Abyei leaving him to wonder. Abebe answers curtly, "We have eaten them, of course. What would you do in America, Mr. Harper?"

After three miles, they stop at a mud brick hutch, square with a thatch roof and a single window in the rear. The door is a thin sheet of unpainted wood. The debris out front has been cleared away. An outdoor pit used for cooking is encircled with clay bricks stacked two feet high. The pit is to the left of the house. Twenty yards further down is the truck with supplies Ani Risha promised.

Benchere gets out of the jeep and walks toward the truck. Inside is a mismatch of metals, scrap sheets and rubbish finds, a butane torch, pieces of rope and rocks, two bags of cement and a sack with files and hammers. The materials present a challenge as few of the metals work well together. Benchere doesn't mention this. He assumes Abebe has helped orchestrate the haul and, not wishing to offend, he touches the closest sheet of tin and thanks him for the effort, does his best to sound enthusiastic. "Wonderful work, Mr. Neen," he says.

Skeptical of Benchere's visit, Abebe does not reply.

The house has been cleaned and set up with the expectation of several more people arriving. Mattresses line the floor, shelves filled with canned meats and vegetables; Jolly Green Giant and Dinty Moore, nothing extravagant yet each a luxury in Abyei. Harper goes outside to the cooking pit which is filled with dry wood.

After traveling all night, he wants to sleep, but is also hungry, tries to decide what to do.

Benchere leaves the truck and walks across what is left of the road. A half house sits abandoned. Additional structures remain further off in equal states of ruin. To the side of the house, grave upon grave, the earth heaped and turned and not quite repaired. Benchere takes stock. The wreckage of the city is disturbing, though less surprising than the silence. From all reports online, Benchere anticipated constant gunfire, sirens blasting and ongoing mayhem. Discovering the area no longer under siege comes as a relief, and yet for reasons of his own he is also disappointed.

He wipes his face with the palm of his hands, thinks of Deyna, considers what Ani Risha has asked him to do, pictures the ghosts in Abyei, the ghosts in his head. *Crazy, crazy, crazy,* he attempts to convince himself. *Here is fine, here is good enough.* He has come as a favor, has come for personal reasons, to give himself distance, and if needed, perhaps more. He looks about, attempts to merge the two purposes of his trip, but can't quite do it, becomes anxious and thinks building a sculpture here in the empty ruins of Abyei is a mistake.

Ahh, Benchere.

From miles away, he listens for sounds of mortars, imagines the gunplay in the hills, the planes overhead and the Northern soldiers in ambush. He remembers the night Deyna came to him, lying there in the dark, holding her awkwardly afterward, over-compensating, making his grip too tight, releasing her, only to reach for her again. He thinks next of Marti, of the times and times and times again, then pictures the fighting further off in Kadugli and Khartoum and tells himself, if nothing else, a sculpture nearer the mountains will serve the canvas of the area better. The challenge of his arrival excites him suddenly. He moves a fly from in front of his face, checks behind what remains of the shattered wall, folds and unfolds his arms, rubs at his chin, puts his hands on his hips and stares east toward the horizon.

Harper watches, sees Benchere clear enough to have a bad feeling. "Hey," he shouts, tries distracting him by tossing a stone. "Come and have some water and cool down," he says. "Come and get some sleep."

The other men watch as well, unsure what is happening as Harper yells, "Come on."

Benchere looks in the direction of the truck, points back at Harper.

"Fuck." Harper shakes his head, tells Benchere, "Hold on now."

Benchere pretends not to hear.

Harper pitches another stone, this time directly at him. "You're crazy," he says.

Benchere howls.

Harper raises his hands, is tempted to flatten the tires on all the vehicles, making it impossible for Benchere to call Abebe over and say in that way he has when posing a question that is no question at all, "So Mr. Neen, how far is it to the Nuba Mountains anyway? How far if we left now in this thing you call a truck?"

DANCY MUND HAS put on a suit, adjusts his tie, parts his hair and polishes his shoes. Gabriella has refreshed her make-up which tends to run in the heat. Near noon, four men and two women arrive in a rented limo. The Munds go and greet their guests together, repeat the word *delighted* nine times.

Two of the guests snap pictures of Benchere's sculpture. The others film with their cell phones. Afterward, everyone heads behind the fence where a table is set with plates and glasses, a pitcher of water, sliced fruit, fried potatoes, a bowl of nuts and sugared candies Gabriella has saved. Dancy arranged the meeting in the days before, had hoped to catch Benchere by surprise and bring further support for developing the area directly to him. With Benchere absent, the Munds look to close the deal on their own. Dancy encourages everyone to fill their plates then moves to the front of the table and begins his presentation.

On hand is a representative from CEDA – The Citizen Entre-preneurial Development Agency – the UNDP – United Nations Development Program – and BOCONGO – Botswana Council of Non-Governmental Organizations. The remaining invitees are agents for Botswana's very deepest pockets; investors made famil-iar with the Munds' idea for a resort and intrigued enough to con-sider involvement.

Deyna and the others watch from the main camp. The Afri-cana stop what they are doing to observe as well. Daimon films. Rose and Stern run photographs through their computer for each of the six arrivals. "Quite the gathering," Stern says.

"Big guns."

"Heavy hitters."

The group talks with Mund of routes and roads, of building a landing strip for commercial planes, of the hotel they will erect in the desert with Benchere's sculpture as the centerpiece. When asked, Dancy apologizes for Benchere's absence, explains that he is off now in the Sudan overseeing another project, but that he feels very strongly about the prospect of inner-desert devel-opment. "No one is more committed to his vision than Michael," Mund says. "Of course," he uses the moment to explain how the sculpture is actually free for all who come to the area to view on their own. "We don't need to license the work from Benchere. The land here is available for purchase. Our including Michael is more of a courtesy. We can build here on our own."

The Munds present their business plan. A decision is made to bring out a surveyor, a geologist and an engineer to determine what is needed. Numbers are discussed, a projection and time-line, as well as a cost analysis the others will take back with them to consider. At the end of the meeting Gabrielle offers the group parting favors: oranges and dried meat for their drive, each packed in sheets of wax paper flown in from Maun.

Handshakes and backslaps are exchanged all around. As they walk to the limousine one of the men points in the direction of the Africana and the storefront, which is partially stocked and prepared for business. Mund takes note, is about to offer assurances that the assemblage is temporary and will be removed once the actual construction of their resort is underway. Instead, each of the others congratulates Mund for his ingenuity and business savvy. "It's generous," the woman from CEDA says and everyone agrees. Mund pivots on his bad leg and replies, "I do what I can." He opens the car door and wishes them all a safe journey.

ABEBE DRIVES THE truck with Benchere and Harper up front. Before leaving Abyei, he radios Juba and reports their change of plans. The radio is ancient. After twenty minutes they receive a one word response from the capital: *Proceed.*

Two of the other men follow behind in the jeep. The road from Abyei is a rough path covered with sand. The trail disappears completely nearer the mountains. Twice a plane flies overhead and Abebe squeezes the wheel tighter, curses beneath his breath. *Voetsek. Fokof. Hol naier.* The truck and jeep have been covered with mud to help camouflage them from the planes but this only helps so much. Not until the *whoosh* of the planes pass does Abebe relax his grip.

Most of the water and canned foods from Abyei is packed in back of the truck with the metals. Extra gas is stored as well. They drive along the west side of the mountains, toward Kadugli and possibly Kordofan. Benchere sits by the door, Harper in the center. The road bounces them from side to side. An hour removed from Abyei they are stopped by Southern fighters. Abebe identifies himself and the Americans. "Yo brothers," he says and gets out of the truck, stretches, explains about Kiir and Risha and Benchere, offers a few cans of food from the back and inquires about the road ahead.

They continue on. Harper naps. Just after dusk the mountains come clearly into view. The landscape rolls higher, the hills in a more severe undulation. The topsoil is dotted with dry yellow grass, thorny trees and shrubs. Abebe stops at a series of abandoned huts that have survived the recent shelling. He gets out of the truck again, calls "Hallo," and waits to hear if anyone is near enough to answer.

Harper and Benchere climb out as well. Abebe calls louder into the hills. When no one shouts back he tells Benchere, "They are further up. It is safer in the mountains."

"We should drive on then."

"No." Abebe says, "We'll stop here." He explains why driving in the dark is a bad idea. The men from the jeep check inside the huts. Benchere and Harper examine the cratered holes in the earth while Abebe walks the length of the area. The absence of any tools, clothing or food suggests the village has either been ransacked or quickly packed up by the original inhabitants and carried off.

Wood is gathered and a fire started. Cans of stewing beef and corn are opened then mixed together in the only pot they've brought. They eat communally this way, with spoons sunk in. Harper has tobacco and papers picked up in Tshane. After their meal he offers the two men a smoke. They take the pouch and papers and show Harper how to roll a cigarette with one hand. Their names are Bako and Jelani. Harper calls them Ben and Jerry. The men don't get the joke but smile just the same. "What is a Harper?" they ask. "Do you play?" Bako mimics the strumming of strings.

Harper interprets the mood of the men as a good sign. After a day of driving only Abebe remains silent. Harper offers him the pouch and papers but he declines. Benchere takes his spoon and stuffs it in his back pocket. He turns to Abebe, asks about Kadugli, wants to know how far off they are and what chance there is they will run into soldiers between here and there.

Abebe holds his rifle in his left hand. The muscles of his forearm are taut strands of rope wrapped around the bone. He turns sideways to Benchere, treats the question as an indicator of the American's obliviousness, has taken to dropping the *Mr.* as he replies, "You had us drive here and now you want to know what might happen, *Bencheer?*"

Benchere nods once as if to show he understands what

Abebe is saying. He rephrases his question, to which Abebe replies, "We can expect to see soldiers."

"And if we stay here, how long before they find us?"

"How long?" he takes out a cigarette from his own pack, lights it and says, "These are questions you wouldn't ask if you understood better the situation."

"Right, but assuming I don't."

Abebe lets the smoke out through his nose. The question irks and Abebe is tempted to say, *If you knew what you are supposed to, Bencheer, you would have stayed in Abyei.* He goes ahead instead and describes the areas near Nuba and further up where they are heading, details the regular attacks, the bombings and the soldiers. In Kadugli, the South attempts to push back the North with limited success. "Not to worry," Abebe mocks now. "I can get you all the way to Kadugli if you want. Beyond Kordofan. We can go to Khartoum and meet al-Bashir for lunch."

Benchere gives the comment a shrug, dismisses the sarcasm while saying, "Khartoum may be a bit far. I bet al-Bashir has plans for lunch, but if you can get us to Kadugli that will be good. Let's shoot for that."

"Shoot, yes." Abebe slips his arm through his rifle strap, slides the gun up over his back then turns his head so that he's looking at Benchere from a different angle. He puffs more smoke, brings his head straight and says of Benchere's decision to leave Abyei, "Tell me again what you will do in Kadugli."

The details of Benchere's plan have already been presented and yet when Benchere answers, "I'm here to build a sculpture," the reaction from Abebe is to laugh.

The men with Harper look over. Abebe stands with Benchere on the opposite side of the fire and asks, "This is what you've come for?"

"It is."

"We've heard this."

"Then you know."

"What am I supposed to know, *Bencheer?*"

"Why I'm here."

"Do you know why you're here?"

"Didn't I just tell you?" Benchere's voice rises. Defensive, he says, "I'm sticking my Goddamn neck out, Abe. You might want to lighten up a bit on the attitude."

Abebe holds to a different view and says, "This neck that is stuck, *Bencheer*, isn't it ours? Taking you where you want to go and for what? To sculpt?" This time when Abebe laughs the other men join him as well. The place they've stopped sits in a hollow between two hills, not quite a valley but low enough to offer shelter. Abebe tugs at his shirt beneath his rifle strap. He stares at Benchere, wonders what the penalty might be if he left the Americans here on their own and was done with them. Of Benchere's plan he says, "Why not bring us something we can use? Food and guns. What are we supposed to do with a sculpture?"

Benchere adjusts his safari hat. The temperature is warm still, though the air through the near-valley after sunset has a hint of something cooled. The question is reasonable. *What are you doing?* He answers not as his students would, does not tell Abebe that building a sculpture is a stick in the eye to al-Bashir, a show of defiance that puts a spine in the center of the South's resolve. Instead, he says, "What you're supposed to do there, Abe, is observe what the sculpture has to offer."

"To observe?"

"That's right." He settles his boots on the sand, takes the spoon from his pocket and waves it like a baton for no particular reason. He forgets how exhausted he is from too little sleep and all the travel, keeps Abebe in front of him, leans forward and says, "Art is what everything else chases. Do you get what I'm saying?"

Abebe answers, "No."

Benchere huffs. He takes the spoon and slaps it inside his left palm, puts it in his front pocket then takes it back out and says, "Think of art as the looking glass. What you are able to see is truth in its most concentrated form. It doesn't matter if you're from the North or South, if you're an innocent or a monster. Everyone when they stop and look at art is confronted by the same thing. This is art's function."

"To show us truth?"

Benchere sounds off like his students, "Art is truth."

Abebe listens, finishes his cigarette and crushes it under the toe of his shoe. Despite his size compared to Benchere, there is a power when he speaks. He responds with denial, challenges Benchere directly. "What are we to see that we don't know now, *Bencheer*? What truth is there that I don't get? There is no other truth than this," he moves his hand about, lets the panorama of where they are settle in. "You can't create truth. A sculpture is cold steel and knows nothing." He points again, shows the craters in the earth's surface, the empty huts beneath the hills and mountains. "This is truth for real," he says. "This is all there is."

"You're wrong," Benchere, provoked, lets Abebe know, "What you describe isn't truth." He digs in and says, "War is real but it's still bullshit. Listen to me. You have all these years of conflict, declarations and treaties and pacts, agreements and referendums, cease-fires and attacks and none of this resolves a damn thing. It's a killing field. It's genocide. It's madness. It's reality, sure. There's no denying. But truth?" Benchere says, "Reality isn't truth, Abe, it's just the thing you live in while you search for something else."

Abebe frowns, does not buy a word. He sees where the conversation is going and shuts Benchere down. "What you make is not truth either, *Bencheer*," he says. "What you make means nothing." To Abebe, art is a luxury, the sort of pretty tapestry purchased for the home when someone has a few extra pennies, and no more representative of the real world than a candy dish or graffiti painted on a rock. "All this is easy for you," he tells Benchere. "Here you come for a visit. You join causes like a man putting on a pair of socks. You will go home all safe and pleased with yourself and where will we go, *Bencheer*?" Of the idea to create a sculpture in Kadugli, he says, "How can you make anything true when five minutes ago you didn't even know if soldiers were near?"

"Bah," Benchere folds his large arms across his middle and stares back at Abebe. He thinks about his answer, about his decision to leave Abyei and move closer to the fight. He attempts to rationalize it all in terms of Deyna and Marti as the fire crackles with the addition of new sticks.

Harper is still standing with the other men. Benchere talks about Kiir and Kadugli, about using his sculpture to steer the spirit away from unseemly disputes and back to the soul, when Abebe interrupts. His eyes are large with a yellow-white shade hosting the lens. His intelligence is forceful, is ancient, like knowledge before it's distilled for mass consumption. He says of Benchere's reference to Ani Risha and Kiir and al-Bashir, "That's not why you're here."

The sun has set behind the hills, leaves the camp in shadows. Abebe shifts his rifle strap across his chest, can see the tension in Benchere's face, the gravity as Benchere puffs his cheeks and tries to explain again why he's come to South Sudan. The difficulty and desperation in Benchere's attempt causes Abebe to look at him differently and with sympathy for the first time. He doesn't know the details, has no idea about Marti or Deyna or any of the rest, but he has lived his life in Abyei, has seen enough of the look, has witnessed it each time a neighbor is forced to wrestle against his own unspeakable form of loss; how each would rush with eyes wide and wet into battle, his cry wretched, a sound the heart registered before anything else.

Abebe sees the same in Benchere, takes a step closer, gets him to go quiet as he asks, "Why are you really here, *Bencheer*? Why is it? What has brought you here now?"

18

STERN COMES FROM HIS CHAIR AND STANDS ATOP THE hill. "Well now," he says.

ONCE THE LIMOUSINE is gone, Deyna along with the BAA students and several of the others from the main camp go and confront the Munds. Dancy stands again at the head of the table, answers questions, says in reference to the six people who've just left, "They were here to help formalize our plan."

What plan? The others say, *There is no plan.*

"Of course there is, dears," Gabriella stands beside her husband. She is wearing a blue and green print sundress, high heels and pearls. Her hair is re-dyed, the orange faded twice now in the sun, the color a yellowish ginger. All the tents in Mund's group are set on deeded plots. The size of each plot varies depending on what the occupant can afford. The larger plots are toward the rear, their view of the desert unencumbered. A numbering system provides an address. A chart is posted with corresponding names, debts and duties owed to the camp. Mund brokers the deals. The money goes toward bettering the group, Dancy says, though he takes his own cut off the top and does not explain what exactly these promised services include.

The water Mund sips is warm and slightly clouded by the iodine crystals. He speaks about developing the area while the others hoot and shout him down. *Not going to happen,* they say.

"Of course it is," Mund appeals to their liberal bent, says

of the Africana and what impressed the six officials before, "You need to consider all the jobs we can generate by building a resort."

What jobs? The others aren't fooled. *You mean for the Africans? But they have their store now. They're independent entrepreneurs. You want to get rid of that and have them come work for you as what? Cheap labor? Bellhops and maids at your hotel?*

"Yes, that. Exactly," both Munds say. "There's nothing wrong with being part of the labor force. America was founded on the value of organized work."

And here you want slaves.

"Hardly. Salaries and benefits and places to live. You progressives," Dancy says. "You spout your rhetoric, and yet at the first opportunity you look down your nose at maids and bellhops and deny these people any fair chance for steady, risk-free employment."

That's not what we're doing and you know it, the others shout back. Deyna stands with Zooie and Daimon. Mindy accuses Mund of using the Africans as pawns to leverage their support. "It's exploitation," she says. "First you want to co-opt Benchere's sculpture, and now you want to create a feudal labor force and take the African's store from them."

"Now that's a bit harsh don't you think, dear?" Gabriella scolds.

The skin at the end of Dancy's nose has dried and peeled. The heat of the desert has had its effect, the weeks of enduring the climate without the most basic of amenities has compromised his temperament, make it more difficult for him to maintain any semblance of cheer. His features are stern and pinched now as he says, "We're being generous, whether you see it that way or not. We're offering opportunity against this little business hutch you've built. How much money do you think your store will generate long term?"

Plenty.

"And who is going to manage the merchandise if not us?"

Kayla Doure can manage quite well on her own.

Deyna warns Mund against making deals with the people from the limo. "You have no authority."

"I have all the authority I need." Dancy wobbles on his bad leg as he says, "If the powers in Botswana want to develop the area, you won't be able to stop them."

But they can't develop here, the others in unison remind Mund that Benchere already has a signed agreement with the regional government, that he has leased the land and owns the rights to his sculpture.

"Please," Mund finds the comment of little consequence. "This is Africa," he says. "Even assuming what you say matters, and it doesn't, how far do you think Benchere's agreement extends? How far from where we are now do you think the sculpture can be seen? Do you really think if we don't put a hotel up here someone else won't a half mile away?"

Heidi in full fury shouts, "That's crap. If Benchere was here ... "

"But he's not, dear," Gabriella notes.

"Until he is," Deyna announces a moratorium on any further conversation.

"What's that?" Dancy scowls in Deyna's direction.

"There's no point in discussing anything further."

"Is that so?"

"It is so," Mindy says in support of Deyna.

At this everyone begins to roar. Several men from Mund's group stand inside the fence listening. The dirt in the compound is a silver sandy tan. Mund tosses his head back and snaps at Deyna. "Has it occurred to you," he says, "that what I'm being is polite and you are actually little more than a nuisance?"

"You're being ridiculous," Deyna says.

"Am I? Ridiculous?" Dancy fumes, "Here I'm presenting you with a great opportunity and you treat me as if I just shot your dog." He moves away from the table, takes to standing on one of the crates, on one leg, like some deformed stork or mad conductor, his arms waving, his face agitated as he points back toward the Africana and says of their store, "It's ok for you to merchandize the area, but not me, is that it?" He lifts his bad leg, lets his voice slip over completely to contempt and barks, "What is it with you people? I've proposed something that is surefire and fair to all and a testament to the free market system, and you tell me that I'm exploitive and to go away. What hypocrisy. How is your treatment of me any different from the fascists you claim to denounce? From Mugabe or al-Bashir or any of the rest? You are depriving me of access to the market on what grounds?"

Deyna doesn't answer. Instead she starts walking toward the fence. Everyone else follows. Dancy is still shouting, even louder here. He looks toward the men from his group, gives the others fair warning, insists his plan will move forward regardless and that, "I don't have to ask you for anything. You can't stop the natural progression of things. You can't impose your will when you have no will to impose. Your position of power no longer exists. You can't block our advance when you have no means to enforce your threat. If you push us, we'll take what we have to. Are you listening? Do you get it?"

Dancy hops about on the crate, announces firmly his own authority, resorts to the standard instrument for seizing control. The method is timeless as Dancy's men produce from beneath their shirts that which was removed from the storage shed last night.

IN THE MORNING Benchere and Harper drive with Abebe toward Kadugli. All three sit in the front of the truck. Bako and Jelani have taken the jeep and headed back to Abyei, unable to go further safely. Soldiers appear on patrol and at checkpoints. Twice the truck is stopped. Ani Risha has provided Benchere with forged papers meant to work in Abyei. He is now a contractor for the North's CBO sent to inspect the area's needs. Al-Bashir's signature appears at the bottom of the page. The soldiers turn the paper over and back, can read only so much. *Dag* brothers, Abebe says as he offers them a cigarette. *Ma'a as-salaama,* once the soldiers wave them on.

Benchere's right arm hangs out the window. A few hours ago, inside one of the remaining huts, he sat against the far wall, removed his boots but not his socks. Starlight entered through the slats of the roof, created charcoal shades. The air was an odd scent, a mix of decaying root and smoky sulfur. Abebe, Bako and Jelani settled into a rotation of dozing and guarding the grounds. A breeze blew across the near valley, moved the thatch and passed between the openings in the walls of the hut. Benchere put his nose to the air like a dog to the wind and thought of his earlier conversation with Abebe.

Why are you really here, Bencheer?

Harper was stretched out on the opposite side of the hut, trying to sleep. Leaves and straw were used as a semi-cushion against the dirt floor. Benchere was restive, told Harper what else Abebe said. *A man comes to the Sudan for only two reasons. A man comes to the desert because he has lost something. Or a man comes to get lost. Sometimes it is both.*

"Can you believe?" Benchere shifted his weight in the dark, supported the small of his back with a handful of straw. Harper listened to the rustle. Occasional gunfire could be heard in the distance. Benchere lit a match, dangerous inside the dry hut. He held it high just the same, could see Harper spread out.

The match burned down to Benchere's fingers and he dropped it. The sound of his own breathing annoyed him. Harper pictured one of those old Disney cartoons where a mad bull snorted steam through its nose. Benchere held his breath for 30 seconds before he quit and lay down on the straw. He closed his eyes, thought of Deyna on the first day they met, how he had gone to set the stakes for his sculpture and she had asked him, *Do you know what you're doing?* There in a nutshell, the universal question. *What don't I?* Benchere thought, and then again.

Laid out on his back, he extended his left arm to the side. His fingers searched the empty space as he used to when in bed after Marti died. Maneuvering across the vacant mattress his loss was clear, yet inside the hut everything felt different. The absence and emptiness were open-ended, spoke to him of voids created and voids to fill.

He stretched further, straightened his arm until his hand hit the wall. The contact with something solid got Benchere's attention. He tested the barrier by pushing back. Everything, Benchere believed, was composed of either resistance or advance. *I won't. I want. I will.* Each was connected to one or the other. He considered this, thought of Deyna again, weighed his options, and reaching with his hand rolled tightly, he confronted the firmness of the wall, pushed until the first of the sticks began to bend and slowly gave way.

INSIDE KADUGLI, WITH the fighting moved inland from the border, almost all traffic flows out of the city in search of safer grounds. Abebe drives the truck against the tide, past the shells of remaining buildings and the recent rubble not yet removed from the streets. The roads are also shelled, the souqs burned down, the soldiers ordered by al-Bashir to cut off utilities and supplies. At the soccer stadium soldiers interrogate anyone suspected of supporting the South, the rebels or SPLA – the Sudan People's Liberation Army. The methodology employed by the soldiers produces tortured screams which the government attempts to drown away by piping Wagner's *Die Walkure* through stereo speakers hung in front.

Those who've not fled remain in makeshift camps in the center of town. People scavenging approach the truck. They look in back, search for food, find only sheets of metal as the canned goods and rifle are hidden beneath. Disappointed, they step away as Abebe drives off.

After a few more miles Benchere has Abebe stop the truck near a roofless brown building which may or may not have once been a school. An explosion has sent bricks and stone and other materials into the street. Benchere climbs out and begins pulling metals from the back of the truck. The plan is to create a fully realized sculpture in under twelve hours. Whether or not the soldiers will allow Benchere to continue is a separate concern. Arriving now, fresh from his night in the hut, he is excited by the prospect of making art.

He sorts through the metals, checks the propane torch and additional tools. People come and watch Benchere work, unsure at first what he's doing. Soldiers in the area inspect the scene, report their findings and then move off. Benchere lays out a flat sheet of tin which he hammers then folds and welds to an elongated piece of piping. "What we need," he says, and asks Harper to find a large cement block from one of the collapsed walls, which will serve as the sculpture's foundation.

Harper uncovers a usable slab, fastens a rope and gets Abebe to drag it over with the truck. Benchere sits atop the slab, his legs out in front as he uses a hammer and chisel to create a hole in the center of the cement. Once the hole is deep enough he gets Harper and Abebe to help him lift the piping and place it inside. The rod is heavy and awkward to hoist. Two men from the crowd step forward and lend a hand.

Benchere works for several hours. The crowd grows and more people volunteer to help. A woman on a tin drum beats out an accompanying rhythm, while a few of the braver children make a game of dancing close to Benchere then dashing back. Benchere laughs. Harper pretends to give chase. Even Abebe is caught up in the scene. Food appears from somewhere as the sculpture acquires shape. Everyone marvels at Benchere's skill. He tells the crowd his name, says, "I am Michael Benchere."

The others repeat as if in song. *Benchere. Benchere. Benchere.*

Soldiers continue to monitor the crowd throughout the day. The conflict as it stands between North and South, between Dinka and Nubans and the Muslim-dominated Northern soldiers, between tribes and sub-tribes and so on and so on renders the dangers in the city feral. And still more people come out.

Benchere makes use of each piece of metal from the truck. His sculpture evolves in layers, as a maze of angled sheets and strips welded like stalks sprung from a single spore. People bring additional materials and lay them nearby, present them as intimate offerings. Benchere incorporates each of everything he receives.

By dusk more than two hundred people have arrived and occupy the area. A source of light is provided from a neighboring rooftop; how exactly Benchere isn't sure. He finishes his work just before 10 pm. Exhausted, his sculpture is beautiful. As he steps back people hand him water, bread and slices of dried meat. The woman playing the tin drum has been joined by other musicians and singers. One man strums a homemade guitar. Everyone is festive. The creation of the sculpture is wildly applauded, produces a clear sense of achievement, possibility and promise.

Benchere is pleased, too, feels in the moment relief. *Here then,* he thinks. The advent of his handiwork has altered his perspective, allows him to appreciate the intimacy gained from a specific sort of audience. All of his earlier distancing falls away, replaced by the compliment of having so many people gathered in a way that is unlike the crowds at galleries and museums and one-man exhibits where his work has been viewed before.

Harper stands to the side of the sculpture, a blue paper hat someone has given him propped on the back of his head. Abebe is dancing near the tin drum. Benchere, too, in the spirit sways and sings with those in the crowd. All is harmony. Everyone is fearless. Benchere celebrates, is excited to tell Deyna, to tell his students and Zooie.

The sound from the music and dancing is such that everyone is focused on the immediacy of their celebration and no one notices the soldiers at first. Only as the soldiers get out of their jeeps and push through the crowd does the music stop. The crowd scatters while the light from the roof is extinguished and the street goes dark. The soldiers wear green uniforms made of cheap Egyptian cotton. Their helmets are ancient, their faces cold as they rush forward. The crowd flees. Startled, Benchere and Harper remain.

Three of the soldiers move directly to the sculpture and set themselves to work, while the remaining four secure the area.

They aim their rifles as Benchere calls out, "Hey now." When he moves too close one of the guards uses the butt of his rifle to strike him hard on the hip, knocking him down.

Fallen, Benchere anticipates a second blow. Instead, after a minute all the soldiers run back to their jeeps and drive off. Benchere scrambles to his knees, looks toward his sculpture and thinks, *Ahh hell.* As quickly as he can, he climbs to his feet and rushes for cover. There is in the moment nothing else to do. Watching him from across the street, three of the children who were dancing just moments ago stare at Benchere from behind a half wall, eye him expectantly.

Benchere spots the children and returns their stare. *Shit now.* Here is the thing about innocence, it knows everything and nothing. *Here is the thing.* Benchere sighs, *Fuck.* What a perfect challenge to his new mindfulness. Here he is, after last night, his hand against the wall of the hut, and through then, finally so, a resolution he did not know was coming and is at last prepared for and now what? So much for what Harper said before, that coming to the Sudan was easier than staying in the desert. What would he say to that now?

Aaarggh.

The children continue to peek from behind the half wall. Benchere pictures his Kadugli sculpture as she was before in the truck; no more than metal scraps and wires. He sees her as she is this evening and soon to be what again? *Shit,* he turns and runs back into the street.

Harper shouts and tries to stop him. Abebe appears suddenly and also tries now, too. Together they call out, but Benchere pays no attention. Huffing, he runs with his bruised hip and mounts the base of the sculpture. The timer has already counted down past 12 … 11 … 10 … The explosive itself is big as a microwave, large enough to blow the sculpture into a thousand jagged pieces. Benchere bends to pick it up, imagines the shrapnel passing through him, tries to understand what is happening, how maybe this was what he wanted once but it isn't anymore, and yet in the moment he can only think, *Well, yes. Here I am.*

The charge is heavy in his hands. He says no prayer, says nothing more than "Fuck." The timer clicks. Harper shouts. Benchere with eyes clenched, throws the explosive into the street.

An eternity of the most absolute silence in the seconds before the children stand.

Slowly, others who have run for cover peek from behind previously damaged walls and inside empty buildings. They, too, are surprised the device has not gone off. They look at the explosive, look for the soldiers, look at the sculpture and at Benchere. One by one they reappear, approach where Benchere remains at the base of his work. Everyone is quiet at first, unsure exactly what they've seen, though knowing they've seen something they surround the sculpture. Benchere tries to speak, tries to make sense of it all. Trembling, he rubs at the soreness in his hip, feels the racing of his heart, shakes his head then starts to laugh. Soon the others join him. There is music again and everyone is dancing and singing even wilder than before.

WHEN THE SOLDIERS return, the reaction from the crowd is different. They do not scatter this time, but remain in the area, laughing and singing even as the soldiers push through. In the chaos, everyone is upbeat, convinced what happened with Benchere is providential and uniquely divined.

Benchere resists attaching miracle status to his good fortune, is content to think of the charge not exploding in his hands as dumb luck and leaves it at that.

The soldiers repair and remount the explosive before returning to their jeeps. From thirty feet away, Benchere resists rushing the sculpture again, understands there is just so much tempting of fate he can get away with. The others, too, seem to realize this. However heartened by their initial triumph, they are realistic now, and knowing what was gained from the sculpture can't be stolen from them, they take shelter.

Benchere runs behind the half wall and ducks down. When he peeks out a second later, the area is cleared. Relieved, he is glad he came, and begins to duck once more. Only here is the reality Abebe spoke of, the way of the world advancing from across the street; the drummer woman and one of the men racing toward the sculpture. The woman has black hair and luminous brown eyes. She mounts the base and tugs at the charge while Benchere in a panic stands and shouts, "No, no, no." The woman turns only for an instant and smiles. The lamp on the rooftop has not come back on. Benchere in the dark howls as loud as he can, calls out just as the explosive gives way and the street is again bathed in light.

19.

STERN WITH ROSE, REVIEWS THEIR NOTES. "THE DAYS
are a daze," he says.

Rose knows. "First one thing."

"And then oh brother."

INSIDE THE TRUCK, the following afternoon, Benchere, Harper
and Abebe leave Kadugli for Abyei. Already the wire services have
picked up the story, have presented theories regarding Benchere's
role and report the possibility of his having died in the blast. A
harsh condemnation of al-Bashir is attached to every article. Salva
Kiir is pleased. Benchere less so. He growls and slaps the dash,
blames himself for the two deaths.

"My fault," he says. What did you expect? Who else is there
to blame? The soldiers? al-Bashir? Kiir and Ani Risha? But they did
not send you to Kadugli. He sits sullenly and says nothing for a long
time, considers his arrogance, attributes the disaster to his ignoring what was right in front of him before he left Abyei and swears
now, "I should not have come."

Abebe disagrees, has changed his opinion completely and
says, "*Shukran, bru*. But did you not see?"

IT TAKES TWO days to reach Abyei. Harper's Maule is where they
left it. Benchere and Harper say goodbye to Abebe, give him the
few dollars they have in their pockets, stumble through some parting words before flying off.

"HOME AGAIN, HOME again," Rose goes with Stern out to the plane.

"A sight for eye's sore."

"These two have cat lives."

"Cat lives for sure."

IN THE LATE afternoon, three days before, the Africana gathered as Mund's men waved their weapons. All threat and bluster, in defense of their friends the Africans mounted a charge, came with knives and sticks and handmade bows and arrows. Caught in the middle, Deyna's group dove for cover. Rose drove the jeep down the hill. Stern stood in the front seat, the Savage FP10 assembled and held in one hand, a bullhorn in the other. He identified himself and Rose as the cavalry, the regional authority and officers from the United States of America. "If you fire another shot," he shouted at Mund's militia, "I will drop you like a tea cup."

A good line. "Like a tea cup," Rose approved.

Seeing the Africana in full assault, Dancy and Gabriella turned and ran. Dancy took an arrow in the ass, fell and flailed around on the ground. Certain he was about to die, he peed himself, offered in heavy whimpers all the current cash he had in reserve if someone would save him. Gabriella sprinted past her husband, headed out into the desert, running as far as the hills until Rose brought her back.

In order to slow the attack, Stern fired a shot through the thigh of a man wielding a Wesson M&P45. The Africans drew up and Mund's men raised their hands. Rose and Stern used zip ties for cuffs, put Mund's group inside the newly built storefront while the Africana were told to pack and go. "Under the circumstances," Stern confirms, "given who did what."

"The counterattack was warranted," Rose adds.

"A righteous aggression."

"A defense of allies."

"Pack and go seems fair."

Stern radioed for transportation, had Mund's crew removed

from camp, taken to hospitals and held by the local authorities in Tshane. Everyone else was encouraged to leave as well. By the time Benchere and Harper returned fifteen people remained: Deyna and Zooie, Julie and Naveed, the BAA students, Daimon and Linda and the Iowa three. As for the Africans, Rose says, "It's fortuitous they only lost the one."

Brought into the shade, the boy was laid out on a tent tarp taken from the main group. Before Kayla and the others prepared the ground to bury the boy beneath the crusted sand of the desert, in a dry brown clay and loam, Deyna knelt and put the boy's head in her lap, cradled him as Jazz paced back and forth, confused and wondering what to do.

QUICKLY EVERYONE GATHERS. The BAA students rush over with the Iowa three. Jazz barks. Benchere looks about, finds Deyna, Zooie and Daimon. He notes the absence of the Africana, sees Mund and his followers are also gone. Stern and Rose are there. Staring back across the expanse of the three camps, Benchere spots the marker where the boy is buried and wonders, "What gives?"

BY THE FIRE, later that night, Benchere sits with Deyna. His hip is bruised and still sore to the touch. He has on his BU sweatshirt and a clean pair of jeans. Deyna wears her leather jacket unzipped. The breeze this evening comes from the north. Deyna talks about the boy. Benchere talks about Kadugli. Both try and explain.

"In the street," Benchere describes the people dancing and singing, how they got him to join them, willingly and completely so. He resists telling her yet about his handling of the charge, does not say that as he lifted the explosive and prepared to toss it in the street, fully expecting the worst and wishing for something else, that he thought of her. He repeats instead what Abebe said after the bomb went off, with Benchere grieving the two people killed, as he railed and wished he'd never left Abyei, Abebe said, *Shukran, bru, did you not see?*

"I think the sentiment is valid," Benchere tells Deyna. "But I can't get there yet."

Deyna listens then says the one thing she can, as has been there since well before Benchere came to the desert, she answers, "You will."

KYLE AND CLOIE rent a U-haul, drive their stuff across town to Broad Street where friends help carry boxes and furniture inside. Construction on the other row houses is now complete and the remaining members of the cooperative also begin moving in. Cloie and Kyle greet them, provide everyone with a notebook containing contact information for each unit, an overview of the co-op's mission, its guidelines and philosophy and what to expect. "Excellent, excellent," the other members are excited and can't wait to begin.

AFTER MIDNIGHT, BENCHERE lies with Deyna in his tent. They are quiet now, in need of a moment. Deyna stretches her feet bare along Benchere's shin. The cot is a snug fit. A fully extended spooning is required, with little room for error. Deyna has her left hip flat, her right hip up where Benchere rests his hand. Her back is to him, curled in. She looks at Jazz on the floor. Benchere says her name. The stillness soothes, allows them a chance to catch up. Alone, they address the personal, ask each other, "How are you?"

ZOOIE LIES WITH Daimon in what is still their tent. Nearly all of their belongings are packed. The moon is lambent, shines white above what remains of the camp. The sculpted moons rise as sentries. Daimon whispers, asks Zooie if she is good. "Are you?"

"I am," she says this.

Inside their sleeping bags combined, he feels her welcoming. Zooie holds Daimon close. She thinks about the Africana and the Munds, about Rose and Stern, about Benchere as he returned. A relief to have him back for sure. She thinks about the wells outside Serowe, about Marti here once, and still here now; the desert so vast it feels capable of holding everything. The internet hints of incidents Benchere experienced in Kadugli, but he has yet to tell her. Zooie thinks of this, too, of how crazy it all is and how much she also has to tell him.

For a while she talks with Daimon about Providence, about what is to come and what they have planned. Their conversation serves as a gift for having traveled this far. Daimon whispers again and Zooie answers. Afterward, they slip even closer together, as wild thatch weaved, then sleep on sands made warm beneath them.

LINDA GIVES HARPER the butt of her smoke. "Last one, sailor," she straightens her shirt, looks for her boots, makes as if to go. Harper lies back, brings the cigarette to his lips, jokes of Linda's need to always make a grand exit. "But of course I do," she fills her reply with an exaggerated Tallulah Bankhead inflection.

In the time Harper was gone, Linda monitored the news for updates. "Crazy man," Linda said of Harper then, says the same now. When others asked, she denied her concern, said hers was nothing more than a casual interest. "Tell me honestly," she wants to know now what really happened in Kadugli.

Harper offers her the full account. Linda considers the narrative, pictures it all in cinematic hues.

"My turn then," Harper says. "I heard you missed me while I was gone."

"In your dreams, flyboy."

"In my dreams, definitely. Tell me," he keeps his free hand behind his head, stretched out on the cot. "Why were you keeping tabs on the news so closely?"

"Who says I was?"

"Mindy and Heidi."

"Don't flatter yourself," Linda pulls on her boot. "I was following the timeline is all. I just wanted to know how the story ends."

"Is that right, Darling?" Harper moves his hand in circles,

creates a trail of smoke. The eternal question. "In that case," he says, "come here and I will tell you."

ONCE DEYNA IS asleep, Benchere gets up and walks outside. Stern is sitting at the foot of the old Africana camp, where he and Rose have relocated their chairs, their table and tent and umbrella. The jeep is parked to the right of the store. Stern closes the lid on his computer as Benchere approaches, settles his arms behind his head.

Benchere sits down in Rose's chair, stretches his legs and rubs at his hip. Rose is inside the tent. The lantern is placed to Stern's left. The light glows around the table. "Who's there?" Rose calls out.

"Our man," Stern answers.

"Man of the hour," Rose in turn. "Can't he sleep?"

"Apparently not," Stern reaches beneath his chair into a cooler, pulls out a bottle of water and tosses it to Benchere. "Grade A filtered," he says. "Perks of the profession."

Benchere removes the cap and drinks.

"So," Stern again, wants to know, "what brings you out this late?"

"Jetlag?" Rose now.

"Could be." Stern says, "It's our job to make sense." He repeats what he said at dinner, explains the reason he and Rose have spent the last ten weeks atop the hill, their training as *assessment specialists* sent in to monitor the effects of Benchere's project.

"Your influence," Rose says.

"And stimulus."

"Given your history."

"And celebrity."

"For example," Rose lists the sculptures that have popped up in Somalia and Zimbabwe, Namibia and Yemen, Egypt, Uganda and Chad.

Stern holds his hand toward the lantern, makes finger puppets in the sand. He talks about the other sculptures, says, "If not for these, you would not have been asked to fly to Abyei."

"And then drive to Kadugli."

"For whatever reason you chose to do that."

"You tell us," Rose goes.

"What exactly were you thinking?"

The curve of Rose's chair fits Benchere's frame. He shifts his back, slips his sore hip into the groove. Still inside the tent, Rose says, "It is a risky proposition to truck around the mountains."

Stern calls it, "A radical departure."

Rose agrees, "Radical, yes."

Benchere lets go a loud sigh, accuses Rose and Stern of delivering a routine they've worked out in advance. "If you two spies are going to keep on like this," he says, "I'll find another place to clear my head."

"Spies is it?"

"And what is this about clearing your head?"

Stern asks, "Is there something on your mind?"

"Something we should know?"

"Tell us then," Rose now pops his head out of the tent, his face red from sleep, his plump cheeks and thinning brown hair spread out as loose strings across the front of his scalp. Exposed this way to the lantern light, Rose appears like Stan Laurel without the moustache. Stern opens the lid on his computer again, finds the latest news from Kadugli, reads an updated account of all the troubles in South Sudan and elsewhere, while Rose attempts to provide perspective, asks Benchere, "Do you know how many coups there have been in Africa in the last 60 years?"

"363," Stern answers.

"And do you know what came of 361 of these coups?"

"Anarchy."

"Extended chaos."

"Constitutions thrown out and re-written."

"A promise of change."

"But no plan in place to effect change."

"Mauritania in 2008," Rose lists.

"Guinea in 2009."

"Niger in 2010."

"Mali now," Stern continues. "Toure replaced by Ampoulo Boucoun. Tandja kicked to the curb by his own military."

"And now Riek Machar in South Sudan."

"In South Sudan, exactly."

"It's an endless cycle," Rose steps completely out of his tent, a green blanket wrapped around his shoulders. He brings the conversation back to Kadugli and says, "Africa's been like this forever."

"Since Hector was a pup."

"Since before Homer and the Kingdom of Kush."

Benchere taps the arms of his chair, impatient now, sensing an ambush, he asks, "Do you boys have a point?"

"Do we?" Stern reaches down and adjusts the flame of the lantern, says to Rose, "I suppose he wants to know why we're telling him all this."

"I think he does." Rose says, "It's important to make sure you understand."

"These sculptures," Stern says.

"The two you made and then the rest."

"They muddy the waters."

"Stir the pot."

"Give people a reason to rally."

"You have to remember," Rose says, "war is tricky business."

"For every Mau Mau there's a dozen disasters."

"A dozen or more."

"Listen," Benchere stops them, stands up and comes from the chair. He looks toward Rose and then at Stern and says, "You make a cute couple, but your chatter is just that."

"Is it?"

"Honestly?"

"But that stings."

"It really does."

"What have we missed?"

"Have we said anything that isn't true?"

"Anything at all?"

"We'd hate to think."

Rose walks around and sits in his chair, the blanket adjusted as a toga over one shoulder, across his chest and down to his thighs. He clarifies Stern's statement with, "He doesn't mean hate to think, he means hate to think."

Benchere flips his water bottle toward the table, folds his arms across his middle and says, "Are you done? If you're trying to warn me off, if my going to Kadugli has you rattled and you'd like me to quit, you can save your breath."

"Can we now?"

"And why is that?"

In the distance the outline of Benchere's sculpture is visible in the dark. The shape beneath the moon gives the desert definition. Benchere stands just inside the lantern light, in front of the chairs. Stern sips again from his water, puts the bottle down on the sand and replies to Benchere, "Not that it matters."

"What's done is done."

"The die is cast."

"And you're wrong if you think we're telling you to quit."

"Why would we want you to do that?" Stern remains in his chair.

Rose tips himself sideways and closer to Stern as he says, "Of course, people did die in Kadugli."

"Yes, yes. May as well shut down after that."

"People have never died before."

"When trying to get out from under."

"Or find a voice."

"Better to turtle."

"And keep away completely."

"Yes that."

"Artists can't be expected to get involved."

"God dammit now," Benchere finds himself fully into the

argument, can't help but snap, "I came here to build a sculpture, that's all."

"And yet?"

Rose says, "Didn't you bring your art along to Kadugli?"

"Isn't that why you went?"

"To build a sculpture?"

"I built a sculpture," Benchere barks, "as a piece of art."

"Which carried a certain meaning."

"Art is all," Benchere once more. "That's the meaning."

"You weren't trying to get anyone worked up?"

"I was hoping for the opposite."

"The opposite now?"

"Were you?"

"Did you say hope?"

"I believe he did."

"So it was hope you were looking to offer?"

Rose smoothes the wrinkles from the blanket wrapped around him, while Stern comes and stands beside Benchere, turns to Rose and says, "Nothing wrong with hope."

"Used to be a little hope could go a long way."

"Remember back in the day?"

"The day, yes."

"Mandela and the UDM."

"Alpha Conde."

"The UDK, MDM and ADM."

"Ghana."

"And Kenya."

"Zambia."

"The SSAA and Lam Tungwar."

"Rashid Diab.

"It can be done."

"It can, it's true."

"Tell me that wasn't a good time."

"The best."

"The best for sure."

"It takes a certain artistry, wouldn't you say?"

"I would say so."

"Unfortunately," Rose goes back into the tent, comes out with a fresh explosive device and a hardhat on his head and says to Benchere, "as far as your sculpture is concerned."

"Regardless of your intention."

"Your intention, yes."

"Others find your sculptures are a bit much."

"You're riling the masses and all."

"Whether you meant to or not."

"Not that we agree," Stern says.

"But our handlers do."

"Our handlers, yes."

"They want to get rid of all this."

"Uproot your influence and cool the pots you've set to boil."

"Wait now," Benchere makes a move toward Rose, who turns his shoulder.

"Not that we're persuaded," Stern confides. "We told our handlers we object."

"Put in a good word."

"Let everyone know what would happen if we made a martyr out of your sculpture."

"We did our best to convince them all," Rose says.

"Yes we did."

"Say what you will, your work is spectacular."

"No one can deny."

Rose takes the wires off the charge, tosses his hardhat back toward the tent. "Pity you're giving it all up."

"I never said," Benchere in protest.

"What's that?" Stern cuts him off. "But didn't you just say we should save our breath?"

"That's not what I meant," Benchere in a huff. "I wasn't talking about sculpting."

"Oh no?"

"Didn't you?"

"Our mistake."

"What then?" Stern asks.

"Yes what?"

"What now?"

"What next?"

Stern waves toward the sculpture again and says, "We thought you meant."

"Enough," Rose nods in the direction of the Sudan.

"Maybe we misconstrued."

"After all these weeks."

"It's been a long haul."

"It has been that."

"So then."

"So, yes," Rose looks at Benchere.

Stern winks, gives hint once more of all things rehearsed. He puts an elbow into Benchere's side and says, "So what then? All our blabber and tell us now what's come from this and what are you really thinking, Benchere?"

20.

IN THE MORNING BENCHERE WAKES BESIDE DEYNA. THEY have moved from the cot, slept on the air mattress, not bothered with netting, have spent the rest of the night exposed this way.

A new group of tourists arrives early and is permitted to walk the grounds. They explore all sides of the sculpture, take photographs, snap pictures of Benchere with Jazz, Benchere near the baobab trees and standing beside and beneath his work. Everyone still on hand is in the process of packing up. The sheds and shelters are torn down, the pits and trenches filled in, the desert put back the way she was before.

Transportation from the desert has been arranged. After some debate, the BAA students have agreed to go; the idea of establishing a lasting community put on hold, idealized into entropy, collapsing inward following the incident between the Africana and the Munds. Still, there is confidence the effect of the sculpture will continue on its own, its individual magnificence as Benchere originally explained. There is talk of returning next spring, of letting the area settle first before starting again. Mindy and Heidi hope, appeal to Benchere about the prospect.

Daimon films the events of the morning. Zooie and Linda help Harper pack and prep the Maule. The media expands its coverage, the incident in Kadugli presented in folkloric hues. Support for South Sudan increases as additional news reaches the States. A successful gambit. Kiir is invited for a goodwill tour. Websites appear offering to raise funds. Students at universities hold rallies and sit-ins, continue to do so until the rift between Kiir and vice-president Machar ends in a permanent fission, divides the newly independent South into its own internal conflict.

Benchere packs his own belongings. Following his talk with Rose and Stern last night, he lay back down beside Deyna, who was awake and waiting. He told her about his conversation, about his thoughts before and after and all points between. He sat up again and made a motion with his hands, spread everything out then brought them back together.

Deyna took note of the way Benchere moved his hands, how they expanded and offered themselves in full, opening up as inclusive as an invitation.

CLOIE AND KYLE follow the news. Shaken by the first reports of Kadugli, Kyle turns to Skype, relieved only as Benchere appears on screen, offering assurances and an explanation for what has happened.

Two nights later, Kyle calls the initial meeting for the Broad Street Cooperative to order. A common area has been constructed in the courtyard, with plans for a kitchen and yoga studio. Chairs have been set in a circle. Both Cloie and Kyle are confident about the cooperative's future, are pleased with their selection process for its members. Everything is meant to affirm what nearly came to pass in the desert. Kyle is open-minded and not alarmed at first when a member stands and introduces himself to the group. Holding up the Broad Street Cooperative Handbook, which he has read several times and marked with notes and filled with yellow stickers, the man says, "I am Owen Robins-Greene and I have a few suggestions. Just a few ideas if you don't mind."

NAVEED HELPS THE others load the bus which has arrived in camp. Dawid drives the truck. Harper flies out with Linda, with Daimon and Zooie who have plans of their own now. Deyna packs her clothes and personal items in the two duffles she has brought. Her tent is folded and kept separately from the others. When everyone is ready and the bus begins pulling away, Benchere and Deyna stand to the side and wave farewell.

THE REST OF the morning is spent packing the second truck with supplies. Gas and water, the rifle and tent, dry food, fruits and seeds, metals and tools are tied down beneath a large tarp. Together Benchere and Deyna plan to drive south, past Kang and Khakea, below Werda and Lobatse, on into South Africa and Swaziland. *Here I am*, Benchere thinks. Life in layers. Jazz rides in back. Deyna checks their map for markers. When the sun sets they stop and make camp for the night. Benchere gathers wood, helps Deyna build a fire.

STERN AND ROSE have packed the rest of their supplies into the back of their jeep. In hardhats they walk from the sculpture, leave the charge against the center. "Too bad," Stern gives Rose the detonator and turns away.

The half crests at the top of the sculpture stare down. Rose stands at a distance, asks Stern, "How far do you think we should go?"

"I think we've gone far enough."

"I mean to be safe."

"I know what you mean."

Rose shrugs his heavy shoulders, "Ours is not to reason why."

Stern disagrees.

Rose changes the subject, says about Benchere, "How far now would you guess?"

"Past Tshane, I'd bet."

"Maybe further."

"Could be."

"At least there's that."

Stern looks back at the sculpture and says, "I still don't think."

"You don't think or you don't think?"

"Goddamn it."

Rose adjusts his hat and says, "I know."

"Such a waste."

"It is what it is."

"And it is something."

"Let's make the best of it." Rose says, "Let's have a blast."

THE NEXT MORNING Benchere and Deyna drive across the border into South Africa. Benchere has his window down. The air is hot. The dust is a gold silt set aglow in the sun. They stop in an open area outside of Perth. Benchere has gathered bits of material along the way; wood and stone mostly. He has brought additional metals from camp, as well as solder and tools for welding. Later they will have to purchase actual supplies, will need to enter cities and improve their scavenging if they're to continue on this way.

A spot is cleared twenty feet from the road. Benchere selects materials from the truck, begins to visualize what he will make. Deyna helps with the construction, gives assistance with the weld. They talk as they work, an easy back-and-forth. They do not try and explain things, allow the moment to provide its own sound reason.

The road as they drive comes and goes, appears and disappears then reappears once more on their map. Occasionally still they talk of what happened with the Munds, the Africana and the others. Benchere talks about Zooie and Kyle and Marti. He discusses art, the soldiers in Kadugli, the woman on the drum and the children dancing. About each he offers a quiet impression. More reflective now, he looks at Deyna and says, "Here is what I can tell you."

IN KURUMAN THEY stop for gas. When the radiator is cool enough they add water to keep the engine going.

JUST PAST KIMBERLEY, Benchere builds another sculpture. The piece is six feet tall, constructed of sticks and wood supported by a center frame of metal left over from the Kalahari. In the middle is a stone. The stone is flat on one side and rounded on the other. Benchere creates a shelf in the center of the metal on which he rests the stone. The stone is then encased by a thin shield of twigs and vines Deyna has gathered. Depending on the angle of the sun, the stone appears as a different shape and texture.

Benchere steps back when the work is complete. The foundation has been buried a foot beneath the soil, with angled stakes submerged on either side as Marti taught him. Deyna tamps down the ground around the sculpture, makes sure everything is secure.

ON THEIR FIFTH day out, Benchere wakes to the sound of Jazz barking. He comes from the tent, finds the sun just high enough to sting the eyes as he stares east. Squinting, he lifts his hands to his brow in order to make out a figure standing between the acacia trees.

Thirty yards from the tent, a boy is in the covering. Alone, he watches Benchere. Where he came from Benchere can't be sure. Deyna leaves the tent and calls to Jazz. Benchere waves the boy over but he does not respond. As Benchere starts walking to the trees, the child moves away. Benchere stops and walks back toward the tent.

Deyna makes a small fire, cooks the potatoes they have left, reheats their coffee in a blue pot. Benchere again invites the boy to join them, but as before he refuses.

They have decided to make their way to Queenstown, to continue south and then afterward work back north toward Soweto and Johannesburg, then east to Zimbabwe and Mozambique and into additional cities. The course of their travels is subject to change, dependent on the news. Deyna keeps a notebook, explores the landscape for variations and potential finds. The open-endedness of their plans suits Benchere. After breakfast, he and Deyna break down the tent, load the truck again. In back are the remaining metals Benchere has brought from the Kalahari, as well as a stack of branches, twigs and stones recently gathered.

Benchere removes a few of the pieces from the back, stares down at them separately before bringing them together. He uses

Deyna's shovel to dig a hole, sets the foundation and works his way upward. The boy watches from the trees, edges slowly forward as Benchere uses the portable torch to melt the solder, fastens the sticks against the metal, the sheets and stone held hard. The boy by now has moved all the way in, stands close enough to take a piece of piping Benchere offers him.

When the piece is finished, Benchere pats the boy's shoulder. He goes back to the truck, empties all the remaining metals and materials he has gathered, is confident they'll be able to get more in Johannesburg. He hands the boy the torch, his ECM portable and one of his propane tanks, some solder and nickel. He shows him again how to use the torch. The boy proves a quick study. Deyna leaves two oranges and a small bag of oats. They get back in the truck then and drive off.

LATER THAT EVENING they stop in an area covered with wild grass and acacia. A flight of birds passes over as they take their water and food, tent and blankets from the truck. They talk quietly. In their tent, after they eat, they lay side by side. Jazz spreads out in a corner. Benchere relaxes, clears his head, tries to solve nothing. In Kadugli a new sculpture has been built from the scraps gathered after the blast. In the Kalahari, too, the shards of metal are reused. In Zambia, Angola and Zaire, in Syria and Sierra Leone, the Nuba Mountains, Mali and Darfur, in Mali and Senegal, Gaborone, Makhado and Francistown, in Spain and England, France and America, Russia and China, North Korea and Cyprus, the effort gains momentum.

Benchere sleeps deeply. Deyna has her hand on his chest, her leg across his thigh.

Acknowledgements

TO THOSE WHO ENDURED ME DURING THE FOUR-PLUS years of writing this book. To friends and foes, the many authors who shared my experience and as I hope I was of service still to them during this time as through Dzanc. To my Dzanc family, Guy and Pat, Dan and Parker and Michelle, and now Gina, thanks for indulging the madness of my schedule. To the great folks at Hawthorne, in particular the inimitable Rhonda Hughes, publisher and editor and as crazy mad about what she does as I am. Thank you. And of course, to my family. Nuclear in every way. Mary, Anna and Zach, all my love and thanks. Without you there is no me. Onward!